After the Crash

Also by Carol Patterson and published by Ginninderra Press
State of the Heart

Carol Patterson

After the Crash

& other Tasmanian stories

After the Crash: & other Tasmanian stories
ISBN 978 1 76109 289 3
Copyright © text Carol Patterson 2022
Cover image: *Nautical Dreaming 11*, by Doreen Locher

First published 2022 by
GINNINDERRA PRESS
PO Box 3461 Port Adelaide 5015
www.ginninderrapress.com.au

Contents

After the Crash	7
Australia Day	17
Bullimore and Vandal	34
Falling up	46
Hound's Tooth	54
Jeopardy	68
Patrimony	79
Overboard	93
Peaches	104
Pentimento	118
Sasha	126
Slip Yards	134
Stillborn	145
The Dead Zone	155
The Quad Squad	171
Surface Tension	183
The Shore	192

After the Crash

For three days now, the plane tree outside Susan's cottage had been thrashed by a gale blowing from the south. She stood at the window, watching the leafy frenzy, and wondered how the leaves hung on.

Susan had come to Hobart for cheap housing, as her ex-husband had lost everything they had in the stock market crash. Nineteen eighty-nine, called Black Monday. Why had it happened to them? Him a top public servant in charge of a department, her an early childhood teacher, they were doing just fine, protected from the vicissitudes of the world by their money. Or so she thought. After all, the shares they had invested in had proliferated like cancer cells on the stock market. But money attracts, and Angus had listened to a financial adviser so helpfully recommended by the bank, who had lost them everything. Not so much investments as divestments, she thought ruefully. And then had come the Crash. With it had gone the house.

Angus. Where was he now? Every night for months after he'd left, he'd come round in the early hours begging her to forgive him and take him back. Yet, when the house was sold, he had already remarried, finding a new wife to buffer him against the cold winds of penury.

The tree outside had held against winds for at least a hundred years, its blotched trunk brawny, branches embracing the street, its canopy splendidly leafy. Herself? Shrinking. For instance, the move from a big house and gardens in Melbourne to a rented cottage of four rooms and a patch in Hobart; from a family to living on her own; from a busy social life to loneliness. With this cottage came a table and two chairs, a kitchen cupboard with packets, bar fridge with eggs and a carton of milk, two mugs, a few knives and forks, bowls and saucepans. Bare, simple, no guises or disguises.

Her emotions? Contrarily, they'd expanded, taking in a world of flee-ing refugees, child victims of war, poverty, abuse, animals kept in horrid captivity, and the pitiful state of the environment. It was if she had lost a protective skin and could no longer harden herself to it. No more watching television or the internet, flicking it off as soon as the ads ap-peared for donations. Yet, to some extent, she was coming to accept it, this rawness, like a carapace, a protective shield, ripped off from her life. But there were still nights, lying in her bed in her attic room, when she would wake suddenly from sleep, gripped by anxiety and a reeling fear that the world was crashing about her and she was one of those desperate people needing help. Her money was running low, what to do? Go back to teaching? But at her age? Fifty-five was nothing, but she quailed at telling that to hard-faced employers. And so her thoughts thrashed round and round.

Across the road in the double-fronted red-brick, the boy learning the drums was practising. Salvos in staccato bursts, rolls of sound drifted over when the howling wind eased a little. From the weatherboard di-agonally opposite, a woman in a red parka took her large dog for a walk on a lead, a red setter, as she did at eleven each day, both buffeted along the footpath by gusts, the dog's plumes streaming. She was glad she could watch the goings on in the street, glad she had beached here, in this safe enclave. Beached? On sunny days there was a seaside feel to the cottage, the sunlight underwater-green beneath the moving swaths of the plane tree, the massed foliage sighing like surf, seagulls crying high up… She liked this house where everything was in reach, reduced to essentials, the garden so simple with its lawn, paving, and an ornamental cherry spread-ing its branches.

Susan turned away from the window. She was due to go see her son, Edward, who lived on Mount Wellington at Ferntree. He thought she was coming in on a plane, travelling into Hobart from the airport after gadding about the world. Her son had come here to attend the univer-sity, to study geology, seemed enthusiastic, and then, well, he'd dropped out. Drugs, she wondered. Or his mental health? The crash, he knew about it of course, but to what extent? In order not to worry him, she dressed when she visited him as if she'd just arrived from overseas via Melbourne. Was this a symptom of a breakdown, she wondered. His or hers? Breakdown. Fall. Crash. Pieces you must put together again. Somehow. No, her retreat to this little town was more an act of sanity. It was tiny, like a place viewed from the wrong end of a telescope, but once here your world expanded as if you'd turned the telescope around, disclosing immense vistas of water and sky, and hidden treasures. Like the plane tree on its grassy reserve in the middle of the road outside.

Mornings, early, she lay in bed listening to local radio. She liked Bob, the presenter. This morning, a mate had come into the studio with a two-kilo Collinsvale swede. Collinsvale at the back of the Mountain being, it seemed, favoured for growing this vegetable. The debate was what to do with this giant swede. A caller said to slice it and put salt on it. Sounded like a punishment, Bob said. How did the swede originate? A cross between a turnip and a cabbage, his mate said. When did those two get together, Bob snorted. The swede was their love child? She'd laughed out loud. And, for those few moments, stopped worrying.

Susan heaved on thick socks, warm pants and leather boots. Then she pulled on a knit top of a tropical flowery hue to give her a devil may care holiday look for Edward's benefit, and a navy polo fleece jacket too big for her that she'd found in an opportunity shop, but warm. She wound a magenta scarf around her neck, pulled on a sunhat and sunglasses, tucked in her hair. Presentable? She took the handle of her travel case, empty of course, but she might find home-grown vegies to buy on the way back home. She turned back to the window to look out for the taxi she'd ordered half an hour before.

In his house in Ferntree, Eddie shuffled from corner to corner of the room, moving his rock collection. It was one big room he'd created by knocking out the walls of this shaky house, precarious on a mountain slope, bought with a loan, a bribe, a payoff, whichever, from his father. Two little bedrooms and a filled-in veranda, which was his study. One bedroom he let out to Vance, who'd been renting the place when he bought it. He was an elderly vet who'd spent time in Changi prison, then on the Burma railway, and he couldn't throw him out. And then, Vance knew so much about Tasmania, its flora, fauna, geology, but also which families lived where in its regions, telling tales of men and women's hardship and courage. Eddie was in awe, loved to sit with a beer, magging on with Vance. This was true learning from those who'd gone before, learning from their life experience, not university study.

Eddie knew his mother worried about him, a dropout, living on what? Where was his life going? He knew all that, but he worried more about her. He was twenty-four, and she still called him Edward, not even Teddie, Ted or Eddie. And when was she going to give up the pretence that she'd just flown in from exotic places OS? She had a place somewhere down in town, must have. He needed to know where, but how could he confront her? Today, he might try. Not directly; you have to go careful with mums. Eddie paused, holding a tray of white and rose quartz crystals. Why not take her out for a walk? A walk on the mountain, that'd be the thing. The wind would blow those fantasies out of her head, and then it would ring true, clear as a bell.

Spiders filled the corners of the room with grey looping nets of web, crouching fat and black in them. He called them all Dante, neutral gender, one name's enough to say g'day to, and Vance agreed, any bloke'd have a hard time telling the difference. Clean them out? That's what Mum would want, mums being like that. But spiders have a right to a roof over their heads, don't they, earning a living catching the blowies cruising through. They were into heavy metal, and when he played bass guitar, the webs quivered. Boom boom! His mother had hated him playing the metal, said smart-arse literary things like, for whom the bell tolls comes from John Donne via Ernest Hemingway. Tell that to the spiders, boom boom. He'd asked the spiders what he should do to help his mum. She needed a web? Well, that was right, he needed to make a web for her. He was her only family, wasn't that the start of a web?

Eddie placed the glistening tray of quartz on a bench made up of a plank on brick towers. They can tell you so much, rocks, and like the spiders, they never let you down, never show a different face, never cheat or steal. Take osmiridium. Made up of two minerals, osmium and iridium. The miners used to call it Ossie, Vance said. Awesome story, about a rush, like a gold rush, people going to the West Coast from all over, selling it for thirty quid, more, an ounce, and some made fortunes. Used for making pen nibs. Watermans fountain pens were the best, Vance said. Pelikan ink, smooth as silk. Then along comes the biro, invented by a Frenchman. End of the fountain pen, end of the rush for Ossie, end of the rush to the West Coast. Now biros have gone, pencils too, writing by hand, you have your computer to do it. Call that progress, Vance scoffed. Surveillance. The government knows where you are, got its eye on you, mobile phones too. No, Eddie didn't call that progress.

Progress was what had broken his family, brought his dad down in the financial crash. The idiot, he coulda told him what was going to happen. He'd looked up the history of crashes, and found one or more every few years somewhere in the world. Crises, booms and busts, depressions, recessions, wars and invasions, the whole system as unstable as a volcanic zone with its earthquakes and eruptions, lava and magma, boiling mud and geysers. Give him geology any time, you knew where you were with geomorphology: the scientific study of the origin and evolution of topographic and bathymetric features created by physical, chemical or biological processes operating at or near the Earth's surface. Yep, he could rattle it off. And don't say technology's the answer. Technology's the problem, he was with Vance on that. So, living on the dole, he'd slowed down his life to match that of the spiders.

He went back to the kitchen and put out a pot of honey, a spoon and a jug of milk to go with the tea. Ruffled his hair, rubbed his face. Normally, he didn't give a fuck about his appearance, but mums like a neat look.

Susan paid the taxi driver, stood shakily as she watched the taxi drive away and was blown down the drive to Edward's front door, her case clattering after her. The door was open, and she entered on a gust, dust blowing ahead of her, calling out 'Edward!', hoping that Vance wasn't about. Yes, she knew, he'd served his country and was to be honoured, she just wished he was honoured somewhere else. Edward looked up to him, and she was sad. Was Vance a substitute dad for her boy?

'Mum?' Eddie emerged from the gloom and they hugged. He took her case and led her through to the kitchen. 'Pretty light travelling, hey, Mum? Not much luggage.'

'Oh yes,' she started guiltily, thinking maybe she should've put some books in the case to give it authenticity.

'Cuppa tea?'

'Thanks, love, fine.' Looking about, shying away from the looping webs, seeing that the floor was swept, the bench cleaned, Edward had made an effort. 'Vance here?'

'No, he's gone north to see Rob. Ex-Changi mate.'

'I see.' Though she didn't. Vance's ways were a mystery to her.

'He's down,' Eddie explained. 'They stand by each other, Mum.'

'That's nice, dear.' Maybe Vance being here was a good thing, when the alternative might be drug dens, crack labs, pimps and such like she'd heard of. And said, 'I can't stay long, my flight. The taxi's coming for me.' To get it over with.

He gave her a look. Flight. Key word there, and he poured boiling water onto the tea bags. Steam billowed up and Susan sensed the spiders shifting in their webs, indulging in a tropical sauna in the hot steam, and giggled.

'Mum?'

'Spiders,' she murmured.

He peered at her. 'You all right?'

She was different today. Was that good or was that bad? His policy was not to analyse. Let it drift. As was his policy in life, but it had got him into trouble at uni, geology needing heaps of analysis.

'Yes, dear.' She shouldn't let her thoughts dwell on the spiders; she was here for her son.

'Finish your tea, we're going for a walk.'

'In this weather?'

'Wind's easing off, no problem. Just across the road to the Pipeline Track. Easy as, then back.'

Susan gazed at him over her steaming mug. His narrow face shadowed, eyes keen, hair an untidy blond mop as always. What was he up to, suggesting a walk? She had to trust him, and sipped the hot tea, her hands warm around the mug. Twisting round, she looked out of the grimy windows at the dark forest rising at the end of a garden. So self-contained, those trees, centuries old as the planet wheeled. Goodness, where were her thoughts taking her today!

'You've got warm gear, good boots?'

She was back with him. 'Suppose I have.' And took off the sunhat and glasses. Her hands shook, she sensed change, as Eddie planted a beanie on her head.

'Oh!' She touched her fringe of blonde hair going grey that was sticking out. 'I've never worn a beanie.'

'Always a first.'

He led her down the long room and out the front door. It slammed in the wind behind them as they battled up the drive, her arm in his bent elbow, into the cul-de-sac, making for the corner. Overlooking the road, a charming church stood out from the forest, and across the way was a quite nice modern tavern. She liked this area, but above soared the Organ Pipes, the sounding instrument of the mountain, and she shivered with the drama of it.

'Eddie, hey, Eddie?'

They turned as two children, warm in red parkas and coloured beanies, ran up the cul-de-sac.

'Hey, guys, this is my mum,' Eddie welcomed them as they arrived, flushed and panting.

They giggled, the boy tugging at Eddie's parka, the girl turning up her petal face, blonde hair in plaits.

'Say hello.'

'Hello,' they breathed. 'You bringing some more rocks for us to look at?'

'You bet. Now, buzz off.'

And they ran off.

'Who are they?' Watching them disappear up a drive between trees.

'Community school,' Eddie said. 'I go in and talk to them about rocks.'

'Oh?' A community school. Would they be needing an early childhood teacher, she wondered? 'What do you tell them?'

'Last time? Osmiridium. Found at the boundary of Cretaceous and Tertiary right around the earth. Evidence of two things: the asteroid crashing into the planet, and the end of the dinosaurs. They love it.'

Of course they do, she knew that at once. 'Do you tell them about your spiders?'

'Sure. They've been in to see them. Adopted them for pets. Feed them flies.'

'No!' Susan laughed. She needn't worry about him. He was all right, her son. He'd fitted in.

They crossed the road, climbed up the steps and onto the track. It was broad, gravelly underfoot, rising away from the road, edged by rhododendrons and banks of ferns above a low mossy wall. The air was sharp, sweet, filled with the moving rustling of wind in the trees. She sensed the city far below, and felt elation at being here, so high in the grasp of this mountain. The track was inset with worn sandstone slabs.

'What are these?'

'The old waterworks pipeline. Water was brought from the head of the North-west Bay river, seventeen kilometres to here, Ferntree…'

'Ferntree,' she echoed.

'Piped down to reservoirs at Ridgeway, for Hobart. Still do. Here's the newer pipeline.' He scuffed dirt from the surface of a concrete pipe.

'Amazing.' To think that life could be so simple: here we will live, and here will be the source of our water. No need for stock markets, booms and crashes.

'Hey, Mum, look here!' Eddie stopped, looking into the under-growth of the bank.

She went to his side and followed his gaze. Under a rotting log green with moss was the most delicate fungus, a silvery white fan reaching out from the dank bark, yearning for light.

'Beautiful, so delicate. It looks almost shy.'

Pleased at her delight, 'It's the best one I've seen, of that sort,' and they walked a bit further along the track. He stopped again, this time to show her a tiny parade of tan toadstools rearing from the leaf mould.

'Gorgeous. Like little soldiers on a march,' she said. 'It's a whole world here.'

They walked on, beneath the trees, pale trunks towering straight and strong, canopies tumbled by gusts. The track curved around the hillside and people passed them, some on bikes, one or two walking little dogs on leads, workmen in orange high-vis, chatting. The road below was out of sight now, the low density of trees angled on the slope, a tangle of dark green, white limbs, silver leaves.

They reached a gravelled open area, Fern Tree Bower, tall trees encircling it. A stone bench was engraved with the words, faint with moss and age, 'Hobart Town Corporation 1861', and a signpost indicated a track to Silver Falls. Beside the track, a creek bounded down the slope, rushing over rocks, a torrent right below where she and her son stood. She looked up the track, dark under overhanging ferns, heard the thunder of the waterfall and was fearful. She knew that if she walked up there to the falls, there would be no taxi, no pretence, no going back, and she, a different person, would be set in stone: Susan Brownlow 1989. Could she handle that?

As she hesitated, three women came past, dour in bulky jackets, boots and beanies, walking three bony greyhounds, black, tan and golden, eyes liquid in pointed faces, stepping delicately along, outfitted in flowery coats, one with striped leggings on its thin front legs. Susan watched them go by, and as they passed, one of the women turned to a lagging greyhound, 'Come along, Esme!' And Susan laughed. Another treasure.

Eddie took her hand. 'You can do it, Mum. It's not too steep, the slope.'

'Can I?' But first, the truth. 'I have to tell you something, Eddie…'

'Give me your address. I'll come, whenever.' She might get into difficulties, have a fall, be unable to pay a bill, she had to be able to call him. 'I'm your safety net, Mum.'

Ah, so he knows. She turned and smiled at him, feeling anxiety subside in her, strain easing away, a pain she didn't even know was there. Eddie. Her dear son. This place. Her cottage. They were all she needed, living their lives after the crash.

'Come on, Mum. After, we'll get a mulled wine at the tavern, warm us up.' And he strode away, Susan trotting with him, sheltered in the serried shade of the man ferns, up to Silver Falls.

'And then home, Eddie.'

Yes, home.

Australia Day

Annie Medhurst turned her hire car into the drive. Crunching over the gravel beneath the old pine tree, she saw, leaning against its bole, a line of cows and calves cut out of corrugated iron, painted black and white. Whose idea was that? She halted the car, got herself together, grabbed her bag and got out. The farmhouse, looking the same as always, and she leaned at the picket fence edging the driveway. The garden stretched beyond the row of crab apples her mother had planted, wanting to make crab apple jelly. Nothing had come of this scheme, but they loved the pink and white blossom in spring. The garden beds were overgrown with petunias, salvia bunched with grass, honesty going wild. No one was doing the gardening, that was clear. The old stables over the way were disappearing below purple bougainvillea and banksia rose. Sheds filled with rubbish, defunct machinery, old building materials, bins. Her father could never throw anything out.

Lifting her case out of the boot, Annie slammed the car door shut, and walked up the steps to the house. Two dogs rushed to the bay window beside the door, setting up a racket. She pushed open the door and called out, 'Anyone home?'

No one answered, no one called for the dogs to be quiet.

Leaving her case there, she went back to the path, going around the back. 'Hello! Dad, Jack?' Was that a tractor she could hear? Surely Dad wasn't up to driving the tractor?

A movement over in a shed and her father, sitting upright on a red three-wheeler bike, pedalled out. He had on a safety helmet and a plaid shirt, workers' overalls, and gumboots.

She laughed out loud as he waved. 'Dad! What are you up to?'

'How yer goin', girl?' He pedalled right to her.

They hugged, Annie feeling her father's chest stiff against hers.

'What's with the bike?'

'How I get around, now my legs've had it. Flight okay?'

'No problems.' She'd flown direct from Sydney.

'Where's your luggage?'

'Round the front. The dogs wouldn't let me in.'

'Poppy and Smut? They won't hurt you.'

'But well…' Living in Sydney, you didn't just march into people's homes. Even this one.

Her father gazed at her, his eyes rheumy beneath the rim of the helmet, and she saw how much he'd aged since she was last here, when her mother had died. And also sensed how much he wanted her here.

'It's good to be back home, Dad.' To the Channel, that magical place, in summer. Woodbridge, Kettering, Bruny Island; her childhood was embedded here.

The tractor engine stopped and she looked around. That must be Jack.

'Help me outa this contraption.'

She gave John, her father, her arm and lifted him. He got one gum-booted leg and then the other down to the ground, and leaned against her. She smelled the tobacco he'd given up smoking, dust, manure, grease, the smells of a farm.

He ruffled her hair. 'Good to see you, girl.'

Jack appeared, striding over from the paddock, in boots, shorts, a ragged singlet, and a bent Akubra askew. 'Hey, Annie!' He strode across and hugged her. 'How's our smart corporate lawyer?' Looking her up and down.

Oh god, he was starting already. 'I'm fine. How are you, Jack?'

'Goin' good. Like a cuppa?'

'Sure.'

Her brother, her pal, and they banged fists in their old welcome.

'Dad, you'd like a drink?'

'Never knock back a cuppa.'

She helped her father up the back steps onto the veranda, Jack following. She looked out over the far side, where scraggy pine trees threw shade. Beyond them, she glimpsed the raw pine of new fencing, and the walls and roofs of new houses.

'What? The cherry orchard's gone?'

'Told ya, Annie.' Jack was blunt.

'Why? They were the best cherries in the Channel, in Tassie!'

'Couldn't keep goin'. No one wants to do the pickin', the prunin', the packin',' her father said.

Was it beyond Jack to do that? The criticism stayed unspoken.

Jack scuffed a boot, head down. 'Got a good offer. Couldn't refuse.'

She looked away. The orchard in clouds of blossom, the scent, the shiny globes, deep red to black, hanging amongst the green leaves, the fun when the pickers came in, backpackers from all over the world… All gone, bulldozed for housing, and they'd never thought to consult her?

Jack went inside, and the dogs came bounding out, two cross border collies by the look of them, with blue eyes. She ignored them, as, quietly fuming, she helped her father along the veranda.

'See the tomatoes, girl? There, on the bench.'

'Sure,' pulling herself together.

In tubs between the veranda posts, they were hanging with fruit. Between was a riot of pot plants, fuchsias, carnations, succulents.

'All I can manage now, with Jack's help.'

'Nice, Dad.'

They walked through open doors into the dark dining room, dominated by a blackwood dresser with glass doors. An old leather sofa slumped, its back to an empty fireplace. The long dining table was jumbled with tools, old-fashioned scales, bits of wood, sandpaper sheets, a hand sander, electrical wiring and wall plates, electrical boards, dismantled motors, collections of nuts and bolts and nails in jars.

'Bit of a workshop,' Jack said, looking down at his hands.

'I'll say. Where do you eat?'

'Kitchen bench, it's easiest,' nodding towards his father.

'Oh?' The dogs bounded about her, barking, 'Girls!' She stooped to ruffle them.

'Get down,' her father growled at them.

'Where's your case, Annie?' Jack asked.

'Outside the front door.'

In the kitchen, the dogs jumped onto a low bench where their beds were laid out, and threw themselves down, panting and watching, tongues hanging, eyes bright. Sun fell through the bay window. The benches were clean, the washing up was done, the newspaper was laid open on the bench top at the sports page. The gas stove sat by the old wood stove, both set into the red-brick chimney rising to the ceiling of celery pine boards. The dresser was higgledy-piggledy with the plates, cups and saucers her mother had loved. The slate floor was worn but clean, there was a basket of clean washing, sheets and towels folded. In this room at least there was order.

'Someone comes in to help out, Dad?'

'Marlene, once a week. Jack keeps it up. Give him a break, you being here.'

'Right…' How short a break she kept to herself, because she hadn't decided. 'Is he okay with you, Dad?'

'Can't complain.'

She wondered what that meant.

Jack came in, wheeling the case. 'You're in your old room?'

'Suppose, Jack.' She felt a twinge of panic, because she would've broken her neck to get out of this place when she left school. She'd had to stick it out while she finished law. Four more years listening in her room to the scrapping, the disagreements, the tension. Now she was back, staying for the first time since their mother had died of cancer, three years before. She'd come back for her mother's funeral, of course, stayed a few days in a hotel in town, then headed back to Sydney. Work was her excuse then. And now what excuse to get away?

Jack filled the jug while she got her father seated in a wicker chair with broken cane. 'He likes the good armchair,' indicating with his head while getting cups from a cupboard.

'I'm all right,' the old man said. 'Stop fussin'.'

'How long're you stayin'?' Jack looked over.

'I've got the hire car for a week.'

'Take it back. You can use the Toyota.'

He hadn't got the message.

'Thanks, but no need.' Leaving it at that.

Jack flung tea bags into the cups and poured boiling water onto them. 'Sugar? Milk?'

'I have it straight.'

He handed her a cup without a saucer, and one to his father, taking a tray over to him. 'Biscuit?' He placed a couple of biscuits on a plate and offered them to her.

'Where's the Anzacs?' Her father was suddenly querulous.

Annie started. Oh no, not that tone.

Jack guffawed. 'No biscuits for you. And it isn't Anzac Day. It's Australia Day and that's tomorrow.'

'Australia Day, who for?' Chuckling, but an anti-immigrant rant was coming, Annie saw, and at the same time Jack gave her a warning look.

'How's business, Annie?' Her brother cut in.

'Oh, you know. Busy.' Telling him nothing about the break-up, the finances, the loss of the business. You can't fight a lawyer, especially a QC who has a new younger partner in life, especially when you've failed to establish a family line, as he put it so charmingly, when it was him who wouldn't countenance IVF as a good Catholic, a key fact she'd overlooked when she'd married him. And so her mind ran on, as Jack's eyes were rested on her, and she knew he guessed, as he always had. But she guessed his ancient grudge still held, that she'd got away to the bigger world of the mainland, and he hadn't. So much for that.

'Drinks at the RSL, later,' he muttered, giving the old man a quick look.

So her brother had turned into a bogan? 'I'll give it a miss, bit tired from the flight,' she said.

'Not an offer,' Jack retorted. 'You gotta be here, do Dad's legs, toilet him, get him to bed,' giving her a grim smile.

She stared at him, then she looked out of the window. She still had the hire car. Head back to the airport and grab the next plane available. The plane back to what? The friends she'd lost because a Queen's Counsel has more pull than her, in Sydney's social circles? The house she'd lost, auctioned away? And the rest? She looked back at Jack.

'I'll give you a hand,' he said quickly.

'Thanks,' said without irony.

And here they were, she and her younger brother staring each other out, both caught in the trap of the past and desperate to free themselves. But hadn't Jack freed himself, by getting rid of the cherry orchard?

'Okay.' She would concede for now, a strategic retreat, but that was all. She finished her tea, set down the cup, took her case by the handle and trundled out and down the hall to her old room.

Annie pushed open the door. It was bare, musty, a single bed hugged the far wall. Curtains stretched dusty lace across the window, a blowfly buzzed and tangled in it. She pushed open the window, pressing it against branches and a vine creeping in over the window ledge, felt a sneeze rising, and when it came, it shook her. She fell onto the bed and lay there. The room was not far enough away from the living area to dull the sound of her parents' fights. Had they ended when her mother had sickened with cancer? She didn't know. So much she didn't know. If she stayed, what was she going to live on? She'd have to get a job, which meant she needed Jack to keep on doing the caring, did he realise that? Would this spoil his plans, if he really wanted to break free? Problems buzzing around like the blowfly caught in web, and she dozed.

Evening, and Jack was at her door. 'Annie?'

'Oh, Jack,' she sat up. 'Look, Jack. I'm here for the week, that's it.'

'A week! I've been here for fuckin' years!'

'You could've left, why didn't you?'

'We had the orchard to run, stupid.'

'Which you've sold.'

'Why did you come back anyway?'

'You know,' lamely.

He sat by her. She shifted her legs and the bed creaked.

'You in trouble, Annie?'

'No!'

'Spit it out.'

'You know…' Defensively. 'What happened to the money?'

'What money?'

'You got when you sold the orchard.'

He jumped up. 'That's what's brought you back, the fuckin' money? What the hell do you think we're livin' on? Dad's pension? You take the cake, always have.'

'Jack, calm down. I just want to know how things are.'

He looked back from the doorway, and he was her brother again, curly black hair tinged with grey now, bright eyes bloodshot, sturdy frame overweight, and she felt sorry.

'Come on. Dad needs lookin' at.'

She got up and followed him back to the kitchen. Her father was sitting in his armchair. Diabetes, his bare legs were red and blotched.

Jack went to the bench, took a tube. 'Okay, Dad.' He rubbed in the cream, his hand smoothing the rough skin as the old man groaned.

She looked away.

'Raw honey, thinkin' of trying that on his legs, hey, Dad?'

'Talk rubbish. Attract the bees.' The old man snorted.

'He has to get out in the fresh air, get the sun.'

'I know that,' Jack's resigned tone, and she was sorry once more.

'Toileting.' Jack helped his father up. 'Wears a nappy,' he murmured. ''S all right, I'll do it.' He steered him through to the bathroom.

Annie followed and stood outside, listening to the murmured words as Jack changed his father and got him into his pyjamas. They came out of the bathroom, soap-scented steam puffing with them, Jack helping the old man, clean and neat in pyjamas and dressing gown, shuffling in his slippers. She followed them back to the kitchen.

'Pills, Dad. Blood sugar test.'

Watching, Annie was amazed. Her brother was so tender with this man who'd always given him a hard time. She wondered for the first time how his life would've been, if he'd left the orchard. But he'd always loved it, hadn't he? This life had been his life, and it had gone now.

'Kath'll come by with his dinner. You want a bite to eat?'

'No, not for me, Jack.'

'She'll have enough for you, change your mind.'

The old man made a lurch for his armchair.

'Hold on, Dad. Just get you into it.' Jack settled him down, straightened his legs, pulled on cotton socks and rested his feet on a leather pouf. 'Here's the remote. He likes to watch the sport.'

'I remember,' Annie said.

'Whisky ready?' Her father gave Annie a cheeky grin. 'Join me in a snifter?'

'Not my drink,' she laughed.

'After your medication, Dad. It's his reward,' Jack murmured as he handed the old man a glass of water and the pills to swallow, then took up a lancet, lifted his hand and pricked his finger with it. He read the result. 'Blood sugar's okay. If he needs a sugar hit, jelly beans are in the jar.' He nodded towards the kitchen shelf. 'But he won't.' He went to the dresser in the living room and took out a crystal whisky glass, and a bottle of Glenfiddich. 'Like a drink?' he waved the bottle.

'No, no. Tastes like medicine to me.'

'It's my medicine, girlie.'

Girlie. 'Dad, don't call me that.' She always hated the word.

Jack over at the sink, laughed. 'He knows how to press your buttons, don't you, Dad?'

'No water, Jack. I've told you before,' the old man croaked.

'Okay, don't lose it.' He handed his father the glass.

He tilted it and sipped.

Annie pulled up a chair and sat by her father.

'You'll be okay, Annie. Just get him to bed.'

'Okay.'

Jack left, the door banging. She heard a car start up and leave. There was silence, apart from the dogs panting.

'You still doin' all right up there in Sydney?'

'Yes, Dad.'

'Bronte Beach, isn't it?' His eyes were sharp, set deep in his wrinkled face.

'Yes, Bronte Beach.' How could she tell him it was sold?

'The QC, how is he?'

'Oh, you know.'

'Other investments doin' okay?'

She shrugged, turning away.

Silence, then, 'Any port in a storm, eh girl?'

'Port?'

'You want port? In the dresser. Got some fine old stuff there.'

She got up, wanting to get clear of his knowing eyes, and went to the dresser. She found the bottle of Mateus, managed to unscrew the top and poured the ruby liquid into a crystal glass, held it up and it caught the light. She went back into the kitchen and sat by her father. He'd turned on the television and was watching the footy. She watched too, sipping the port, the liquid warming her.

'You're like your mother, Annie.'

She nodded.

'You go for it.'

She tensed, knowing what was coming.

'Things fall apart, just get up and dust yourself off.'

Was that all he was going to say? She glanced at him.

'You're welcome here, always, you know that.'

'Dad, I'm here for a week, is all.'

'That's what your mother said. She stayed forty year.'

Annie was silent.

'Miss her, Annie. I miss my Sal.'

'Dad?' She took his hand.

'I know we had our fallin's out, I'm sorry for that…'

'Oh, Dad…'

'We loved each other,' he beseeched her.

She let go his hand and gulped her port. Why hadn't they let that love guide their lives? Did he think of her and Jack, during their arguments? At least she and Max hadn't argued. The end was the end, coming when Magenta had appeared on the scene. What a name, sounded like a poison. Max and Magenta! She tipped back the port. Good luck to them.

'Annie? I'm on the way to joinin' her.'

'What, Dad?

'Long Point, t'other side.'

What was he saying? She shifted closer, took his other hand. Long Point was the far end of the bay.

'We always said, one day, when it's all over, we'll meet at Long Point. Sal and me, where we first met, the old picnic spot…' His voice was frantic.

'Dad, calm down. I'm here, Jack's here…' Trembling at the passion in his voice.

He waved his glass. 'Just a snifter more, eh?' Gazed at her, and he was back to his old self.

She took up the whisky bottle and poured a finger, the tawny liquid splashing.

'Jack. He's done good. Give him that.' He eyed her. 'He needs a man's job. I'm nothing but a weight around his neck.'

'What does he want to do?'

'Nuthin' here.'

What could he do, when he had his father to care for? She felt such shame. There was a knock on the kitchen door, the dogs jumped off their bench, barked and swirled as a woman came in, carrying a dish wrapped in a tea towel. She had tight white curls and wore a pink jump-suit and ugg boots.

Annie jumped up. 'Hi…'

'You're Annie? I'm Kath. Here's your dad's vegetable casserole. Still warm. He doesn't like it too hot. Plenty for you, too.'

'Oh, thank you. You'll stay?'

'No, no. Hello, John, you're okay?' Speaking as she got a plate from the dresser, wiped it and dished the casserole onto it, carrot and pumpkin with mashed potato and gravy.

The smells rose, and the dogs whirled around, frantic.

She plonked the plate of food onto a tray and took it over to John. 'Here you go.' She had a napkin round his neck and a spoon in his hand in no time. 'You've fed Poppy and Smut? I'll do that, don't you worry.' A whirlwind of energy, she was spilling dried food into their bowls for the dogs, splashing water into a bucket. 'You right to get the old fella to bed?'

Annie looked uncertain, and then felt awkward. Couldn't she do anything for her father? 'Sure. We're fine.'

'My phone number is on the list on the fridge. Give me a call if you have any trouble.'

'Thank you, Kath.'

'Bye!' And she was gone.

After John had eaten his dinner, Annie cleared away his plate and his napkin.

'There you go. She's nice, Kath,' but he wasn't talking. 'I'll just rinse a few things in the sink.'

There was no dishwasher, so she washed the plate and cups and knife and fork and wiped them dry. Next time she looked at her father, he was dozing. The television was still going, but as she bent to put things away, she heard a sudden gulping groan and a glass clattering to the floor.

'Dad!' She dashed over to him. 'You okay? Dad…'

He started awake.

'Let's get you to bed.'

He was uncomplaining as she helped him out of the chair and led him down the hall to the bedroom.

'Here we go.' She turned back the coverlet and steered him into bed, lifting his legs in.

His head flopped onto the pillow, she tucked the sheet around his neck, and he was already snoring.

Back in the kitchen, Annie sat around, thought of watching the news, instead decided on a shower. In the bathroom, she stripped and got in under the hot stream, thinking over her father's words. Was he foreseeing his death? Is that what happened, with old age? A vision of her mother, busy, smiling came to her and, missing her, Annie let the water flow over her face to wash away the sadness.

Getting out of the shower, she caught sight of herself in the mirror. Thin, gaunt almost, breasts slack, what a sight! The same curly black hair as Jack, same dark eyes but it was as though she was just a receptacle that her old self had poured out of and drained away. With it her desire, for sex, for passion and for life? She grimaced as she rubbed her hair, dried her body and put on her nightgown. No sound, just darkness, a distant dog barking, now and then a car passing.

Thinking that she might have to get up to her father, she went to bed early. Patting the dogs, she murmured, 'Goodnight, good girls,' and went through to her bedroom, pausing at her father's door. No sound, not even snoring, just his presence. In her room, she left on the night light, opened the window, made sure the fly wire was tight, got into bed and fell asleep.

Annie awoke to darkness. A door had banged and she raised herself, her heart thumping. She reached for the lamp switch, it clicked on and off, the power was off. Easing out of bed, her eyes wide, she felt her way out of the room and down the passage. A light was glimmering in the kitchen. She stood at the door. The dogs saw her, their eyes catching the light, and their tails thumped. She walked over to the sink and turned on the tap, holding a glass under it.

'Hi, sis.'

She turned, the glass in her hand. Jack was lying on the sofa in the dining room. Two lit candles shone on the table.

'Power's off.'

'Maybe a car's collected a pole.' She sat on the sofa, leaning against his legs. 'Woke up. Thought I was back then.'

'Ah, the wunnerful world of back then.' He reached for the glass of whisky by him on the floor, and drank. The teardrop candlelight was reflected in the glass, the dresser and his eyes. 'You okay?'

'I'm fine.' She was silent for a few minutes, then, 'Jack, what really happened?' her voice shook, the candles wavered, the shadows jumped. 'The property.'

'Nuthin' out of the ordinary. We went broke.'

'But why? People still buy cherries, especially our cherries.'

'You seen the size of the outfits in the Derwent Valley, Campania? Massive. Chinese market, fuck, they're even owned by the Chinese. Couldn't compete.'

'So?

'The old bastard had mortgaged the place to the hilt, throwin' money at it. Lucky to keep the house.'

'The paddock?'

'Sold off to Fred next door. I was mowin' it, keepin' down the bracken.'

'Oh, Jack…'

'Got enough to live on with Dad's pension, bit of fallback, about it.'

'What's going to happen?'

'Nuthin'. Not until the old bugger falls off the twig.'

Annie drank from her glass. The house ticked away, a dog groaned. It was Australia Day now, a day of celebration?

'What's your story, Annie?'

She glanced at him as he crunched a pillow under his head.

'Gotta say, whatever, you're lookin' good. Age, what, fifty?'

'No way,' she snapped.

'Forty-nine, it suits you, sis.'

She humphed and grinned.

'C'mon, spit it out. What's happened?'

'I've left Sydney for good.'

'Route complete?'

'Absolutely.'

'Fuckin' bastard, that lawyer.' He drank. 'Tellin' you, I had a gutful of lawyers over this place.'

'Suppose you did.'

'No kids do it?'

'No, no… Would've been worse if I'd had any.' Was that true? Once, she'd longed for a baby with passion. Hard to remember why, now. But her life, herself, back then, she barely recognised.

'Business?'

'Folded. House sold. He fixed it so I got nothing.'

'Your career?'

'Years representing toerags without the wit to organise their own lives.' She sighed. 'I used to sneer at them. I'm no better.'

'You're bloody brilliant, Annie. Don't you let anyone say otherwise.' He looked around the room as if the detractors might be lurking in the shadows. 'So why are you plannin' on goin' back?'

'Got to.'

'Bad move, Annie. Stay here.'

'And do what?'

'Roof over your head, that's what.'

She gave him a look.

'An it's not, I'm not, look… I can manage the old man. No worries.'

'No, honestly, I wasn't thinking that,' though she was.

'I got my life organised.'

'Doing what?' And bit her tongue. She was still sneering at her brother? He ignored that. 'Ag science. Third year.'

'At the uni?'

'Yep.'

'That's great!' And felt absurd delight. 'Doing all right?'

'Dropped out. The old man. Might've ended up workin' for the Chinese!' He chuckled, reached for the whisky bottle and poured himself a finger.

'So unfair. How've you managed, with Dad and all?'

'Kath and Marlene help out. Good sticks. Dad's only been this bad since last July. He ain't too good. He knows it, too.'

'Said something weird to me. About Mum.'

He looked up. 'What?'

'Wants me to take him to Long Point.'

'Down the bay?'

'Yep. Reckoned he and Mum'd always said they'd meet there, when the time came.'

'Yeah? Hard to believe.'

'They really loved each other, hey?'

'Couldn't they have lived in peace with it?'

'I know. Seeing them fight, you get it all wrong, about relationships.'

'That's us, ain't it?' Suddenly bitter.

'That's us.'

'Typical Aussies. Onto a bad thing, stick to it. The old Aussie oy oy oy.'

'Yeah?' Only half listening, resting there in the candlelight, the shadows, in this dark, old place she'd grown up in, breaking her neck to reach the light, only to wilt, her stem weak from going too fast, too far.

'Buncha card sharps'd do better than our pollies for this country.'

'Poker players?'

'Check your hand, what you got there. Korea? Pass. Vietnam? Pass. Iraq? Pass. Afghanistan? Pass. Nuthin' in those wars for us, just a human sacrifice to the great fuckin' power, the US of A, as simple as that. Here, have a few young blokes, that'll keep you on side for when the big bust up comes.'

'They say that up at the Returned Servicemen's League?'

'You bet.'

She lay back on the sofa, arching her body over his legs. Up on the wall was the huge circular saw blade her father's dead sister Maude had painted, the metal surface bright with idealised rural scenes: the little farmer, his wife, cows and sheep, the ducks and chooks, fences, pasture and paddocks. and the farmhouse and stables, just like their own farm, she'd believed, loving it as a girl. Now she would call it kitsch or, at best, folk art. And the reality? So different. Firelight glinted on the jagged teeth of the saw, and she imagined it ripping through the pristine forests, birds and animals screaming. Another dud hand, the environment, another sacrifice to wealth and power. Oy oy oy.

'Who did the cows out the front?'

'Dad. Joke at the RSL: he needs to do a bull, those cows'll go off the milk, get restless.'

She laughed. 'We'll do it, okay? Take Dad out for an Australia Day treat.'

'Sure. Why not?'

'Then I'm going to clear this table of junk!'

Jack jerked upright. 'No way, sis! Everything here's in its place.'

She laughed, stood. 'I'm off to bed.' She took the whisky bottle, replacing it on the bottom shelf of the cabinet.

'Bossing me again. Good you're back, Sis.'

'Yeah. Catch you in the morning.'

Mid-morning, after breakfast, Jack and Annie had driven down to the bay, the folding wheelchair in the car, the dogs too. Now, they stood beside it, their father seated, the dogs circling and tangling in their leads.

'Poppy, Smut…' Jack tried to untangle them.

Annie started the wheelchair. It jammed.

'Now, no bingles, you two.' The old man looked anxious.

'Don't worry, Dad, we're only going along the esplanade.'

'In this contraption?'

'That's right, Dad.' She pushed him along, the wheels squeaking, Jack following with the dogs.

Pines threw shadows across the sand down to the tangling foaming wavelets, and Bruny Island scorched brown was somnolent across the water. A jet ski bounced up North West Bay, trailing an Australian flag from its stern.

There was movement along the shore. Half a dozen people appeared, small dogs, kids running ahead in T-shirts and shorts, wearing hats with little flags on the crowns. The adults lined up the kids, got the little ones to raise their hands, and snapped pictures with their phones. 'Aussie

Aussie Aussie oy oy oy,' rang out and the kids ran away, splashing into the water as their parents walked along, chatting.

'See that, Dad?'

'What's that?'

'Mums and Dads having a good time,' Jack giving Annie a sly grin.

Family, in Australia. This was her place, Annie knew now, to make her own.

'Take the dogs.' Jack handed her the leads, took the handles of the wheelchair and powered the old man along.

Annie chased after him, the dogs barking, the sun shining, and Jack turned back and grinned as they wheeled their father along the esplanade towards Long Point. To where the concrete ended and the headland fell into a jumble of rocks, with pounding waves shattering high into crystalline fragments, like light, like life.

Bullimore and Vandal

The two girls, Sophie and Jan, were bickering as they stood on the side of the road waiting for a lift, their packs at their feet. Well, Jan was bickering, Sophie was easy. Because Sophie, small and blonde, was always easy, while Jan, thin and dark, was all nervous intelligence. The air was scored with the cries of crows, across the road grey companies of sheep stood, and far off were the purple flanks, patchy with cloud shadow, of the Western Tiers, like giant beasts asleep.

'We should've stuck to the Midland Highway, there's more traffic.' Jan said. 'How are we going to get to Campbell Town?'

'This way's beautiful, I so love it.' Sophie sighed.

'Why didn't you tell Keith we need the car to get home?' As if it wasn't obvious, but Jan had found that with people like Keith and Sophie, nothing was obvious.

'He needs to use the car.'

Sophie had met Keith at a forest festival outside of Deloraine three months before. Dancing, vegetarian cook-ups, stalls with forest products, naked splashing in a freezing river, is how she'd described it, enthusiastically, to Jan. They'd driven up to see Keith in his owner-built cabin in the forest, spent the night, uncomfortably for Jan on the sofa, and left the car with him.

'It's all right, you've got your car. What's the problem?'

That was an explanation? Unsaid was that if Keith didn't have a car, he couldn't drive down to see Sophie. And she wanted to see him, but her job in a plant nursery meant she couldn't just drop everything and head north. He, as a matter of principle (capital letters) didn't work, and could drive down anytime to see her, at the house they shared. He'd driven them to Longford in Sophie's car to start hitching down to Hobart. But so far they'd got only one short lift, having taken the back road via Cressy.

Jan and Sophie shared house with three others, close in to Hobart. Krishna and Karuna were orange people, they kept the garden beds full of herbs and vegies. Then there was Mick, an architecture student who'd managed to set fire to his bedroom. But they were fun, and Jan liked living with them all, while she got through university.

Way off up the road a car approached, with it the faint sound of baying dogs. They stared as an old Mini Moke like a matchbook on wheels sped closer, appearing to be driven by dogs.

'We aren't getting in that?' Jan clutched Sophie's arm.

'Cool!' was Sophie's response as the Moke swerved in to the gravel shoulder.

A tiny woman hidden under a broad hat looked up at them, two hounds dribbling at her shoulders. 'You get in, nu?' the woman said.

Jan stepped back as Sophie stepped forward, her hand out to the dogs.

'Sophie!'

'Sensational!' Sophie swinging her pack plopped in the front beside the woman.

Jan pushed into a space next to a dog. 'Where's she's going, Sophie?'

'Campbell Town,' Sophie assured her. 'These your hounds?' she asked the woman. 'What's their names?'

'Bullimore, Vandal,' the woman indicated each.

'Great names.' Laughing, Sophie ducked Vandal's swiping tongue.

Both were lithe with tan hides, brown muzzles and melting brown eyes.

'Excuse me,' Jan asked, 'where are you heading?'

'Lower Fens,' the woman answered, her accent so thick below the sound of the engine Jan thought she said Fence.

Sophie, chatting away, wasn't even listening. This was an adventure, she loved adventures, and off they went, all talk stopped by the wind rushing through the Moke. They careered down the highway, and Jan relaxed, they were on their way. She'd only come with Sophie because

Karuna had made her, otherwise Sophie would be hitching back on her own. Too bad about her study timetable, Jan had grumbled. But Karuna, severe, decisive, was not to be denied, she had Sei Baba on her side.

Suddenly, with a wrench of the steering wheel, the woman turned off onto a dirt road.

'This isn't the way to Campbell Town!' Jan called to Sophie, her voice muffled by the flank of a dog.

'Go with it…'

Sensing they were nearing home, the dogs started up their baying, and a little while later they swerved through iron gates, one stone post of which bore a faded name, Lower and the other Fens. The driveway was overhung with a density of deciduous trees, but after a few minutes it opened out, and they bounced over a causeway, crossing a bulrush-crowded pond. A large house appeared on a rise, a two-storey square of old sandstone, in the centre a round portico two storeys high was supported by sandstone pillars. Black pines, shattered and leaning, were reflected in the windows.

'God!' Jan gasped, and Sophie laughed.

The Moke slowed, spun around an entrance circle and stopped by a curve of steps, gravel crunching. Silence. Then the wind swept through the pines, roaring down and the dogs leapt out.

The woman climbed out and staggered over to the steps. She held out a tiny hand as the girls got out, and waved them after her. 'Come in, it is cold, a hot drink, nu?'

Looking up, her hair flattened to her face by the wind, Jan saw boarded-up windows and broken panes, and felt a sense of foreboding. What was this place? What were they doing here?

They walked after the old lady up the steps to the impressive portico. She pushed open double wooden doors flanked by stained glass side panels with coloured parrots and waratahs amongst gum leaves. A tiled entrance hall with a domed ceiling high up allowed light to flood down, and a wooden staircase with an ornate carved banister tacked upwards.

The hall was lined with books on shelves, but the books had the dusty, self-absorbed look of never being read. Jan thought of the book burnings in the square, under Hitler. These books would burn too, if this place caught fire.

Sophie nudged Jan, and they caught up with the woman as she hobbled through a door on the right. It led into a kitchen with slate floors, worn wooden bench tops and a black many-doored wood burning stove squatting in a chimney alcove.

'Come in. I am Cornelia.'

Jan didn't answer but her friend smiled, 'I'm Sophie.'

They sat at a wooden table with rush-seated chairs at angles, taking up the central space. The dogs drank noisily from two bowls, spraying arcs of drops, then leapt onto an old leather sofa pushed against the wall, and watched, tongues lolling. Two old dressers stacked with china, and knick-knacks took up two walls, and above the sink was the only window, long, square-paned. Jan glimpsed a view of paddocks stretching to grassy hills cut across by a long building like a stables, the brickwork disintegrating at its end.

Cornelia took three glasses from a dresser and plonked them on the table. She took a half-bottle of red wine and poured one glass, almost spilling it, her hands shaky. 'You like wine?'

'No, water please.' Jan was firm. Whatever happened next, they wouldn't be getting drunk.

Cornelia took the glasses and filled them with tap water. 'Water is good. From the tank. Best water.'

'Thank you.' Sophie took a glass and made big eyes at Jan over the rim.

This, Jan could see, was an experience. Who knows when they would get back, but Sophie would regale everyone in the house with it. She winced at the thought.

'You have pain?' Cornelia opposite them, lifted her glass. 'You name?'

'Jan. No, no pain.'

'Wow, this house is so…!' Sophie was prattling on, but Jan wanted to hear what this woman had to say.

Her clothes were odd, but no weirder than Sophie's. She was old, but Jan couldn't imagine her as young.

'How long have you lived here? Is it in your family forever?' Sophie chatted on.

'My family, yes.'

'You came here, from where?' Jan asked.

'Europe, yes. With baby.' Nodding to an old pram in the corner.

It had spoked wheels, a scoop of seat, and a hood of some old material hanging in strips. A tortoiseshell cat lay in it, curled up, its tail twitching annoyance at the noise they were making.

'Oh, wow! Is that all?'

'One suitcase. What more you want? Things. They do not matter.'

Jan knew about ruined cities and people leaving in carts and cars and trucks, whole towns fleeing on foot. So long ago, and Cornelia had been one of them?

'It's like Edward Scissor Hands,' Sophie breathed.

'What are you talking about?' Sophie was too much. 'How are we going to get home?'

But she was away in her fantasy and Cornelia watched her, smiling.

She turned to Jan. 'You must trust. Life can take you anywhere you go,' and reached for Jan's hand.

Jan clenched, trying to withdraw it. She was wary now, of this woman who could guess her thoughts. 'Sophie. Let's go.' Jan stood, the chair scraped backwards. She heard a distant shriek. Birds?

'I haven't finished my water.' Sophie turned her blue eyes on her.

Jan shifted towards the door. A dog slid off the sofa, padded across and leaned against her.

'Bullimore like you,' Cornelia said. 'He does not want you to go.'

'I need the toilet.' Sophie got up.

'Sophie, no wait…'

'Don't worry, I'll find it.' She left the room, Vandal following her.

'In your life, who has spoken kind words?' Pinning Jan in place with the question. Was she a mad woman, was this a madhouse? 'Fond words unsaid, a kind touch speaks.'

Jan sat down, intrigued now. The words, a hidden meaning, what else was hidden in this house?

'Tell me where you from.'

'Nowhere special. Hobart.'

'Ah, the Hobart. A know-nothing town, I think.'

Jan laughed, nervous. What would she think of the area she had grown up in, a workers' suburb north of the city, a place where, Saturday nights a bus collecting the adults, dolled up, took them to the casino where they sat in front of the pokies in the same order as the streets they lived in. A suburb where mothers expected their daughters to have a baby early and live on welfare. She had been such a baby, loved and ignored equally by a mother who was only seventeen years older than her. She had grandparents who lived in a tiny two-storey house squeezed down a back lane edged with showrooms, car yards and depots, and the air smelled of chemicals. She'd spent weekends with them, Nana and Mac, a Friday night dinner of roast chicken, roast potatoes and cauliflower cheese that she loved.

'You a thinker, nu?'

Jan shrugged. Brains had been her escape. They had made her an outsider, at school and in the bare streets of small houses with no trees, burned-out cars in the front yards, discarded mattresses… Was it possible where she'd grown up, to hear a fond word unsaid, a kind touch spoken? Cornelia. Had she once been a poet, an artist, a chef?

'How come you are here?'

'The planes with the bombs. We run, they bomb us in the ditches. My son in the pram, we run into the field.' Cornelia gestured to the old pram in the corner. 'They strafe. My man is dead, my baby I shield…'

'Oh!' A pain pierced Jan's forehead above her left eye, a shard of clarity like glass, and knew that the old woman's life and all she'd understood to be true was shattered by the bombs and had been brought to this old house, kept together with odds and ends, patched and replaced.

'On the ship, me, my son, we come. My next husband, he too gone. And now…'

They sat in silence, and Jan longed now for the shared house, the people, the home she had made for herself. Feared her future might be staring at her, right here.

'We really need to go.' Jan got up again for the door, but Bullimore stood in the way. Jan turned back as Cornelia looked on, amused. What were these dogs? Familiars, guards, people in animal form? How were they to leave, walk back to the highway?

Cornelia slumped back in her chair. 'Why you go?' A peremptory spurt of red wine into her glass.

Jan eased down, tense, and in the silence started to hear, in the lightness of air sounds scratched on a vastness of space and time, a waiting. For what?

'You hear it, now?'

'Something's coming…' She heard the screams, the cries, the fury of war, and jumped up.

Tears were trickling in the furrows of Cornelia's face. Bullimore whined, looked at his mistress and back at Jan.

'You go. No worry about me.'

'You sure you're all right?' Though clearly, she was desolated. She'd wanted to share this, a catharsis?

A dismissive wave of her hand indicated the back door and Jan crept away, the dog padding after her. Outside were sheds attached to the house, broken concrete, doors hanging off, a wire gate held together by a single strand. The pines held the wind as it roared to break free, afternoon shadows trembled on the grass, and it felt like hours had passed, time slipping away like water. Across the way were the old stone buildings.

'Sophie!' Jan called, the sound torn away by escaping gusts.

She walked across the grass to the stables and looked inside. A long room with stalls for the horses, dusty, straw strewn. Motes hung in the air, blowflies buzzed. Fatigue overcame her and she found hay bales stacked against the wall, and rested on them. Bullimore curled up with her and drowsily, she heard her mother's voice calling her to come in for tea and cake. But her mother never made tea or cake; she'd buy a sponge and bottle of Fanta and plop them down on the old laminex table telling her not to spill it, kind, anxious, and a painful ache took over Jan. She had despised her mother for her showy hairstyles, cheap tights and tops stretched over her bulging body, her coarse voice. Hadn't she, somehow, been born into the wrong family? It meant that university had been hard, an act of mimicry as she copied the talk, more, obsessions of those around her, but so exhausting, as exhausting as she felt now, and Bullimore whined, looking up with his melting eyes, and licked her hand. It was easier in the shared house, a retreat where she could be herself. Well, her reconstructed self, her new image as a top student bound for a life in academia.

Sophie, where was Sophie? Jan got up and went across the grass to the house, Bullimore pushing at a door, and she followed him inside, through to the hall, and stood under the skylight with light flooding down, looking this way and that. There were the stairs, and she dashed up them to the gallery and saw five doors.

Jan went into the room on the left. The window was broken, glass lay on the boards, but as she listened the air filled with the tinkle of music, of frosty forests hung with snow and frozen waterfalls shattering, a vision of the Europe these forebears had left behind? Could she get lost in this other time and space?

'Sophie, where are you!'

At once the vision dissolved and she was in a bare room with a broken window. She backed out and, across the way, was another door. What was behind that? A vision of this place as it was before Europeans had arrived, the local people's country, its wildlife, rivers and forests? And what else, hunting parties massacring them? Jan darted into the room opposite the stairs, a dimly lit hexagonal room set with chairs and small tables for afternoon tea or card games, and a tall cabinet of glasses, a black chandelier hanging like a huge spider on a thread. Piano music sounded, calm and plangent in the deepening afternoon from somewhere and she tiptoed across to a window. She forced it up and leaned out, the wind lifted her hair, and she saw orchards and pasture to the foot of the hills. Just below the window was a tree, huge, very old, its trunk and cracked branches black and blotched with pale lichen, the fronds of its leaves thin. She started, glimpsing through the twigs a shimmer of silk, a scrim of scarf drifting in the air.

Sophie? That was her scarf! Jan jerked back from the window, her hand to her mouth. Who else was here in this house? What unknown tragedies were layered here? She didn't want to know! At once, the sound of a vehicle arriving, a truck or a four-wheel drive and Bullimore started and loped to the door, looked back quizzically, padding away as a door slammed downstairs. Jan left the room, going back down the stairs, down into the hall. The front door was closed, and she eased open the kitchen door.

Cornelia was still at the table, looking weary, the bottle empty. She looked up. 'Always something it happens.'

Sophie came in.

'Sophie! Oh god, I thought…'

Her silk scarf was loosely tied around her neck, and Jan smiled, realising how much she liked her friend, and hugged her.

'Jan…' Sophie held her at arm's length, laughing. 'I've been playing pool.'

'Who with?'

'Oh, I don't know, some locals?'

Two men had come in after her.

'This is Seb, and this is Marco.'

'Oh, hi…'

Each grunted and looked away, broad faces stern. They were dark, heavy, heavy-browed, alike in stained shorts and T-shirts, worker's boots and socks above which brown calves swelled. Jan saw how the dogs' names – Bullimore and Vandal – actually suited the men. And where were the dogs?

'Believe you're needin' a ride to the city?' Seb said.

Both looked at her, brown eyes intent.

'Oh yes, if you're going, thanks,' Jan smiled at Sophie. Thank goodness. She longed to get away from here.

Marco spoke. 'We'll be headin' off, Gran. Get the kangaroo down to Jake's.'

'Is fine, I am tickety boo.' Cornelia waved a tiny hand.

'You're hunters?' Sophie asked, aghast.

'Nah,' Seb chuckled. 'Picked up a coupla carcasses from a mate dropped 'em this mornin'. Bringin' 'em down for his brother.'

'Take you girls right to the door,' Marco said.

'Terrific. Thank you for your hospitality.' Sophie now full of incongruous charm.

'You ever have tea here?' Jan asked suddenly. 'Tea and cake?'

'You want tea, now? You are going, nu?'

'We'll stop for a coffee in Campbell Town, Jan. It's getting late.'

'No, it's fine.' Jan had her answer. 'Thank you, Cornelia.'

'Cornelia!' Seb snorted. 'You been puttin' it on again, Gran?'

'Don't believe a word she says, the old ratbag,' and Jan watched as Marco bent to fondly touch her shoulder, a tail wagging.

His tail wagging! Why had that come into her head! Again, where were the dogs?

'Nice meeting you,' Sophie cooed.

Seb ushered them out to the jeep parked outside in the drive, opened the doors and Marco got into the passenger seat.

With relief, Jan got in, buckled her seat belt and, as they as drove away, the old house receded, finally disappearing into shadow under the old, shattered pines.

By the time they got back to the house, it was late. The jeep parked under a street light, and as the girls were getting out, Seb glanced at them.

'Thanks for spendin' time with Gran.'

'Lovely old lady,' Sophie smiled.

'She came here from Europe?' Jan asked quickly.

'Yeah, Holland. She's a survivor all right, met our Grandad here. Don't take her stories for real, know what I mean? Alzheimers.'

'Old-timers,' Marco added.

Jan didn't believe them. Nothing was as it seemed in that place.

'Anytime you're up our way, call in, hey, Sophie!'

Sophie laughed again, 'Sure, guys! Thanks for the ride!'

But Jan knew she wouldn't be going to Lower Fens any time soon, and she climbed out of the jeep.

'Hey, like some kanga patties?'

Sophie and Jan stood on the pavement, unsure. Quick as a flash, Seb was out and round to the back.

''S goin' on?' Mick came out of the house as Seb hauled out a dead kangaroo, skinning it on the spot. Wolfishly.

'Don't you worry about the skin and the lights, put 'em in a bin, local dogs'll get 'em.' He handed the carcass to Jan in a sack.

'Great idea,' Mick smirked.

Sophie shrugged a horrified look at Jan, who looked up and down the neat, orderly street, imagining the scene.

'Stick the carcass on the Hill's hoist. Give it a whirl, drain the blood, be right for tomorrow.'

'Will do. Thanks a lot, mate,' Mick taking the sack as Seb climbed back into the jeep.

'Thanks for the lift,' Jan called, and they sped off with a toot of the horn.

'The orange people will love this,' Mick said. 'Rampant vegetarians.'

Sophie laughed. 'Had an amazing time, didn't we, Jan? This great house, this awesome old lady, and these dogs, Bullimore and Vandal, they adopted us, didn't they, Jan?'

They certainly did, Jan thought. But what did it mean? Strands of the past fraying in the wind, events repeating down history, dogs turning into humans… Sophie clearly had not seen what she had seen.

They went inside and Jan went upstairs to her room. She sat on her bed, the racket downstairs rising, the laughter, Sophie's raised voice. Jan knew what she'd experienced and felt a cold shiver of fear, uncertainty about everything, what was real, what wasn't?

She took out her mobile and tapped. Waited. 'Mum? It's me.' She listened. 'Goin' good?' Listened. Her mother was talking non-stop. 'Chantelle's coming over, to do what? Hair colouring? What're you goin' for, Mum? Pink and purple, wild! How is Chantelle... Another baby! Sure she loves 'em, but Mum...' She listened. 'Better let you get on with it, hey? Yes, Mum, love you too.' Jan closed the mobile, and lay back on her bed.

Everything had changed but nothing had changed; her mother was as ever. Nana and Mac? They'd be watching television, drinking hot cocoa before toddling off to bed. What had happened at Lower Fens, somehow, Cornelia and the dogs, were a drift, a lag, slippage of past from present, audio from visual, smell and senses, and it would become a story she would tell, about the time she and Sophie hitched down from Longford, and found Cornelia and Bullimore and Vandal. An experience whose colour and warmth were immediately snuffed out by a presentiment as cold and dark as the night.

Jan leapt off the bed, and bounded downstairs. 'Sophie!'

She turned a pink, laughing face. 'Mick's found an old meat grinder. Tomorrow we'll be eating kangaroo patties.'

'But Sophie?'

'What?'

'I, just, look...' but what could she say? You're going to die soon? She didn't even know that. Any more than that, in the interim, they were going to do and experience amazing things in this world.

'Thank you for coming with me, Jan! What an adventure!' Sophie hugged Jan and Jan hugged her back, her dear friend.

It was all she could do.

Falling up

Shena is sitting high up in her friend Hennie's house that Hennie's dad is building. She'd gone to find Hennie, banging on the door of the shack they live in, and the shack shook and groaned and said it was empty. So she'd climbed up into the house being built beside the shack, to read while she waited for Hennie to come home. The timber is rough on her legs, and she hitches up her shorts so they don't tear on nails, bending her plimsolled feet as she climbs up window frames and wall frames to the roofline. Her back against the brick chimney, she can see everything and no one can see her. It's like when she's reading *Alice in Wonderland*, she sinks into the book and no one knows where she is, even though they can see her, sitting right there in her mum's favourite armchair by the wood stove.

From here, the houses, shacks, old buses and caravans on their blocks of land are glazed yellow from the afternoon sun sliding down towards Mount Wellington like an egg in a pan. She sees tiny movements, far off a dog behind their house rolling in the dirt, that's Laddie, who isn't their dog, he's a stray they feed. Their dog is Rona, and she's limping down to the main road, which means the bus is coming soon. Mum is on the bus, and Rona always comes to meet her, knowing with her doggie sense what bus she will be getting off. Everyone will be coming home on this bus or the next bus from school, from shopping, from work.

Shena's at home on her own, because she has a bad chest and needs a day off from school. Mum thinks she's in bed, getting better. She holds her hand over her mouth as she coughs, but she doesn't feel sick at all. It's quiet, birds twittering, a warm breeze, it lifts her long hair. Mum wants to cut it with her sewing scissors, saying a young lady has neat hair but Shena screams, hanging onto her head, she doesn't want to be a young lady.

Sounds. Cars are passing, just one or two on the main road to the Signal Station at the top, where it ends.

Up here in the house, so airy and sunny, she feels like the Cheshire Cat from Alice because no one can see her, and she can see everyone, so small like toys. People go to work, kids to school, mums stay at home or go shopping. But she isn't at school, some mums aren't at home, some men don't go to work, and this is where the stories are, and she loves the stories.

Across the main road, Mr Schwarz, who always stays at home, comes out of his house and stands on the front step. He's tall and thin and his pyjamas are flappy; he wears them all the time. His two kids are Rebecca and Lizzie, and Shena gets around with them sometimes. They go to a Catholic school, she goes to a state school. Next year, she goes to high school, but after that, what? She can't see to high school, and what that will be like, even though her two brothers are there, but they are boys and boys are different. To her, it's a fog as thick as the Jerry that rolls down the river in winter. They are so high up here, it's sunny and they look down on the rolling white billows, but at school it's grey and damp, hands freezing, legs too, chilblains. Then, by midday it's a lovely sunny day and she eats her lunch with Hennie, leaning against a warm brick wall in the playground.

Lizzie and Rebecca's mother has disappeared, and it's not because she hasn't come back from shopping. She's in their house only sometimes, and it isn't homey, not like their place. She doesn't cook nice puddings and cakes, like her mum. Hennie's mum too, she cooks Dutch cakes called olleybollens. Mrs Jones down the main road, she sells cut flowers and makes a delicious butter and current cake that she hands out in slabs. These local women, Mum says, make lovely things, you should see their crocheting, and Mum knits all the harder clackety clack, jumpers for them the boys don't like. But not Mrs Schwartz. Shena heard her dad say to her mum that he'd seen her on the steps of the post office in town, waiting. What, for a letter? They have got their own post office. Pearl and Ruby are the postmistresses, two old ladies from England, the West Country, with slow rolling West Country voices. They are sisters, and she always has a chat with them when she goes to get the mail. It takes six weeks to come from England but only twenty minutes for her to run to the post office and back and, breathless, give the letters to her mother because she longs for the letters from Home. Maybe Mrs Schwartz too is longing for news from Home as she waits on the post office steps.

Mr Schwartz walks down his front steps. Oh, this is interesting. His steps are wobbly, because he is old with a shock of white hair, almost too old to be a dad, more like a granddad. He crosses the road and heads down the track to an old bus parked amongst a few stringy barks where Matt lives on his own. Everyone is building, the noise of banging and hammering goes on all the time, but not Matt. She wonders, why not? He doesn't work, either. Next to Matt is the Miraldos' place. Mick Miraldo did the plastering on their new house and Dad did his brick foundations and chimney, as he built this chimney too for Hennie's dad. Dad has almost finished their own house and they will be moving in, which is good because they are so squeezed up in the shack.

Shena heard her mum and dad talking after Mr Schwartz called on them. He's getting people to help the family who are renting a shack next to Matt. It needs fixing up for the family living there, everyone should help with materials to make it weatherproof. Why is Mr Schwartz helping them, she asks her mum. Because he knows when people need help, she says. How does he know? No answer. Next, her dad and Hennie's dad and Mick Miraldo and Mr Schwartz will hammer new boards on the roof and walls to keep the people renting it dry and warm and safe.

Shena heard her mum say these people are from the islands, down for a child who's in the hospital in town. They are Tasmanian Aborigines, even though at school they said there aren't any. They are real, she's seen them; there's a mum, and two kids go to school, so why say they aren't? How can you be and not be at the same time? Is it like the Cheshire Cat?

They are here for a few months, then they are going back to the islands, Mum says. She knows because she talks to everyone on the bus, and their mum told her. Shena wants to know what islands, but no one in the family knows. Not her brother Geoff, nor her brother Ian, but her brother Doug says he thinks up north and Geoff tells him not to be a know-all. Geoff has a job, so he is the boss of them. Ian is finishing school. They've only been in Tasmania for four years, they don't know everything about this place, but they love it.

Mick Miraldo brought them half a deer he had hunted on the Central Plateau. Where's that she asked her brothers. Middle of Tassie, Doug said. Dad hung the deer and it got maggoty and then he cleaned it off and cooked it. That's what you do, Dad said, on the grand manors of the aristocracy. The what! Geoff said. Lord Dad. And he and the boys laughed. Mum was disgusted, but they all had a slice when it was cooked. Shena had some too; it was delicious.

Shena looks into the house below her, trying to work out what will be Hennie's bedroom, her sisters' bedrooms and what will be the kitchen and the living room, but it's too open still. It needs to be closed in with walls and a roof and floors, but Hennie's dad, Mr Kyma, is slower than her dad. Their house is brick with three bedrooms, one each for her and Doug, a loft Ian has bagged, and Geoff is leaving home anyway. Mr Kyma's house is weatherboard and Hennie and her three sisters are so excited. She's excited too and sings out, We've got a new house! I've got my own bedroom! With my own door! In the shack, her bed is in a little space behind her mum and dad's bedroom, with only a curtain. That's why she wants a door, and a window and white painted walls and a white painted ceiling.

They will have water put on, too, when they move into their new house. Nutty Denholm delivers water to their tank with his water cart, water sloshing over its sides. The boys run along with him and help with the hose. It's exciting getting water like that, but better when it's inside the house, along with the toilet and bathroom. Right now, they are in a shed outside the shack and it's awful. Dad and the boys take turns to bury the dunny can down the end of their half-acre block. So everyone does that? Shena looks over the scene, the shacks and old buses and caravans and half-finished houses, and imagines at night all these men sneaking out in the dark and digging a hole for the dunny can.

Shena stands against the chimney and cranes her neck, trying to see to the Top, to the Signal Station where Mr Blott, the Signal Station master, flings out flags to guide the boats sailing from Storm Bay, dodging around Bruny Island and into the port, where the apple boats come in late summer and autumn and the trucks loaded with boxes of apples from the Huon line right up Davey Street in the city. Every year they get a lovely case of apples wrapped in tissue, given to them by the people her mother cleans for, the Peacocks. Mrs Peacock isn't well enough to do her housework so Mum helps her one day a week. She's always home in time to get the dinner on the table for the boys and her dad, who is a brickie, and worn out when he comes home. Mum does everything else, baking on a Sunday, two dozen cupcakes, a date loaf, a fruit cake and a sponge and they have slices in their lunch all week. She always has a cupcake, still warm and dripping with icing for her friend Hennie, and any of the local kids, the Warnes and the Learys, who creep out of the shanties and farmhouses like shy bush animals, though they aren't shy when they go possum shooting at night and she hears the guns pop off.

The bus lumbers up the main road, and stops at the bus stop. Her mother gets off and there's Rona, wagging her tail. She limps because she got hit by a car when Doug was out early delivering papers. Mum pats Rona and behind her Mr Burke falls out of the bus, drunk, into a ditch below the road. Rona barks, her mother ignores him, and the people on the bus watch, and then the bus takes off up the main road to the next stop. Shena hopes that Mr Schwartz will see and come to help Mr Burke, but he doesn't notice, he's still talking to Matt. Mr Schwartz won't tell off Mr Burke, because, Shena sees, if it's all right to get around in your pyjamas, it's all right to sleep in a ditch.

Shena's other friends, Pip and Jude, live further up the main road nearer the Top. They have long plaits and wear cowgirl outfits, and their little dog is called Woody. Rona and Laddie are friends with Woody, and when she walks to the Top with Pip and Jude and Hennie, the three dogs come along. Last time, though, Laddie caught the little black cat that lives at the nuns' house, the Little Company of Mary. She doesn't think Laddie killed it – they screamed at him to drop! – but he could have and the nuns were cross. As far as nuns can be cross. Next to the nuns' house are the Poultneys, who live in a shack with a dirt floor. There are lots of Poultneys, they are fierce, and she and Pip and Jude steer clear of them.

They have a favourite tree in the bush, a big white gum all spreading and twisting and they call it the love tree and climb into it. She loves walking through the bush after rain when the leaves and branches are hung with silver droplets that catch the sun and sparkle with rainbows. And she loves the bush animals, the bandicoots and kangaroo rats, the birds, the mountain dragons sunning themselves on warm rocks, their pet blue tongue that lives under the shack with their pet duck that turned up one day and moved in. Winter, the black cockatoos float in mobs above and call, and the wind is so fierce it sounds like a train roaring through the trees and everything in the shack lifts and moves, and she can see the stars through the boards that have stamped on them Queens-bridge Motors, because they are the packing cases cars were once packed in.

The Signal Station is great. The Blotts live there, in a house that comes with the Signal Station, six kids racketing around the bare rooms and verandas. On hot days, they all run down through the bush, shout-ing and careering through the she-oak groves, and over granite boulders to Nutgrove Beach, and have a swim. Sometimes they muck around all day at the beach and walk through the old cemetery, chasing around its broken graves and statues, and they pick cherry plums from the trees at the back of the houses and mulberries from the tree in the big paddock on number one bend (there are seven bends), and faces and hands stained red with juice they walk up the bendy road, all the way back home. Shena sighs loudly thinking about it, such fun. Some nights, she and the boys lie on this road and it's so black and the stars so many and so bright wheeling above – there's Orion, there's the Seven Sisters! it feels like they're falling up into the night sky.

At the Signal Station there is a metal plate with a map showing what you can see, way across the Derwent and all the islands and peninsulas to the Tasman Peninsula. The convicts were chained up there, guarded by a line of fierce dogs and she can almost hear them barking. Dad and Mum are friends with Jude and Pip's mum and dad. Shena heard Dad say to Mr Weatherby once that he didn't realise he'd left England to come to an ex-prison camp, and Mr Weatherby says you can say that about the whole of Australia. Glum. He's always so glum, she hears Mum say to Dad. It's his war injuries. But every Christmas they have a party at the Weatherbys and Mum makes a Christmas cake, and they wear party hats and play musical chairs, and get presents, and hers was a Readers Digest condensed book called *The Magic Mountain* by Thomas Mann and she found it much harder than *Alice*.

Shena's legs start to ache and she eases them off the wooden beam, holding onto another beam, Alice clutched tight in her hand. She watches her mother start down the track, she coughs, feeling dizzy, and she sees her afternoon all over again. Getting out of bed, running down the track to Hennie's, seeing Laddie, Mr Schwarz, Rona, the bus, and time slips and slides away.

They fell down a hole Mum and Dad, Geoff, Ian and Doug and herself when they emigrated, tumbling though darkness into a place that has black swans instead of white, Christmas in summer with a long school holiday and the test on the radio. We are upside down in the Antipodes, Doug says, which means opposite feet in Greek. What's more, in England all their neighbours were English. Here, there's Hennie's family the Kymas, they're Dutch, Roman and Mia are Polish and German, there's a Maltese family, and Mr Schwarz who is Jewish with Rebecca and Lizzie, the Miraldos are Italian, and there are Tasmanians and Tasmanian Aborigines. Shena likes it that there are so many different people. She feels dizzy again, and suddenly she feels wet between her legs. She pushes her hands into her knickers and fingers the wet, looks, and sees blood. She's hurt. Her tummy hurts too. Her mum is walking by, her arms dragged down with shopping bags, Rona limping along with her.

She stops. 'Shena,' she calls, 'what are you doing up there? Come down at once!'

'Mum!' Shena drops the book, its pages fanning open and she goes to grab it and slips, falling and hitting the wooden beams, falling, falling into blackness.

When she wakes up, she is in a white painted room with a door, and a proper ceiling and a window with a curtain, and she sees as she stares around that she has landed in a completely different world.

Hound's Tooth

After the concert, the sisters Ida and Sara decided to have a drink in the bar next to the concert hall. It was smart, sophisticated and Ida, who had driven from Launceston that morning, zipping down the Midland Highway in her little red car, appreciated it. Sara had rung inviting her to go with her to the concert as Simon, her husband, had opted out. Ida needed to get out of Lonnie, Sara stated. As she had many times before, Ida reflected. And then, why not stay the weekend with us? Ida considered the offer. Was Sara lonely now that her two daughters had left home? No, it was Sara being the good sister, yet again. So Ida had given in, headed south suitably dressed in a black evening coat, heeled leather boots, gloves. Now she was tired, so she sipped her gin and tonic and left chat about Brahms's Second Piano Concerto to Sara. She had loved the drama and lyricism of the piece, she said, the brilliance of the Tasmanian orchestra, the superb playing of the young female pianist.

Ida agreed without thinking. Actually, she loved the solitude of books and the garden of her house in West Launceston best. She'd lived there for thirty years now, working at the Launceston Public Library. This was after a period in a fashion chain in Hobart selling dresses she hated, while studying librarianship at night, aching to leave this place, family, friends, after what had happened. Finishing her librarianship studies, she'd moved to Launceston, making it her own, her retreat, her refuge.

The library, the intellectual rigour of categorising each new book according to the Dewey System, the rows of books, each with their special place on the shelves, the smell and feel of books and binding and glue, the satisfied faces of people returning their loans and taking out new ones, she loved it all. In the library's calm and order, she'd progressed, establishing a children's corner, a school holiday program, historical displays, film afternoons, finally the digitisation of the collections.

Ida had first rented, then bought her house from the landlord. It was quaint, the comfortable living room had views over the city, and with just two bedrooms it was quite big enough. Over time, she'd put in a new bathroom, and upgraded the kitchen, and she'd installed a wood stove to defeat Launceston's damp winter days, and a heat pump in the bedroom. And she lived quietly day to day, month to month, and the years passed. Not like Sara, always the busy one, getting honours then a PhD in history, raising a noisy family, and writing local histories which were generally acclaimed and gave her a small income. In other words, she was successful, accomplished, appreciated.

Ida remembered a time when she had been noisy and boisterous and high-achieving like her sister and was destined for a similarly successful life. Until Bruny.

Shaking the ice in her glass, Sara gave Ida a look. 'The Bruny property is up for sale.'

Ida glanced up, then stared into her gin and tonic. She knew what Sara was referring to and wished she wouldn't: the time she'd spent at that property on Bruny Island in the school holidays with the Birchmont family.

'Hadn't it already changed hands?'

'After?' Sara didn't need to say after what, but she tried. 'You know, I mean…'

'Mean what?' Ida was stony.

Sara subsided. Tragedy was the word she couldn't say. Both sipped their drinks.

'I could write up a Bruny Island history,' Sara perked up. 'Cook, Bligh twice, Baudin, Furneaux…'

'It's been done,' Ida snapped.

'A local history. Local characters. Why not?'

Ida smacked down the glass.

Sara recoiled. She followed her as she abruptly shifted off her stool to leave. 'Ida, I didn't mean…' she bleated as she followed her sister out, and down the steps of the hotel.

Mean what, exactly? Ida said to herself.

They stood there, on the hotel steps. The night was mild for late autumn, lights glowing around Constitution Dock and the waterfront, the fishing boats flying their flags raffishly, people walking over from Salamanca Place, where the lights looped on the plane trees glimmered. Off to the west, Mount Wellington loomed against the night sky and Ida glanced at it. How much she missed it, its moods and colours, but she had created her life in Launceston, and there was no changing that.

The car was parked on the wharves opposite.

'Come on!' Sara grabbed Ida's arm, and they dashed across Davey Street ahead of the oncoming traffic.

Ida was sombre as they drove through the quiet city, happy for Sara to talk on and on about the concert. At last, they turned into the driveway of the house, lit cheerfully, got out and went inside.

Simon welcomed them. 'Good concert?'

'Wonderful, wasn't it, Ida? It was well worth coming down to Hobart to catch it.'

Speaking for her again and irritated, Ida shifted away.

Sara noticed and touched her hand. 'Hot chocolate?'

'Nice.'

They had it by the living room fire, and then at last Ida was able to retreat to bed. She pulled the curtain closed to block out the night, put on her nightgown, and got into the warm bed. She crunched the pillow under her head and tried to still her thoughts, but they circled round and round like a dog settling until she drifted into sleep.

Later, much later, she woke from a dream, a voice calling Jenny! Jenny come on! She started upright, staring into the blackness, then lay flat, wide awake. That dream! Triggered by Sara's comment about the Birchmont's house on Bruny Island. For heaven's sake!

Jenny Birchmont had been her best friend at high school. Living so close, just along Meath Avenue, it was easy to go to her house after school and catch a late bus home. Jenny lived with her parents, the father an academic at the university, mother at home, a writer, poetry. To Ida, coming from an ordinary family, her father a builder, and her mother a dress shop assistant, the Birchmonts were exotic. Next, she'd been invited to the family shack at Adventure Bay for the school holidays. Well, shack? It sprawled graciously in a bushy acre of land with its tall trees.

Her stays had been fun and special for her, the big girl in the class, unaccountably favoured by popular Jennifer. But then, that last summer holiday, Rick, an older brother who was studying at university on the mainland, had come back home, and everything had changed. Change, changeling, challenge, the words clanged through Ida's mind as she tossed and turned, eventually dozing off.

Next morning, at breakfast of pancakes and coffee, Sara sprung it on her: why not go down to Bruny instead of heading straight back to Lonnie? Check out the sights, go for a walk. 'I really want to follow up the local history idea.'

'Sara…' Ida was tired and irritable, and with a feeling of foreboding, she looked out of the windows where fog rolled over the streets below, giving the rooftops a slick gleam as if slugs had slithered by in the night.

'Come on, you can help me.'

Simon was eager, too. 'Why not go?' His back to the wood stove, bouncing on his heels, hands in his pockets, his plain face cheerful. 'It's a nice day for a trip,' though it wasn't, to Ida's mind.

She gazed at her sister over the rim of her mug, imagining herself in her little red car speeding up the highway, home to safety, like a beetle up a tree trunk. But, in the face of Sara's bright smile, and Simon's encouragement, she acquiesced.

They left to catch the ten a.m. ferry to Bruny at Kettering, driving carefully, shivering in the car until the warm air kicked in.

'It won't get down the river as far as Bruny,' Sara said of the fog. 'It'll be a sunny day for us.'

The route down the Southern Outlet was fast. Sara drove on, bypassing the southern conurbation of outer Hobart, and reached Margate, a messy stretch of a town, the first town of the Channel.

Through the car windows, Ida viewed the scenery, distant water, green hills luminous in the grey atmosphere, small holdings, their colours muted by the fog. Cruising through Snug, they reached Kettering and drove down Jetty Road.

'Oh, god,' Sara said, speeding up, 'the ferry's already in!'

They joined the queue, of a few cars, a truck and a van that were boarding. With a clatter, Sara drove over the iron ramp and into the ferry's hull, parking where the ferry worker indicated. She wound down her window as he reached her, rummaged in her bag and asked for a return ticket.

'Return trip?' The man stared at her as he tore off her ticket.

'Yes, just for the day.'

The engines were rumbling, shaking the ferry. The entrance gate clanked shut, and a few minutes later, Ida sensed forward movement, the timbers of the jetty sliding past. She got out of her car, climbed the iron steps and walked across to the railing, pulling up the hood of the raincoat Sara had found for her. Ripples ribbed with light fanned across black water, rocking the white yachts at their moorings as they chugged out of the bay.

Sara stood beside her. 'You aren't angry, are you, Ida?'

She shrugged a no. What was the use? Sara was in charge, it was why she was here.

Twenty minutes later, the ferry was close to the island, the engine note changing down as it slowed past Robert's Point. Ida and Sara hurried back down the iron stairs to the car and got in, slamming shut the car door. The ferry came to a stop at the jetty, the gates were opened and the ramp was lowered for the vehicles to leave. Sara drove behind the car in front of her onto land and followed it up a rise, leaving the bay behind.

'The road's good. Get the signage!' Ida exclaimed. 'It never was this smart.'

'Tourism,' Sara said. 'Packed in summer, I believe.'

They drove away, through pasture and forests, following the waters of the Channel on the left, reaching the left turn to Dennes Point where a number of vehicles peeled off. They drove on, heading for South Bruny and Adventure Bay.

The island had changed, not just with the upgraded roads. Shacks had given way to houses, new businesses established. Bruny Island House of Whisky, Bruny Island Cheese, Bruny Island Beer. However, at Great Bay there were still shacks creeping close to the water as if to warm the spirit, as you creep close to a fire to warm your body.

Before reaching the Neck that linked North and South Bruny, Sara pulled over and parked at a place called Bruny Island Honey. 'Hot coffee?'

'Sure.'

They got out and walked across a huge car park, to newly built premises.

'God, tourism's really arrived.' Sara hugged Ida's arm as they walked up the steps.

Inside, they were greeted by a woman behind a stack of colourful honey tins, who told them no, no coffee, they could get coffee at Adventure Bay. Shaking her head, Sara walked out, Ida close behind.

'We needed Bruny Island Coffee,' Ida said.

As they reached the car, Sara stopped. 'Isn't that the track to the Cape across the road?'

Ida glanced over. 'That's it. Let's go.' The bad dream of the night before refluxing, she dived into the car.

'The sign says to Cape Queen Elizabeth,' Sara said as she turned to drive past it.

'And to Hound's Tooth,' Ida muttered.

A few kilometres further on, they reached the Neck linking North and South Bruny, cruising close to the water, dunes rising on their left.

'This is all new,' Sara said. 'Get the view!'

Mist, the last of the Jerry, shrouded bays and headlands north up the estuary to distant Mount Wellington/kunanyi.

'Gorgeous.'

'But where are the man ferns?' Ida said. They had once had crowded the Neck.

'What's that?' Sara slowed. 'Look, a car park? Viewing platform?'

Ida craned. 'It says penguin rookery.' A set of wooden ladders climbed the dunes. 'Whose idea was that?'

They glanced at each other, dismayed.

'The tourists have to have something to do,' Sara said, 'or they won't spend their money.'

Sara drove another twenty kilometres and took the turn left to Adventure Bay. She accelerated up hill, the road winding through tall groups of gums, ragged pines, a few houses. Pastured hills sloped down to the water, and ferns and man ferns crowded in clefts and gullies, looking to Ida like refugees seeking sanctuary from the developers. They drove down into Adventure Bay and slowed, cruising around the neatly landscaped verge lining the beach, the calm waters of the bay shimmering beyond.

Ida checked the beach houses on the right. Again, the shacks had been upgraded, added to, painted, giving the place a smarter tone than its former holiday scruffiness. They crossed the bridge over the Captain Cook Creek, drove past the café and the shop, then the Bligh Museum and continued, Adventure Bay on their left guarded by distant headlands.

'There it is.'

The house was off the road, most of the trees had been cleared, a gravel drive leading into it formed a circle with a palm tree.

'Oh, my god, positively Californian,' Sara said.

'It didn't used to be like that.' Ida couldn't identify with it at all.

Even the roofline was different, a bulky storey having been added. A real estate sign offered for sale a substantial weatherboard home, two living areas, four bedrooms, two bathrooms, and an entertainment area. The acre of land was still attached, running back into the bush.

'It'll go for a million,' Sara said and took out her mobile. 'Read me the contact number.'

'Why?'

'Get a viewing.'

'Sara, put that away, I do not want to go in there!'

'Okay okay… Coffee?'

'Hanging out for it.'

They drove back and turned in at the café. Ida walked across to the verge to sit at a table, brushing moisture off a bench as Sara went inside to order coffees. She looked out across the bay. Far off, there was the headland of Cape Queen Elizabeth, and at its end the abrupt spike of the Hound's Tooth. She got up abruptly and sat with her back to it.

Her first stay at Adventure Bay, Hugh had collected them from the ferry and driven them home in a rackety old Volvo, the family car. Jenny's older brother, he was studying pharmacy, and Ida at once took a liking to him. Jenny's father, Professor Birchmont, was in the front garden, that first visit. A gruff welcome from the tall man in brown corduroys, his shirt loose, a terry-towelling hat pulled low. Mrs Birchmont, grey-haired but gay in a summer dress, was kind, easing her into the household, and Ida felt welcomed. She shared Jenny's bedroom and they stayed awake chatting late, ignoring Mrs Birchmont's admonitions to, now girls, get to sleep, until they did fall asleep, tired out. The next day started off with a noisy breakfast at a table in the sunroom, loud discussions about international politics, and it was exciting to Ida, being part of this family.

'Here you go. Coffee.' Sara was back.

'Thanks.' Ida took the mug from her and prised off the lid. Steam warmed her cheeks.

'Tell me about it,' Sara said. 'When you stayed there in that house.'

'I've told you.'

'Not really.'

'What more? Walks with Hugh. The Captain Cook tree, the Bligh Museum. We went to the Lighthouse, that was an adventure. The road's been fixed up, I guess. Cloudy Bay… Jenny and I just hung out, swimming, sunbaking, walking along this beach. Nothing to add.'

'Hugh's younger brother, when did he show up?'

'The next Christmas. Jenny and I were in B Class, then.' And the holiday changed for her and Jenny. From a girly sharing of hopes and dreams, lots of giggling, obsessing over make-up and body shape to something wilder, more serious.

'What was he like?'

'Slight, sinewy, always on the move, high energy.' Ida was blitzed by his charm and his looks, but she wasn't about to say that.

'How did he fit into the family?'

'His mother's favourite.'

'Is that all?'

'No…definitely a problem.'

It had started immediately. Rick making fun of his father behind his back. Old bastard, he'd mutter, go jump, when his father asked him to do a job. Mrs Birchmont always looked away, never telling Rick to behave. Ida had sensed mute agreement, amusement even, and realised that Professor and Mrs Birchmont might not be the ideal couple they appeared to be.

'Not like Hugh…?' Sara let her question hang.

'No. Hugh was cautious. Rick was a risk-taker.'

'Like how?'

'Diving deep under water, taking the dinghy down the Captain Cook Creek catching eels that he threw at us, lighting fires in the bush.'

'Didn't he go off with his mates?'

'He didn't have mates.'

'Go on,' Sara sipped her coffee.

'He started playing us off against each other, me and Jenny.'

'How?'

Ida thought back to that time. 'Making rude remarks about me, and Jenny would laugh, then jibing at Jenny, she'd almost be in tears. I couldn't cope. Then he told me things. Made me feel special.'

'Like what?'

'He said he needed a pal, would I be his pal?'

'Manipulating.'

'I thought girlfriend, you know?'

'Of course, at that age you would.'

'Things deteriorated between me and Jenny. She couldn't stand him liking me. And the mother… She noticed, I'm absolutely sure. He'd do things, like help put on our shell necklaces we'd made, sort of fondling us both.'

'Sexy, then?'

'Yep.'

One day, lying on the beach in the sun, he'd inched his foot up Ida's leg, up to the edge of her bikini. Did Jenny, lying on the other side, notice? Ida, hugging the sand with embarrassment and desire, didn't even think of Jenny. Then, I need my towel. Jen, go and get it for me. Obediently, the girl had jumped up, run along the beach and crossed the road to the house.

'He leapt on me, on the beach. Saying you want it, you're mine, what're you gonna do for me?'

'Shit! What did you say?'

'Nothing. I said nothing.'

'That's harassment!'

'Yep. Then, payback. Remarks about my weight, what size bikini did I wear, in front of everyone, Sara. And Mrs Birchmont just wafted around.'

'Nasty piece of work.'

'Then Rick said, let's walk to the Hound's Tooth.' Ida turned, and she and Sara looked across the bay. There it was, silhouetted against the sky.

'So?'

'Hugh gave us a lift.'

'Right…'

'On the way, Rick set a challenge: to get across the rocks from one bay to the next before the tide came in. Who'd be first, who last? Hugh said not to if the tide was up, it was dangerous, but Rick pooh-poohed him and we went for it.'

'Was the tide up?'

Ida shook her head. 'No...I can't remember. It's a blur...'

'Let's go take a look on the way back to the ferry. Won't take long.'

Ida gazed at Sara, then away, suppressing panic, but feeling an awful inevitability. Maybe it needed to be done.

Finishing their coffees and tossing the cups into a bin, they got into the car and set off, driving back the way they'd come.

Opposite Bruny Island Honey, Sara drove into the parking area for Cape Queen Elizabeth. The track lay ahead, there was no boom gate across it, and further along were pools of water, muddy tracks.

'Hey,' Sara said, 'let's drive further in, save time.' She started the car forward, easing it along the track.

After a few minutes, it became dryer, firmer, winding through the coastal scrub and she speeded up. After three or so kilometres, the track narrowed to a path, and they got out.

'Where is the beach?'

'Not far.'

They started forward along the path. After ten minutes, they reached a junction. A noticeboard indicated Mars Bluff to the left, Moorina Beach to the right. It also stated access only at low tide.

'Is it low tide?' Sara asked.

'Haven't a clue.'

'Ida... Are you okay?'

Now was the time to ask?

Sara took her sister's arm. 'Come on, I'm with you.'

They came out of the scrub into a landscape of sound and fury, the waves breaking with a roar along the flat shore of the bay. The tide was low, and on their left was the headland. Ida gasped. She'd forgotten the drama of this place, the great tilting headland disintegrating, tumbling down into piles of boulders, a cleft, a great arch over a dark chasm, the stack of the Hound's Tooth.

'That's the Hound's Tooth.'

'Amazing! Where's the other beach?'

'Through the arch.'

Sara headed across the sand, Ida following her, clambering through the cleft, under the huge archway. The rock close up was striated in lines of pitted sediment, grey, black, orange, so coarse to the touch it would tear, had torn, the skin. The roar of the ocean resounded, and Ida panicked, dashing out of the far side, falling onto the sand where rocks were frozen in strata of molten mounds like memories, and she sat there, trembling.

Sara dropped beside her. 'It's so wild,' she said, 'the drama! Just like Brahms's music!'

Ida turned on her sister. Only horror could happen here. 'It's like the Earth is swallowed into the void,' taking all her hopes and dreams, with only a tenuous link keeping her out of it.

'Ida?'

She didn't hear her sister's voice, as she remembered what had happened that day.

Jenny, Jenny come on! The tide! Ida following Rick as he scrambled back through the arch. She slipped, cracking her knee and staggered upright, her lungs aching, and was off again, scrambling as waves pounded. She reached Rick and he grabbed her, pulling her to him, tearing at her shorts, her blouse, his hands on her bare skin, reaching between her legs, pushing against her. She tore away, scratching at him, fighting him.

He taunted her. Come on, bitch! You want it! She shoved him away, her weight a benefit now, and crying, staggered away.

Ida! A thin cry. The roar filling the air, seagulls crying above, Ida scrambled back to the cleft, her hands tearing on the rocks.

Jenny! The streaming wind picked up her words and flung them back, Jenny, Jenny… Where's Jenny! Rick threw himself into the surge. She glimpsed his black head bobbing, then nothing, then he was surfacing in the foam of boiling waters. Hugh was there, rushing into the water, dragging at a body, dragging it out. Hugh had Rick flat, coughing up water, then upright. They started along the beach to the path, the boy half conscious, bleeding from lacerations, blood and water pouring down his chest. Hugh rushed back, disappeared and she waited until he came back, minutes? Hours? Staggering through rising water. Where was Jenny? There was no Jenny.

'It wasn't your fault, Ida,' Sara said. 'None of us blamed you.'

Ida knew those words, said so often, back then. 'But Sara, they did. The parents. He did.'

'He was out of control. They should've seen he was a danger, those people. You were teenagers, coping with him? Dad was so angry. And Mum. It was in the newspapers!'

'I know that, Sara.' She'd been sent straight back home, had had a breakdown, unable to come out of her room or to get out of bed, let alone finish school. It was as if a door had slammed shut on her life. Then awful jobs, a future blotted out.

'You've done so well… Would you ever come back to Hobart?'

Maybe she could have been like her sister, successful, achieving, accepted. Loved by her parents, for she felt she had lost their love. And that of any man. That had been her life so far. She turned on her sister. 'I like Lonnie. I wish you'd just stop!'

'Ida? I'm sorry…'

She stormed off, Sara stumbling after her. She turned. 'Bringing things up. Who do you think you are!' Shot back through the arch and out into the pounding chaos of the shore, skidding to a stop, awed by the massive headland, the drama of its eroded dismemberment.

Sara hurried after her. 'I missed you, Ida, I still miss you.' Linking her fingers with hers.

Ida pulled away. It was why she always came when Sara called. What had happened had deeply hurt Sara, so this whole trip was a catharsis for her? Was that the point? Was it time for her to be the strong one?

Sara followed her up the beach to the path. 'You'll still come down?'

When her sister called? 'Of course I'll come down.' Impatient.

Sara needed her, this supposedly successful, competent woman, Ida knew that, she'd always known it. Now it was out there.

'We should get the two o'clock ferry back,' Sara said and Ida smiled.

Her sister was in charge again, and she anticipated Sara beside her at the rails, the ferry chugging across sunlit waters approaching the far shore.

'Time to get back to Lonnie.' To her place, to the library, to her world.

Together they strode into the coastal scrub, back to the car, and drove away from the fury of Cape Queen Elizabeth, to catch the ferry home.

Jeopardy

Henry stood on the front veranda of his cottage, his backpack at his feet. He was about to leave, to find a way into the wider, sure-footed world beyond this shifting vaporous northern city, though he didn't know quite where. He looked out at the view he knew so well, for the last time. The streets disappearing in low hills muffled in darkness where cloud occluded; the river lost in its search for the coast that did not know its banks, narrowing then widening amongst swamps and wetlands, with here and there a silver sheen; the city that did not know its boundaries, streets and houses that could be inundated, swampland invading offices, supermarkets, garages, car sales yards, depots and warehouses, all subsiding despite dredging and levees and barriers. While in the city park monkeys huddled together, dreaming of heat and humidity and the cacophony of a tropical jungle where they could swing free.

Alice had left him. That morning she'd come into the bedroom and said, Get up, Henry. Get up? He always slept in, weekends. The fence with the banksia rose had fallen down, it needed fixing, she'd said. But he always slept in! Right now. It needs fixing, or the dog will get out. Jep will run away, he'll get lost. Alice! Let me be, go! And she had gone, taking a case stuffed with clothes. Her make-up. Her laptop. And Jep. I'm going to Katie's were her last words. I'm out of here. Doors slammed. Silence in the still house. He lay there anxious, and deep down inside something dislodged from the sediment of his emotions, bubbled up to the surface and burst. Grief. It washed through him with an acid flood to his mouth. He choked, got up to get a glass of water, got dressed and waited. All day he waited for Alice to come back. Realised when she didn't, that he must leave too.

Alice. For years, Henry had watched her as she went about the house, pausing to straighten a place mat, replace a glass in the cupboard, take a cloth and dust a ledge, wipe a spot, rub a smear, doing what was left to do after the cleaning lady had been in. He appreciated her precise movements, her swift glances, her humming, her calm, neat way. And then, work. She was well regarded, bringing in the dosh, paying for restaurant meals, entertainment, art, he knew that. He protected his ego by paying the bills, all the insurances, renovations, but a monthly reconciliation with bank statements confirmed that her wage kept them afloat. Now, he stood there, waiting for the taxi to a hotel.

Henry's job? It was what he got up for every morning, otherwise he'd stay in bed. Supervising the workers sorting the mail at the postal distribution centre. Every day he arrived there at eight, and was on the backs of those slackers grabbing a coffee, scanning the headlines, having a piss, fixing their hair, changing their shoes, putting on a dust coat before starting work, while the mail, the letters, the bills, the parcels were building up, waiting to slide along the assembly line to be sorted into postcode pigeonholes and onto trolleys, and out to the waiting vans, towards their destinations. He was into it at once, it was the only way to stop the thoughts. What thoughts? What no one talks about, not to anyone, not out loud, the quiet times and the busy times in the mail sorting room, as out went the letters from one person to another, from one town to another, from one country to another, from loved ones to loved ones. Like the postcards from his mother to a six-year-old left in the care of elderly people he did not know, those were the thoughts he had to suppress, and tears wet his face.

Back then, the bed was the only place he felt safe from the ache, the loss, the fear. It was a boat sailing through the night amongst the stars, taking him home, back to his parents, back to his brother William. How could he tell this to Alice? Barely able to face it himself, of course he couldn't tell her.

The river lost in its search for the coast that did not know its banks.

The city that did not know its boundaries, streets and houses.

The monkeys huddled together, dreaming of heat and humidity and the cacophony.

Alice. She soothed her feet with an aromatic foot bath after dinner, the dishes stacked in the dishwasher, relaxing on the leather chesterfield, a glass of amber whisky in her hand, her blonde hair unleashed. Beautiful Alice, unable to fill the emptiness in him with her love. In bed? Together but apart. Each had a separate mattress which could be raised and lowered with a hand control to allow for late-night reading. A hand control for the sound system. A hand control for the heat pump. No hand control for the past, nor the grief that welled up in him. Why had this realisation come so late? Why now?

Because of the shock, the disorder to their lives following the arrival of Jeopardy, a black Labrador. Four Saturdays ago, Alice had brought him home from her Saturday afternoon where she spent her time with a group of women, knitting rugs for refugees. Katie, one of the knitting front line, had needed a home for the dog. He had been her mother-in-law's but she was now in a nursing home, linked to an oxygen bottle, having survived her husband, who had died of emphysema, and was no longer in touch with adult children who'd fled the place. That was how things went in this fulminous city – people either fled or died. So Jeopardy had come with a bed and two bowls and a bag of meaty bites. He'd wagged his tail and inspected each of them, sniffing their legs, examined the house and garden, and decided to stay. You see, Alice was triumphant, a rescued dog: some good comes of my knitting circle friends.

Henry had warned Alice that meeting in the town's mall to knit together and to give out pamphlets was asking for trouble, a risk to her health. It's my conscience food, she'd retorted. You should try it instead of lying in bed all weekend.

Actually, he resented the time she spent with them, that was the truth. But now, he had Jeopardy to take for a walk every day, observing his excited sniffing at tree trunks and gateposts, his strained effort at doing a poo, his delight at meeting other dogs and after a volley of barks and tail wagging, sniffing their bums, or rolling over to display his private parts; and he loved the dog's warm eager eyes, sitting so obediently, tail sweeping as he waited for a treat. If only people could be so innocent and natural! He would miss the dog, his cheerful eyes, tongue lolling, wagging tail knocking over vases, spilling books and coffee cups off the coffee table. He would miss his excited barking at mealtimes, his mischievous games, gnawing the carpet, dragging down the tablecloth, pawing at his leg for attention. Jeopardy demanded to be noticed, there was no way he could be ignored, as, Henry felt, his emotional needs were ignored by Alice. As his needs had been ignored by his mother and father. What he couldn't explain was how could he jeopardise what he had with her by accepting love? He couldn't trust to love, because look what happened when you did. You were sent away. Abandoned.

He blinked and gazed up the street for his taxi. It was darkening, the street lights came on, luminous in the lingering dusk, and still no sign of it. What should he do, ring for an Uber?

The river lost in its search for the coast that did not

The city that did not know its boundaries

The monkeys huddled together, dreaming of heat and humidity

Alice sat with Katie in the studio. Both were seated in comfortable wicker garden chairs, baskets of coloured balls of wool at their feet. Alice enjoyed the knitting get-togethers, and the talk to do with following a pattern. Ply, tension, gauge. She loved the precise instructions for creating something beautiful, like the lovely little hats and jackets the older women knitted for their grandchildren. One row of a pattern might read, *Row 1(WS): k1, drop yo, kfbf, purl to the last 3 stitches, kfbf, drop yo, k1, (4stitches inc'd.)* a code as or more intricate than computer coding in her opinion, with stitches called moss stitch, cable stitch, stocking stitch. All were antidote to the jargon and politicking and workplace bullying and endless meetings that constituted her daily work life. She loved too the calm chat that went with the click clack of needles as the coloured wools slipped through her friends' fingers, about this and that. She wondered when would she and Henry have children; she was in her mid-thirties now, Henry older, but he'd shown no interest. Through the windows, trees darkened with damp dripped and the grass was soggy.

It was a big house, as old as Alice's, but on a grander scale, as was Katie, voluminous in a pink woollen tent dress, knitted of course, her hair loose, earrings in the shape of parrots dangling through grey strands like bright birds in a dead tree. Alice felt boring in comparison, neat in a navy jumper, jeans tucked into boots. Fastidious, and she wondered how she would fit in, living here with Katie.

'What did he say again?' Katie stacked some knitted squares, readying them to be sewn together.

Alice took a shuddering breath. 'Sent me a text, that's all. Going. Taking a break. That's it, no explanation.'

'Really?' Katie lowered a look. 'There must be more.' Alice was wasted on Henry. Moving in here, she would come home from work exhausted and Katie would care for her and they could knit together, after a delicious dinner. And a few drinks. 'Like a small glass of something, dear? I've a very nice Pinot Grigio.'

'Katie, he never takes a break. It's all I can do to get him away for a long weekend, like the house might disappear behind his back, poof!'

'So insecure. Where does it come from?'

'Childhood. Doesn't it always?'

'That's for sure. What happened back then, exactly?'

'I don't know, Henry doesn't talk. His dad was an oil executive. They were English, upper class. They treat their kids badly.'

'Indeed. Dogs get it better,' with a disapproving glance at Jeopardy. 'Come on inside.'

They got up, walked out of the studio and squelched across the lawn to the house.

Katie went back to her previous thought. 'Wasted. You're wasted on him.'

Alice bristled. She understood the small elisions and glances that telegraphed the message to her, that their marriage was alive, even without effusive expressions, even without love? Love. Was that why she was here? Jeopardy lolloped after them.

'Stay as long as you like, you know that.' Katie tried patting the dog to make more headway with Alice. He jumped up, his boofhead hitting her on the chin, his tongue curling over her lips. 'Oooh!' Disgusted. The dog would have to go.

'Down, Jep.' Alice collared the dog and they went inside.

Waiting for his taxi, Henry thought, what else was he to do? His foe was Katie, who acted like a little girl, instead of Katherine, a woman. Her house had a studio out the back where they knitted away at their squares for refugees. Would Alice have loved him if he were a refugee? But he was: he'd sought refuge, a safe place, here in his life with Alice. Now, he knew this life was as ephemeral as the foggy miasmas of this city. So the decision to leave, what else could he do? She needed the house once they were divorced, and he choked on the word. He'd always liked this house, its steep little roof, steep little garden overgrown with flowering shrubs and a magnolia, a pool for frogs, but comfortable inside and light, with french doors and a skylight. His nest, his retreat, his bolt-hole. More sorrow dislodged, rose to the surface and burst, and he stifled a sob.

The river lost in its search for the coast
The city that did not know its boundaries
The monkeys huddled together, dreaming of heat

Alice and Katie were at the kitchen table, sorting the pamphlets to hand out the next Friday in the mall. Alice usually took a late lunch from her job to join her friends, who continued knitting while handing the pamphlets to passers-by. They hoped to influence government to free the people in detention. Mums and dads, women and men, children. They needed care, support, love, why couldn't those in power see it? Those inadequate men the politicians would never respond to an asylum seeker's needs, because they didn't feel love, empathy, compassion. Alice's inner terrorist fantasised about attacking them with a flame thrower. That might work.

'Okay, so…' Katie wanted to drive home her advantage over Henry.

Possession is nine tenths of the law. 'He's leaving you. Face up to it, Alice. Move on.'

'Katie, you are too much.' Alice stormed out of the kitchen and outside.

Jeopardy started up, following her, his nails clicking on the quarry tiles. Out on the grass, Alice fumbled her mobile out of her pocket and rang home.

'Sorry Alice, I didn't mean to upset you.' Katie was at the back door. 'Come on in, I'll make us a nice cuppa.'

The phone rang inside the house, the landline. Henry started. He'd locked up the house, he couldn't go back inside. It rang on, persistent. Was it Alice? He couldn't face talking to her. He yanked up his backpack and walked down the drive to the footpath. He could still hear the ringing. It went on and on. He waited, thought again about ringing for Uber, then he did so. The driver said he would be fifteen minutes, and then Henry worried that both cars might turn up, and there would be a fight. He and Alice never fought, but he had to admit to tension, exasperation at times, demands he couldn't meet. Get out of bed, the fence with the banksia rose, and so on…. Now that she'd gone, he dreaded the fights, the accusations, the loss that went with marriage break-ups.

Henry's thoughts went back to his childhood, to that house with those people who said they were his mother and father now. That's what they said, mother and father, when he knew they weren't. His own parents had given him to them. Just for a time, they'd said, waving as they drove away, leaving him screaming. In this new home, he had to say thank you, mama, thank you, papa, and they spoke in a strange way and washed him in the bath and dried him, and he didn't like it, and they watched him try to put on his pyjamas and watched him when he cried. He started to speak like them and then he knew, he always would be their little boy. So he'd run away to find his own parents, to tell them, I want to come back. The police had found him and he felt again the pain of returning to that house where his bed was his only refuge, where he hid and pretended to sail away back home.

Henry's mobile rang, but deep in his memories he didn't notice until it stopped. Checked. It was Alice. Not Alice! What could he say to her now? He tramped down to the corner of the street. Cars went by mournfully, headlights swinging around as they took the corner. He leaned against a wall, the damp penetrating his jacket, and he slumped to the pavement. William, his brother. What had happened to him as an eight-year-old, when he too had been fostered out? Uncontrollable as a teenager, he'd tried to burn down the house with his parents in it. Driven the car down the drive and crashed it into the house. Turning his anger on them, it was obvious, whereas he'd internalised his anger. He'd lost touch with Willie years ago, after he'd disappeared into India. And his parents, who'd died in London.

Henry heard a dog barking way off in the night. Jeopardy? No, the dog was safe with Alice. He wasn't deserting him, he wasn't abandoning him, was he? Henry stared into the darkening night, longing for Jeopardy.

The river lost in its search
The city that did not know
The monkeys huddled together

Alice, standing outside Katie's house, wondered why she'd left Henry at this point, when he'd been the same for years. Because of Jeopardy. She saw what love was in the way Henry loved the dog and felt that she wasn't loved, not in the same way. Sex, the big question. It happened, a lot then a little, but she couldn't tell him she loved him, even in the midst of passion. He froze at the words. If she was affectionate, he eased away from her, he didn't like her too close. So she'd retreated, found affection in her friends, got on with her colleagues, thin gruel compared to grand passion, but something, as she knitted love into the rugs to keep warm stateless people. Yet Henry was devoted, she knew that, feeling wretched. She looked down at Jeopardy. He wagged his tail and looked expectant, wanting to go home. But how? Because Katie was right. How was anything ever going to change with Henry?

The house looked lonely, with no lights in its windows, closed in, abandoned. Outside in the cold, that was his true place, Henry felt, because the warmth and love of a home was an illusion. He'd waited and always would be waiting, for someone to come for him, who didn't come because he didn't deserve it, didn't deserve to be loved, that was the darkness his parents had shown him as a child. Then, there was his job. They didn't like his accent, his stiffness, his, well, officiousness. Why hadn't he realised that? And Alice had left him because she preferred Katie, who'd always be up and about, doing things, not lying in bed. His mind snagged on the word 'preferred', as if Katie were his wife's choice of breakfast cereal. His Alice, now was her Alice, and Henry dropped his head in his hands.

The river lost
The city that did not
The monkeys huddled

Jeopardy sniffed the air and started off around the side of the house. He made for the gate, lolloping along, his ears alert. It was shut and with an effort he heaved his fat body over the picket fence, and loped away up the street.

'Jep! Come back, Jeopardy! Come now!' Alice wrenched open the gate, and watched him go. 'Jeopardy…' More a wail than a command.

Katie joined her. 'Where's he going?'

'Back home, to his old home, I don't know. Henry will be devastated if I lose him.' As he had lost her. Oh, god, what had she done!

'Get the car. Alice, come on.'

'My keys, my bag's in the studio.'

'Get in mine, it's right here. I've got my keys.'

They piled into Katie's car, started it, and drove off.

Under the street light, Henry waited. He couldn't go forward and he couldn't go back; the darkness had him in its icy grip. Sunday nights, Alice always made pizza with a tomato base and anchovies, olives, pickled artichokes, chorizo slices, and the house was filled with delicious smells and they sat together and watched a video. Had he ever told her how much he loved their Sunday nights? Shame paralysed him. Bitter regret at what he'd lost. A car caught him in its headlights and screeched to a stop. The taxi? No, the Uber car?

The passenger door swung open and Alice got out and dashed over to the footpath.

'Alice!' Relief, shame, gratitude.

'What are you doing out here, Henry? Have you seen Jeopardy?'

'Jep? Why, where is he?' He looked into the car, thinking he was on the back seat.

'He's gone. I was at Katie's,' as the woman parked the car, 'and Jeopardy, well, I just turned my back for a minute, and…'

'And what?' But knowing, with horror.

'He took off over the fence.' Katie was blunt as she heaved out of the car. 'Couldn't catch him.'

'You've lost him?' He glared at Katie. She was to blame, taking his wife away from him with her knitting, losing his dog.

'I called and called…' Alice looked up and down the street, helpless.

'It's only a dog,' Katie said.

'Only a dog!' Furious, Henry kicked out, smacking the open car door with his boot, and again.

'Hey! What the hell are you doing? I didn't lose the damned dog.'

Henry swung away, colliding with her in blind fury, after all that had happened propelling him, but Katie barrelled into him and, winded, he fell against Alice.

'Henry, Katie, please!'

'You'll be hearing from me, and my lawyer!' Katie got into her car and drove forward, hitting the kerb, then back, U-turned and accelerated away.

Together, they watched the car disappear down the hill. Silence fell as they stood under the bleak street light.

'You all right?' Alice whispered.

Henry couldn't speak. His anger gone, he trembled in the darkness. 'Jep,' he stuttered.

'We'll go find him, Henry. But the car's at Katie's.'

'A taxi?' Maybe the one he'd booked in some distant past.

'No. We can't go looking. He might come back here to the house.'

'Then what?'

'We'll wait here for him,' Alice said. 'And there's a website for lost and found animals. We'll get him back, don't worry.'

Alice was back. She'd chosen him over Katie. He was her favourite breakfast cereal and he leaned, taking in her scent, her breath, the warmth of her body.

'Where were you going, Henry?'

'Were you leaving me, Alice.'

Together, they crab-walked along the footpath, up the steps to the veranda. Henry unlocked the door and they went inside. The lights turned on.

'Leave the door ajar for Jeopardy, dear.'

Leave the door ajar, and the light would defeat the darkness and guide Jeopardy back to the warmth and order and love of his home.

'All right,' Henry murmured. 'My love,' he whispered.

The river

The city

The monkeys…

… All receded as Jeopardy padded along the street and up the steps to the open door, sniffed it and bounded inside, barking a welcome.

Patrimony

A month after her husband Jamie's death, Amanda received an invitation. It had come from Bill Richards, an old friend of Jamie's, for her to visit him in Melbourne. But why the black scalloped edging on the silky square of cardboard? Amanda looked out of the windows of the cottage where she was staying at her cousin Ann's place. Beyond the bunched flourish of gardens and European trees, pasture as smooth as velour rose to hills, and a blue sky. Old established farming country, Flowerdale, a nurturing place where she was facing the loss of her husband.

Her eyes went back to the card. Bill and Jamie, friends at university, both lovers of learning, literature, politics, history, arguing as they sat in the student refectory or walked the campus between lectures. Bill was brilliant, a thinker challenging everything, larger than life, but doomed, in the way that big thinkers and drinkers were, she felt back then as she got to know the pair. Jamie, mild, russet-haired, a bloom of ginger on his skin, stepped from the shower like a ripe peach from a tree, fell into her bed, damp and luscious. It had been immediate, their love for each other, but they had to include Bill in their lives, it went without saying. Jamie was Bill's conscience, while Bill was his tempter, his accomplice, his mate; their relationship her burden.

Then Bill found Lyn, who was working in the university library, a slight, fair, quiet girl. Or Lyn found him, Amanda guessed, because student politics came first for Bill. Following graduation, they had moved to Melbourne, becoming inner-city types, wearing black, drinking coffee, while Jamie had stayed in Hobart, going on to postgraduate studies and teaching at the university.

After the horror of renting flats, and with a deposit from her parents, Amanda had insisted on them buying a newly built house. Flinty, white concrete, with bare Tas oak floors and a stainless-steel kitchen, it had huge windows giving a view of the Mountain's scree slopes, and the harbour far off a metallic blue. A low-care garden of boulders and native grasses set off the house's angled lines and concrete surrounds. Interior design? Amanda had insisted on minimal furniture. Jamie's books, papers and journals were banished to his office at the university, she didn't want them spread untidily through the rooms.

The end result: Amanda loved this house, but Jamie didn't feel at home in it, she knew that, saw him wince as sun shafting through the glass assaulted his skin. He preferred his brother Ron's place, hidden in an overgrown garden down a street of overarching trees, with rooms full of books, pictures, collectables that she regarded, well, not quite as rubbish.

Now that Jamie had gone, she felt some regret. Why hadn't she just given in or at least encouraged him to buy a beach shack where he could do what he liked? Perhaps that was the reason he'd travelled to Melbourne so often, staying with Bill and Lyn in Northcote. He went overseas as well, pursuing research, attending conferences, collaborating with other university faculties, and she sometimes went with him. But it was years since she'd been to Melbourne, long before Lyn who, close to forty had had her baby, rather sweetly named Jamie. After her husband? Obviously, and Jamie had been so chuffed. There'd been talk of them being godparents but it had come to nothing. Then Lyn had died of ovarian cancer when her boy was how old? Amanda didn't remember. She hadn't attended her funeral as she had a broken leg in a plaster cast at the time, having fallen on the concrete steps at home, and couldn't face plane travel. Jamie had gone, of course. Truth was, she felt she had nothing in common with Bill, and had long been out of touch with Lyn. She had her own career at the university, administering the affairs of the arts faculty. Managing a bunch of academics was like herding cats, she said with a laugh. And Bill, what had he made of his life? Teaching in a state high school, Jamie had told her. A high school? She found that hard to take, this brilliant man a teacher.

Jamie's career had flourished, appointed to the Sydney Sparkes Orr Chair of Philosophy at the university as professor. She'd been so proud.

But almost at once liver cancer cells proliferated, his pale body shrinking, his porcelain skin blue in the clefts, the freckles standing out in eggshell blotches on his shoulders mimicking the decay within. She did her best, but the house was unsuitable for the intensive care that he needed. They had turned to palliative care, found a hospice, and were impressed with the staff, the surroundings, the gardens. She was with him every day as he shrank into emaciation, skin stretched over his bones, hair gone, his kind eyes huge. His only solace was his beloved Brahms and Schubert playing quietly through earbuds, taking him away, well, from her. His last wish? When she was able, to visit Bill in Victoria. He only had the boy, now a teenager. She had reassured him, yes, she would go as she held the bunch of bones that was his hand.

Jamie's memorial was crowded, and it was right that it was so, her husband had been the kindest man, a music lover, an intellectual, and she wept. Bill had not attended, but had posted a poem eulogising a shared boyhood into manhood, marriage, family. A memento of a unique, life-long friendship.

Grief, those long sleepless nights, its filigree of memories patterning the night sky beyond her bedroom window. Grief insidious, ambushing her with a smell, a cadence of music, an old jumper of Jamie's held to her face. Grief the invader, penetrating with well-wishers' words of sympathy bringing her to tears. So, she avoided people, didn't go back to work, found that she had enough to live on with Jamie's super pension. She retreated to her cousin Ann's place in Flowerdale to mourn her husband in the quiet of country life.

Earlier that morning, Ann had called in, yellow shirt tucked into blue jeans, the sun catching her white hair, outlining her slight figure. A similar body shape to Amanda's; after all, their mothers were sisters, though she was dark, brown-eyed rather than blonde.

Ann had picked up the card from the table. 'What's this? A late condolence card?'

'It's from Bill Richards, Jamie's old friend in Melbourne. Did you know him? He came from up this way.'

'Bill Richards? I was at high school with him. He came to the funeral? I don't remember seeing him.'

'I read out his poem.' Amanda took back the card. 'I promised Jamie I'd visit him and his son. He's on his own.'

'It might help, get away, a change of scenery…'

'I love it here.' She'd gone to the windows. The wooden shutters had Charles Rennie MacIntosh style cutouts, matching the lilac and green stained glass in the windows.

'You'd have lots to chat about, university days, people you knew…'

'I expect so,' grudgingly.

'Mum?' Kathy, Ann's eldest daughter appeared over in the farmhouse doorway.

'Coming! I'd better give her a hand, she's making quince paste, it's touchy.'

You just couldn't have a chat with Ann without her children interrupting. Jamie's two brothers were the same. Look at how their children had behaved at the wake, teenagers stuffing themselves, wives rabbiting on about the seven stages of grieving, for heaven's sake, or was it five? The fewer the better. She stroked the black-edged invitation. A visit to Bill in Melbourne. Why not? It would do her good to get away from families. Not Ann, of course she didn't mean her. She could always come back to stay, couldn't she?

The plane was delayed, no one was there to meet Amanda as she got off the Skybus at Southern Cross Station. Pulling along her wheeled case, she walked out onto the streets, into the cacophony of traffic, humid air, people passing and colliding. Disoriented, she looked about. No sign of Bill but she had his address in Northcote. She hailed a taxi, the driver stowed her case in the boot and they shot off, through the city streets. She'd booked a bed and breakfast a few streets away for two nights, close enough to easily see Bill and his son for the one visit. Her duty would be done and she could head back home.

The taxi drew up at the address, she paid and got out, and the taxi driver lifted her case from the boot. Number sixty-three? She found number sixty-five, Berit's Bottle Shop and Liquor, indicated in a neon sign. Next to it was a single-storey shopfront with a crooked Venetian blind hanging inside the window, and a rackety old air conditioner projecting above the door. Number sixty-one was a cottage, one of several. So this shopfront was number sixty-three? Couldn't be right. Amanda went into the liquor store. The walls were shelved with bottles of wine and spirits glowing in the light from the open doorway. Behind the counter, a young guy watched her, and another wheeling a case on a trolley, looked around.

'Excuse me, I'm looking for Bill Richards. Do you know where I can find him?'

'We know a Bill Richards?' one said to the other.

'Must be Bill.'

''S right, Bill.' Tossing the comments one to the other. Eventually, 'Next door, love.'

'Next door?'

'Count on it,' the fellow called to the other as he wheeled the trolley into the depths of the store.

'Thank you.'

She backed out along the footpath, tripping over her case and flustered, reached the door and banged on it. Nothing. Backing away, Amanda thought of ringing Bill to make sure of the address. She should have done that at Spencer Street, instead of heading out here. She was about to take out her phone when the door opened and Bill stood there.

'Bill?' It was definitely him.

'Amanda! Come on in. I thought it was god botherers.'

She hardly recognised him as he peered through rimless glasses, bobbed grey hair falling forward, a camel hair coat stretched over his stomach, and a patterned waistcoat over a white shirt, an erudite if dishevelled look.

'I was about to head off to meet you at Southern Cross.'

'I got a taxi here.'

'Good on you. The time!' He looked up and down the street as if it might be lurking nearby. 'Come in, come in,' turning back.

She hesitated, then stumbled after him, an arm closing the door behind her. A hand on her shoulder urged her forward into the gloom, a smell of rising damp, something chemical, mothballs, and bookcases towering to the ceiling, an abstract wall of lettering and colours. At the foot of these cliffs of knowledge angled an armchair, a rug, a lamp, and as they passed she imagined Bill sitting in the armchair under the lamp reading these books, evening after evening. They shunted forward, past bookshelves creating a space with a neatly made double bed. A bedroom in a library? Through a door and into a kitchen with bench tops and shelves, a sink, a wooden table and wicker chairs, lit by grey light from a window. So this was Bill and Lyn's place? Why hadn't Jamie ever told her? What else hadn't he told her, she wondered, with a twinge of anxiety. She lowered herself to a chair, her case hard against her legs and with furtive glances tried to accommodate to her surroundings.

'So…' she couldn't think of the right question.

'Pizzeria,' Bill said. 'I converted it.'

Or the right answer.

'Show you your room.' He left, went out the door and she followed him, trundling her case past a space with a bath, a shower curtain, hand-washed things dangling from a rail. This was the bathroom? A barrier of stacked wine cartons partly screened it.

'Wolf Blass, Kanundra, Penfolds,' she read aloud.

'Books,' Bill explained. 'Storage.'

Bought from the bottle shop next door, the contents drunk, she guessed. Above them was a leaf-strewn clerestory and in the courtyard that they were entering, a huge fig, its canopy merging overhead with the clerestory. The bole of the fig was bolstered with granite boulders between which red geraniums bloomed.

'Jamie and his Mum's. Former garage. I converted it.' They had stopped at an addition to the premises, an entrance way. 'You can use her room.'

'Bill, I've booked a bed and breakfast a few streets away.' Stay in his dead wife's room?

He peered at her over his glasses, his hair falling forward. 'No need.'

Amanda wished she had checked in to the bed and breakfast before coming here.

'Where's your boy Jamie, then?'

'At a mate's.'

'I was hoping to catch up with him.'

'He'll be home for dinner.'

She followed Bill through the entrance into a pleasant, light room, with a sofa, a sideboard, a television. He opened one of two doors. A skylight lit a small room with a double bed and a clothes cupboard.

'Bathroom's next door,' he indicated with a vague lift of his hand. 'Wash up. Come over when you're ready.'

'In a little while, yes…' talking to his back as he left.

She slumped onto the bed. What was going on here? Her Jamie, where had he stayed when he visited? He had never said a word about this strange set-up. Darkness flowed below this friendship of Bill and Jamie, like an underground current she had never sensed before in her bare white house, her bright, successful life. Would it have made a difference if she hadn't come here? Jamie wouldn't have known. Jamie! Grief gripping her, she fell back on the coverlet, staring through tears up at the skylight, feeling the contours of her relationship with him, his presence once so familiar, dissolving into opaque blue.

An hour later, Amanda felt better, enough to brush her hair and cross the courtyard. She'd decided to wait for Bill's son, then leave. She would go into the city in the morning, visit the art galleries, stay another night and then head home.

Bill was at the bench cooking when she came in, a glass of red wine by his elbow, a large pot on an old electric stove. She stared at him for a minute, amazed. Bill, cooking?

He turned. 'Hungry?'

Not really, watching onions and garlic being sliced and thrown into the sizzling pan. Then cubes of meat and handfuls of spices from jars he took down from the shelves, one by one. Dicing carrot, a whole chilli, raisins, and Bill stirred vigorously as he sloshed back the red wine. Spicy scents rose with the steam.

'Indian tonight. You fine with that?'

A burst of manners, 'Very nice.'

'Take a pew.'

Gingerly she pulled out a chair and sat by the table, realising she had just committed herself to staying, at least for a meal. But what could go wrong? What life-changing event could happen that hadn't already happened to her?

'When did you learn to cook, Bill?'

He shrugged. 'Wine?' He poured some into a glass.

She picked up the glass and studied its red glow, and looked around. The room had a late-night feel reminding her of those years in the flat above the shop in Hobart that Jamie had shared with Bill, before he had moved in with her. Was this it, the end for university students, living alone in run-down ex-pizza shops making cheap curries?

'You're retired, Bill, from teaching?'

'Got out as soon as I could.' He took a jar from the fridge and poured liquid into the pot. Stock, she guessed as he smacked a lid back on the pot. He rubbed the bench down with a wet cloth, threw it into the sink and sat opposite her, the glass in his hand. 'Took my super and ran.' He looked at her, over his glass.

They both drank. The wine warmed Amanda, and she perked up.

'So then, teaching?'

'Preston College, organising support teams for kids with special needs. Inclusion programs. They didn't know what else to do with me.'

'You were happy, in a caring role?'

'That's right,' acknowledging the irony with a tilt of his glass.

She remembered the time Jamie had come back shattered from a party, after hitting Bill over the head with a bottle to stop him fighting. Always fights once he was drunk, and Jamie had despaired.

Bill lumbered up, went to the cupboard and got out a packet of rice. He put on the water to heat, stirring the curry with a wooden spoon. She watched as he got together side dishes. Cucumber and yoghurt, grated carrot with cumin, beetroot and sour cream.

'How are you coping?' A glance at her.

Coping? She looked at him, he lowered his eyes and drank again.

'Grief's another country, you can't leave when you want to.'

'Lyn.'

'Blessed are they who mourn, for they will be comforted. The Beatitudes.'

'Is that so? But you had your boy.'

He nodded. 'He was only five. Ten years ago, Lyn departed.'

They each raised a glass and steam billowing, she caught the odour of rice. Bill got up to turn down the heat on the stove. He clattered plates, dumped a mix of cutlery on the table, placed a jug of water and glasses, napkins. She ordered them into two sets of each, then three, a place for his son. Bill transferred the curry and rice to heated Bendigo pottery pots and placed them on the table, then the side dishes, and a plate of nan bread and sat opposite her. He offered the food with a gesture.

'Won't we wait for Jamie?'

'He'll come in his own time.'

Amanda served herself, poured the water into the glasses. Bill lit candles, left a light over the bench and turned off the main light. Amanda shifted on the seat. The night was turning into something else. But what? The man plopped a ladleful of rice beside the rich brown of the curry.

She mixed it, added banana slices and yoghurt, spooned it into her mouth. 'Delicious, Bill.'

He tilted his head in acknowledgement. 'You're remaining in the house?'

'For now. I thought I might sell up. He never liked our house.' Sorrow flooded, and she dabbed her eyes, lips, with the napkin. 'You could never move from here, all these books.

''S right.'

They ate on and Amanda wondered, when would Jamie show?

Bill waved a fork. '*Patrimony*. The Philip Roth book. You know it?'

'Long time since I've read anything, I'm sorry to say.'

'A memoir, really, on the death of his father. Just read you part of a review.' He got up and walked into the main room, returning with a printed page. 'It's about managing terminal illness, the family.'

'Okay…'

He read aloud, 'the agonized, sometimes comic labor of a family and a dying parent…is dictated by the invasive, also benign pressures of modern medicine and its technologies, bureaucratically organized. The struggle that Mr Roth portrays…' He paused, looking at her over his glasses. '…is the effort to keep death as it once was – a phenomenon of one particular human body and soul. Death as it once was, and was allowed to be, special to one person. The right to die in one's own way…'

'You mean Lyn?'

'Ah…' He slumped in his chair. 'We went through the interventionist hoops. I wish I could've just let her die in her own way.'

'Did she wish for that?'

'She wished for life… I couldn't bear to see her…' He looked up suddenly, pain in his voice.

'Morphine?'

'The works.' He choked.

She topped up his glass of water and he swallowed, then mopped his face with his napkin.

'I'm so sorry, Bill.'

He looked across at her. 'How was it for Jamie?'

'His cancer was a fast mover, there wasn't time for medical technology to obliterate who he was. Though I would've gone with it, anything… You do.'

'You do.'

'The funeral… Bill, your poem was lovely. I read it out.'

'Uh huh.'

They were silent for a few minutes, eating together.

'You know, I wasn't in the prime of life when Lyn wanted a child.' He looked up. 'Potency, vigour, all that…'

'But you managed it.'

'What I'm saying, if death is a phenomenon of one particular human body and soul, surely life is, too?'

'You mean birth?'

'Exactly.' A pause. 'No kids of his own… Jamie.'

'That wasn't the reason,' for what? Somehow the conversation had gone off track.

'He couldn't forgive you, Amanda.' The statement was a blow, like a bottle cracking over her head.

She fell back in her chair. 'But we agreed to no children. Jamie and I agreed.'

'Did you?'

She stared at him.

'Lyn and I wanted a baby,' he choked. 'But no IVF, no surrogacy, no adoption. It had to happen as it chose to happen.'

She shook her head. This man, peeling back the skin to the bones of his emotions, she didn't want to know.

'We did it, got there with Jamie's help.'

Her mouth fell open. 'You mean, sperm donation. From my Jamie?'

'Ah, no. Like I said, nothing artificial, not with our child.'

The truth of his words hit, and hand to her mouth she stared at him across the table, the plates, the food, the Bendigo pottery, the glasses of wine, the wine bottle, a still life in the candlelight. Like her still life, confronting her now.

'I've got to go.' She started up.

'Hold it, Amanda, wait.'

The front door banged. The candles wavered in the draught, shadows licking up the walls, and she was drowning, Bill reaching across to her, to lift her clear, or push her down…

'Hey, Dad! Sorry I'm late. Curry, eh?'

The boy striding into the room was rangy, russet-haired, and Amanda could see him coming out of the shower burnished as a ripe peach. 'Jamie?'

'This is Amanda, Jamie.' Bill spoke quickly.

'Hi, Amanda.'

He had the warm eyes of her husband, a smile she knew so well, and she sat slowly, slumping into her chair, her eyes turning to Bill. She shook her head in disbelief, lifted a hand and let it drop. Jamie, Bill's old friend for whom he would do anything, even betray her. She felt a mass of anger growing, and anguish. How long had it taken for Lyn to fall pregnant, weeks, months, years? She tried to get up, she had to go from this strange place, but she was leaden, the boy holding her here. His Jamie, her Jamie, his voice so like her dead husband's, the tone, the inflections, the words he might use. Bill's eyes behind his glasses were on her, as he topped up her glass of wine.

'You're staying long?' She glanced at the boy as he spoke and lowered her eyes. When would he realise who she was, who his father was? Would she tell him?

'Long as you want, Amanda.' Bill said. 'Home away from home.'

A vision of her home came to her, smart, sharp-edged in the sunlight. She eyed Bill, and he flinched. Shame?

'Actually, I was staying with my cousin in Flowerdale,' and felt a piercing desire to return, to another time, another place where she was safe. But how could she return, she wasn't that person any more, the wife of the esteemed, recently deceased professor.

'My old territory.' Bill filled her glass, ignoring the hand she stretched to cover it.

Yes, he held all the cards, everything was his, her husband and his son, her marriage merely a backdrop to his life, here in Melbourne. What did Bill have in mind for her, a stepmother? A stand-in wife? She watched Jamie as he ate, and beneath his rangy, relaxed demeanour saw how careful, neat and self-absorbed he was, just like her Jamie, and with it a thought.

'Jamie, have you ever been to Hobart?'

'No,' he said. 'Dad and Mum always said another time.'

'Come for a visit, so much to see and do, wilderness, national parks, surfing.'

'Surfing! Hey, Dad?'

'Whenever,' an edgy shifting across the table, Bill uncertain now.

'Your next school break, maybe.'

'His friends are all here,' Bill interrupted.

'You could meet Jamie's family.' She eyed Bill. 'Your uncles,' goading him, now. His Jamie could easily become her Jamie.

'Cool! Dad, you never said I had uncles down in Tassie.'

Bill shrugged.

'Your dad's best friend, Jamie, his brothers…'

'Sorta uncles,' Bill grunted.

'Jamie? Yeah, he died.'

'My husband.'

'Unreal. So sorry, he was way cool.'

She turned the knife. 'He would've wanted that, wouldn't he, Bill?'

No response from Bill. What did he fear but the truth? She saw it in his glance, his eyes resting on Jamie, his beloved son.

'Let's do it, Dad.'

He smacked his hands flat on the table.

She jumped, there was tension, now. She got up. 'The toilet.' Hurried out, across the courtyard to the annex, went inside and fetched her case.

Back in the courtyard, the massed leaves of the fig, lit lime-green by streetlight, shivered and she felt all her certainties shivering too, into pieces. Could she really take Jamie away from this man, who to him was his father? Make him hers, who'd never wanted a son? Heat rose from her breast, into her throat, her face, she choked, the curry, it must be the curry and she almost vomited. Her Jamie's rights, his patrimony, what about them?

Bill appeared. 'You okay, Amanda?'

'A taxi. I need to get to the bed and breakfast.'

'Look, sure, a break in Tassie, do him good to get away from me,' heard the plea in his voice.

Her case, dragging across the pavers, snagged a boulder. She stopped at the deep red of the geraniums, wrenched the case free.

The man turned back, bulky against the lit interior. She followed him inside, where Jamie was lounging, legs outstretched, picking at the food on his plate.

'Amanda's heading off,' Bill said. 'Ring for a taxi, mate.'

'I'll Uber.' He grabbed his phone from the table and clicked away.

'Bill, Jamie…' Words stuck in her throat, what could she say?

'Nice meeting you, Amanda.' Jamie lifted a casual hand.

Bill started towards her. She backed away, wanting to kiss Jamie's peach-smooth cheek, but the boy started back, surprised.

'Goodbye.' She stumbled down that long room, the smell of camphor catching in her throat, bookcases towering as if to fall on her. She tore at the door, wrenched it open and fell, gasping for air, into the street.

'The Uber…' Jamie called, as he followed her out.

She turned in the pool of street light to his voice, uncertain who was calling her, the voice coming from far away. The bottle shop's neon sign blinked on and off, a tawdry brooch pinned to the black facade of the shops, and she knew now, she had been nothing more than a showy façade for her husband's life – what other dark secrets had he hidden from her? Her grief for Jamie swept away, a receding tide, leaving her heart a bare shore on which no one had walked.

Bill lumbered out into the street. 'Stay on, no problem,' he rumbled.

Stay. For what? 'Just a few streets away, no bother,' and Amanda veered away, her case clacking along behind her like a reluctant child.

'I'll come with you…' The boy loped after the woman, his hands thrust into the back pockets of his jeans, eager as a dog and Bill watched them disappear into the darkness.

When the night was still, he stood there for a few minutes, thought about getting the guys next door to fix their sign, then turned to go inside, the door slamming shut behind him.

Overboard

Skateboarding home along the streets gives me time to think it through: how, since it happened, Mum's all over the place. I get it, I'm all over the place too, but that's cool, being seventeen. And Mickey, my bro? Two years ago, he had his drama, nearly drowned. Fell off our grand-dad's boat, *Pineapple*. Mum jumped in to save him and that was the start of it, for her. I check my mobile. From Mum, a text: *In court 11 tomorrow. Chicken stew on stove. Make sure Mickey's home, may be late.*

See what I mean? Here we friggin' go again. Mum and her confrontations with life. Booked for parking on the footpath, and she's appealed. Who in their tiny mind would appeal a fine like that? Not me, I'm a skateboardin' dude, final year of college, I aim to nail it. Then, I'm outa here, going surfing up the coast, Coles Bay my heartland, where we always go, Christmas, summer. Pushing on my skateboard, I move it. Mickey will be home already from school.

I've posted on an internet site: *Looking to buy an acoustic guitar if anyone is selling. Shit nylon string with nice low action preferred but open to anything x. Contact Josh.*

A chick called Sally texted me: *Selling a decent Ibanez slimline nylon string yours for $300.*

That's the baby! *Catch you later, my soul machine. Josh.*

Mum works. She does jobs for six months, three months, some sort of study or something, then she's out of work. Says she likes it that way, can't hack routine, being pinned down. She didn't used to be like that, was a regular twenty-four/seven mum. Drop us off at school, do things about the place, be happy… Nice. You'd think my dad, well, he might stick around for her, but after Mickey fell overboard, everything went overboard and him, too.

That day, Granddad decided to motor up the Derwent beyond New Norfolk. A picnic on the river, Gran said. The water was brown, flooded, flowing fast, trees, poplars going by, coots, ducks, swans under overgrown banks, a great scene. The boat, an old fishing boat, gets caught in a current and before we can get it under control, Granddad's yelling Mickey's fallen in! Next thing, Mum's running for the rail and jumping over. Why didn't she wait for me? I run to the rail, and Mickey's floating away, held up by his jumper, his eyes wild as. Mum gets to him so fast, and Gran throws in the lifebelt, way off, we yell at Mum to get it, but I can see she can't hear a friggin' thing, because Mickey's struggling and they both sink! Mickey comes up, but Mum? Where's Mum! A guy fishing on the bank yells, drops his rod and shunts a dinghy into the water. Then I see Mickey pulling Mum's head up, and the dinghy gets to them, the guy drags them in, Mickey then Mum and rows them over to us. We drag them into the boat and he rows off with a mouthful to us about water safety and life jackets we shoulda known better, then everyone's in the cabin. Mickey sopping wet, crying, Mum sopping wet, crying. A few minutes more, it could have been a drama on the news. Mother, son drown Derwent at New Norfolk, that was the reality that day and, though they were saved, we're all living the consequences.

One of which I guess is Mum's court case. Nothing really, she's no criminal. The road outside our place is so narrow, no off-street parking, a grassy verge in the middle so the asphalt goes round two sides. Mum puts her wheels up on the footpath, who wants to get sideswiped? So then, Sergeant Maloney, with nothing in his tiny filth mind at three a.m. on a Sunday morning, books Mum with a fine. Who ignores it. Who gets booked another two times because she says she's gonna park where she feels safe. See what I mean? Her world is shattered. She won't – no, can't – conform because look what happens when she does. She and her precious son nearly drown and her husband, my dad, pisses off and gets us outa our house so he can sell it and shack up with some other chick. She has to go to court for being booked, not once but three times. Like she says, first hearing tomorrow.

I drop my skateboard and dive inside, banging my head on the doorway, it's so low and I'm so tall. 'Chizz, Mickey.' Chatter of the cartoons. I get us some food together, dishing up the chicken stew. Mickey comes to the table, grabs his plate and heads back to the cartoons, me sitting with him.

About seven, Mum comes in, drops her bag, shopping, stands there. 'Hi, kids, thanks for getting tea, Josh,' and disappears into the kitchen.

Mickey follows her, lookin' for treats in the shopping. I check the scene and head back upstairs, I'm into studying for the night.

Next day, after a coupla hours' study, I skateboard into town and find the law courts where Mum's case is being heard. She's waiting out the front, come in from work. She looks friggin' smart, like, professional.

'Hi, Mum, how're you feeling?'

'Nervous, Josh. Last time I was anywhere like this was for a mediation session.'

She means for the divorce, and I hug her. 'You'll be fine. No worries Mum, you're in the right.'

Inside this room, no windows, it's all wood and benches and this quiet solemnity so you only speak in whispers. There's only two other blokes waiting for a judgement and Mum's standing up, first off the rank. The judge is shuffling papers, no wig, suit, pretty old. The judge's assistant reads out the case and the judge looks up, shit stern like a primary school headmaster and asks for her plea. Mum says guilty, because, well, she did actually park on the footpath, but extenuating circumstances. The narrow street, sideswiping risk, no off-street space, yada yada. The judge thinks for a bit, no previous record and she gets a telling off and he puts her on probation. We get up, bow to the judge and leave.

Mum says, 'That wasn't too bad? Not even a fine.'

'No, Mum, but you've got two more times to go. How does probation fit into that scenario?'

'You are so negative,' she says and hugs me. 'I'm off to work now. I won't be late home.'

'See you, Mum,' and I skate off, back home. Apart from study, I have this Ibanez to check out with Sally.

As I'm coming round to the cottage, there's laughing, shouts. A party back of our place? I sneak up the lane and in the back gate, and Mickey and about six of his mates are sitting around the outside table going for it. Is that a joint being handed around?

I loom. 'What the fuck's goin' on here!'

And they go, disappearing in all directions, like mercury slides away when you drop it.

'Shit, Josh, chill. They're cool dudes.'

Suddenly Mickey's got the lingo?

I sit down with him. 'Mickey, you're too young for dope.' I rough his blond mop; he looks like a teddy bear. 'Listening, dude?'

He gazes at me with his round blue eyes and I see again those eyes friggin' terrified when he was floating away from us. 'You're only ten, for fuck's sake. Where did you collect those leeches? This isn't a druggies' house, don't make it one.'

'I'm not ten, I'm twelve.'

'Kiddin' me!'

'And they're my mates from school.'

'Shit, sorry, mate,' and I go to rough him up again, but he writhes out of reach. And I realise, he was stuck in my head at age ten when he fell in the river. How's that for psychology? But shit, hadn't I got him presents for his two birthdays since? His own surfboard? Wetsuit? Had him naggin me to take him surfing but I don't have a driver's licence, so how's that gonna work?

'Where's that joint?'

'Score your own.'

Then my head's back with Sally and the Ibanez. If I don't make a move, the Ibanez will be snaffled. I go inside, Mickey follows.

He sits at the table, looking at me as I get a coffee going. 'You heading off this Christmas?'

'That's the plan.'

'Coles Bay?'

'Yep.'

'I'm coming too.'

I'm about to hit this idea for six, look over at him, and decide no, not right now. 'I'll think about it.'

'You for real?' He's stunned.

'I said, think about it, is all.' I make the coffee and tap out a yes message to Sally. And that's it, as Mum comes home, and we settle for the evening.

Next time at court with Mum, there's a different judge, got this mouldy-lookin' wig on his head. After Mum tells her story and pleads guilty, he's flickin' through these big books, looking for something called precedence, all the way back to 1923. Decides the grassy verge edged with concrete is in fact a park, which affects the parking regs, but same outcome, a telling off and Mum's on probation again.

'Two down and one to go,' I say as we leave the court.

'Piece of cake,' Mum says. Then says she's applied to the council for the two stretches of road around the verge to be made one-way which should solve the parking problem. Good on you, Mum.

Two weeks later, my exams are over. Nailed it, I reckon. I've met Sally down in Battery Point. She's a cool, cheeky woman, like me right into surfing, diving, kayaking, and she's already at uni. Took two hundred for the Ibanez, cool! We get on, and she's gonna be joining me up at Coles Bay. Which means Mickey is a no-go, but when and how to tell him? Thinking about it, he's been real good, no more dope scenes, helping out around the place, making me coffee, and Mum's real pleased. At last he's settling down here, she says, because he missed our old house the most. And our dad. He goes to stay with him now, every other weekend, works well.

Then, that night I have this dream, nightmare really. Mickey's fallen in and this time it's me who goes overboard. I plunge down into that filthy, roiling brown water, bubbles escaping, weed grabbing and surge up, breaking the surface, and Mickey grabs me and we struggle and it's frantic and I go under the slimy water and I don't come up. I start awake, shouting, and Mum runs up the stairs into my room and grabs me, and I'm still in the dream and now I know, I understand what she went through.

'Sorry, sorry, Mum, I shoulda gone in for Mickey.'

'Shhh, Josh. Shhh. I've got you.'

'Where was Dad? Why wasn't Dad with us?'

'He wasn't ever with us.' And she leans back and looks bleak and I'm sorry I woke her.

'I'm okay, Mum.'

Then she says, 'Mickey.'

Oh, shit, I know what she's gonna say.

'Take him, please. I'm working still. I'll bring him back here after Christmas.'

So that's how it works out. Not the best for me and Sally, but she's cool, so we cruise up in her car, with Mickey and the Ibanez in the back. The shack is on the edge of Moulting Lagoon, a way down River and Rocks Road. It's set back from the beach and I just love that walk down to the water through the coastal bush, coupla rods and a net to do some fishing. And the birdlife! Sally, studying zoology, knows Moulting Lagoon too. It's habitat for duck, teal, cormorants, plovers, terns, lapwings and black swans. And it supports the largest flock of common greenshanks in Tasmania, Sally says. Pity they have a shoot every year, and Sally and I decide we're gonna interrupt the next season big time. Those birds need protecting from the bogans with guns.

Sally drives us over to Friendlies for the surf and Mickey's going real well, catches a few, dumped a few times, the usual, but he's hollerin' and laughin' and runnin' around like a mad thing and I guess he's over his drowning trauma. Too stuffed by the end of the day, he sleeps like a friggin' log.

Sally finds a fisherman mate and we go diving off Schouten, Mickey on board, and we're out there in the fresh blue air, seabirds wheeling.

For early morning dips, we go over to Wineglass, do the walk up to the Lookout and down to that friggin' ace beach and one day there's dolphins and we run along the beach as they cruise along, swimming too fast for us to keep up and leaping out of the surf, magic! Think about doing the walk round Hazards Beach and back, or Mount Amos but we're too lazy, having too much fun. But Honeymoon Bay, Richardson's Beach, yeah, we swim there, and breakfast outside the bakery, a buzzy scene in the morning sun. Evenings out on the deck, I explore the Ibanez just like I'd like to explore Sally, testing her strings for vibes and tone but she's holding me off, because Mickey's there. The waiting for her is killing me! So I try a few notes, Mickey gives the bongo a bash, and Sally croons along and together we knock out a few beats and a rhythm. Time passes, and it's like we've gone back to living an earlier, simpler existence.

Mum comes up for Christmas, like she promised, loaded! So, after present opening, and a lazy swim, lots of splashing and laughter, we're sitting around the table for lunch. It's piled with food, a coupla crays for a seafood salad, prawns, trays of local oysters, friggin' magnificent! Mum's brought her special cooked Italian potato salad she makes every Christmas, leafy greens, wine, drinks, Christmas pud, ice cream and strawberry coolis and its unreal the warm day unpeeling around us like a ripe fruit, and we're so cool, happy, relaxed.

Then, Mum drops her bombshell. 'Oh,' she says, 'I missed the last court appearance.'

'Shit, Mum!'

'Fined sixty dollars.'

'Sixty dollars? Not too bad.' And I relax. It's over.

'What's this?' Sally needs to know, so I explain the whole thing, about the parking, the court appearances and the rest of the shenanigans and we have a huge laugh and I hope she doesn't think our family is wacko.

'Your mum is so cool,' Sally says and I can see they like each other, so I relax.

Mickey can see it too, his round blue eyes shining.

'So that's all over, hey, Mum?"

'No way,' she said. 'I went in to the Court of Petty Sessions and asked them to set the ruling aside. And the fine. I haven't paid it.'

'You did what!'

'I want my day in court, Josh.'

'You've had two already,' Mickey pipes up.

'Spot on, Mickey.'

'A last win against Sergeant Maloney.'

'Mum…' Just when I thought she was settling into our new life, she does this. Or is this her new life, non-stop friggin' trouble?

'Well… I'm due in court next week.'

'And you want me to come with you?'

'We'll do that.' Sally turns to me. 'Won't we, Josh?'

'No. I'm not doing this again.'

'Joshy, it's your mum.'

'I'm not going back home!' Mickey's arcing up now.

'Okay, I'll go! Down and back in a day, you bring me back, Mum, that's the deal.'

'I'll do that,' and Mum sits back in her chair, smiles her freckly smile, the sun lighting her brown hair, looking tanned in her summer flowery thing and I love her though she sends me spare.

'I'll keep an eye on Mickey,' Sally says. So it's fixed.

Day of the hearing, Court of Petty Sessions, Mum's smart, me neat, we go inside and find the lists of hearings pinned on a board. There's Mum's name, she's due in Court 2.

When we go in, a shock. A full court is sitting, with rows of lawyers sitting at the table and a fierce-looking judge already under way. Mum checks her name with a clerk and we sit down and listen to people's stories. Pretty funny, like, a guy charged with not wearing a seat belt, and his plea is that he was wearing a seat belt but it was the same colour as his shirt! He got off, so I feel a bit more confident for Mum.

Her turn comes, name is called out and she stands. The judge asks her why she didn't attend the last sitting and she blithely says she was away on holiday, and I can see the judge is friggin' pissed off. Then he asks her how she's going to plead. Guilty, says Mum. All these lawyer heads shoot up and stare at her. Guilty, you plead guilty after getting the ruling set aside that found you guilty! The judge glares at her. He asks the prosecuting lawyer (or maybe it was the defence lawyer) if he has her file. Uh oh, if he does, there'll be the evidence of Mum being on probation two previous times. No, says the lawyer, but he can get it. Whoo, relief and I see Mum relax a bit. Right, so the judge wants to see it, Mum'll have to come back for another court hearing. Now, says the judge, next time how will you plead? Mum is silent, and I know what she's thinking: guilty didn't go down too well. Mum, don't say it! I beam to her. Not guilty, she says. Oh shit! Again, up jerk the lawyers' heads and I shrink down in my seat. Not guilty! The judge tells her off, wasting the court's time! To make sure she comes back at the next date, when's that? he asks a clerk, in a week's time. The judge dismisses us, we leave.

'Mum...'

'Don't say a word,' she says and heads over to the counter. 'Excuse me...' she calls over a clerk. 'You know how I was fined sixty dollars and asked for the ruling to be set aside?'

'Yes,' says the clerk.

'I'd rather pay the fine. Can I do that now?'

'Certainly,' says the clerk and Mum hands over the money.

'And I won't have to come in next week?' She says, as she takes the receipt. 'That's cancelled?'

'Absolutely,' says the clerk and we're out of there, no looking back.

'You see,' says Mum, 'the law is on my side.'

Mum and I head back up to Coles Bay and she takes Mickey back with her, so happy ending.

I had a fab few weeks with Sally, but then, one day I come back from catching waves at Friendlies with me mates, and she's gone, the Ibanez too.

End of story? No. Mum bells me and says she's received a payment of sixty dollars from the Court of Petty Sessions, and when she rang to find out why, did she have to go to court again, no, they said, hadn't she requested the ruling to be set aside? Yes, originally she did. It has been set aside *sine die*, they say. What does *sine die* mean, she asks? It means for ever. Don't you worry about that. Well, that was a win for Mum and piss on his boots for Sergeant Maloney. And we laugh ourselves stupid.

Has Mum settled down? The marriage break-up with our dad, leaving the house, none of us handled it, how could we? Sally helped; my time with her was great. Mickey's calmer now, ready to start high school. I passed my pre-tertiaries with distinctions and enrolled in university, hoping to check out Sally on campus; she owes me the Ibanez. Tell you, though. When I arrived from up the coast, I had Mickey round my neck, and Mum urging us out the front door. There, at the entrance to the road on each side is a sign: keep left.

'What! The council's approved the change?'

'You bet,' Mum says. 'I have had an impact on society!'

And I'm so friggin' pleased for her. Like, at last her life is steadied and she's safe and back on board. How good is that?

Those are my last words? No way. A week later, Mum has a bloke call in.

'This is Derek,' she says. 'He fished us out of the river,' laughing, taking his arm.

We all look at each other. He's short and dark and friendly but I'm not fooled.

When did this happen? When Mickey and Sally and I were up at Coles Bay? How friggin' cunning is that. I storm out, Mum calling after me, but I don't want to know. Mickey's jogging alongside, panting, dragging at me.

'Fuck off, Mickey.'

'He's all right, Josh.'

'Taking friggin' advantage? Moving in on our mum. Who the fuck does he think he is? I look out for Mum. We don't need some short-arse called Derek.'

'He saved us. We would've drowned.'

Mickey gazes up at me, so truthful and honest, my little bro. And it's true. You've got to thank him. But I won't, still I can't.

'You are crazy! He'll friggin' move in, can't you see that comin?'

'No, but Josh…' Mickey stops short. He's gonna cry now?

And it hits me, an echo of that drama two years ago when I nearly lost my little bro Mickey and my mum in that filthy flooded river. Eyes stinging, this feeling, is it grief? And love. Enough to make fish weep.

'Christ's sake!' I give him a shove. 'Coming down the Waratah, catch a game of pool?'

'Oh yeah, Josh!' And he's so friggin' pleased, he's jumpin' around me.

So we head down to the Waratah Pub, two brothers, out to waste some cool time together.

Peaches

Merryl, turning over, dragged the doona up to her chin and snuggled up to Alan. Glimmering light through the windows, a hush of water down on the shore, that midnight sound, she loved it.

'I'm sorry, what could I say?' she murmured into Alan's back.

'One word: no,' his voice muffled.

She rolled onto her back, properly awake now. 'Xanthe's my oldest friend, Alan.'

'So?'

They had no children themselves and that made Alan somewhat intolerant, in Merryl's view. Not that she was always welcoming of them, they were often quite uncontrolled. Tormenting Daisy the dog, racing around the house, clanging her wind chimes in the garden, while the parents looked on.

He turned over. 'When did we see her last? Oh. Don't remind me. That dreadful visit to her place in Perth that time.'

'She always was a free spirit…'

'Free spirit? Pissed. Couldn't get the food on the table.'

Pissed, like she and Xanthe had got pissed in Jimmy Williams and Marcus Brown's student flat all those years ago. He'd made a play for her, Jimmy, but she'd gone for safety and security with Alan, an engineering student who took her bushwalking. A good choice, he had made a secure career working for the Hydro, and here she was, in her comfortable house in Lindisfarne.

'Anyway, she's living in Launceston now.'

'Why us to take on her granddaughter?'

'It's only until she can get student accommodation,' she wheedled. 'I'm sure it won't be for long…'

But Alan had turned back over and was drifting off to sleep.

They had been best friends at school, then at university on student teacher scholarships. Xanthe was thin and wild. Original was the kindest way to describe her. They were both doing arts and loved the freedom of university, frittering so much time between lectures she'd barely scraped through. Xanthe, so bright, got distinctions with little effort, to Merryl's chagrin. She was political, too, dragging her off to student rep. meetings, talks and union stuff but then dismissing them as more blah blah from the men in control. She would always do well, Merryl had believed, but that wasn't how it had turned out. Xanthe left for Western Australia with a fisherman. She had her daughter Mandy, father long gone. Mandy married Don, a nice, quiet man Merryl had only met once and then along came Peaches, and the two boys following. They were all back, and were living in the north, in Launceston, Xanthe too, elderly now. As old as me, Merryl reflected.

One day she remembered, she and Xanthe had gone looking for rooms to rent in Battery Point. They'd strolled through the old streets looking for notices in windows, with no luck. Walking down Kelly Street and into MacGregor, they'd come across a bunch of women chatting, arms crossed over heavy breasts, cigarettes dangling from mouths and fingers. Merryl hung back. They looked tough. Battery Point was tough back then. Blithely, Xanthe trotted over, asked if they knew of any place that had rooms to rent.

The women eyed them. 'Yes, dearie,' one of them said. 'See that place just up there?' Nodding towards South Street, opposite. 'Blue-painted place? Rooms there for nice young ladies like you.'

So off they went up South Street, Merryl disturbed somewhat by the women's smirks. In the drive beside the cottage, she noticed black underwear dangling from a line as Xanthe banged on the blue-painted door. It was opened by a youngish bloke in a navy singlet, black boxers above hairy legs, a tousle of black hair and a love bite on his neck. Xanthe asked about rooms, and he eyed them up and down. No, he said, he had rooms but they weren't suitable. Merryl backed away, but Xanthe was exasperated, demanding to know why they weren't suitable, only getting half-amused answers. Who'd told them to come to here, he asked.

'Those women down there,' Xanthe said and they all turned.

There they were, those women, watching the goings-on, killing themselves. Oh did they, he said, and gave them the finger. That was when the penny dropped, and Merryl and Xanthe retreated out of there and shot off up South Street.

Now, lying in bed, Merryl chuckled.

'What's funny?' Alan murmured.

'The things we got up to…' She snuggled against him and fell asleep.

Peaches came with very little luggage, just the one case, a bag, a laptop and a large folder. Alan and Merryl picked her up from the coach at the terminus. Merryl recognised her at once, she was so like the young Xanthe and felt a twinge of alarm. She waved and the girl came over.

'Welcome, Peaches dear.'

'Hi, Merryl. Thank you for having me.' They hugged. 'Hi, Alan,' and thrust her hand through Alan's arm, waltzing away with him, her wheeled case clattering after her.

Amused, Merryl followed with the bag and the folder to the car.

'My portfolio!' She turned. 'Oh, you've got it,' and laughed.

The girl was dressed gauzily, certainly not warm enough for late winter. Her room with its en suite was warm, the bed had an electric blanket, she would be comfortable. Would it be too comfortable? Would they have trouble limiting her stay to only a few weeks? They drove across the bridge and into Lindisfarne, cruising along the Esplanade around the bay, and past the marina to Anzac Park, Peaches exclaiming all the way, because this was her first visit to Hobart, it was all new.

Once inside the house, Merryl showed Peaches to her room. She felt pride, but also satisfaction that she could accommodate her friend's daughter so comfortably.

'I love it!' Peaches threw herself onto the bed. 'Thank you, Merryl. Thank you, Alan!'

Their dog, Daisy, was a hit. Peaches insisted on taking her for a walk, and Alan went with her, walking over the park to the tennis courts and back. Merryl was glad to see her go, already exhausted by coping with the girl. They had an early meal, chicken stew, and Peaches fortunately decided to get an early night.

Upstairs, Merryl stood at the bedroom windows. Straight ahead the lights of the bridge arching high, were reflected in the water in streamers of colour, red, blue, white, yellow against the blackness of sky and river, and Wrest Point Casino was a gold maypole against the lights of the suburbs rising up the hills.

In bed, Merryl cuddled Alan's back as usual. 'Well, she's fitting in, love. No need to worry.'

'We'll see,' he said, grumpily.

Merryl sighed. 'What's wrong?'

'She's spoiling Daisy.'

'Is that all? She's a sweetie.' And turned over to sleep.

Next morning, Peaches came into the kitchen early and placed a carton of soy milk and a packet of muesli on the bench.

'You shouldn't. We have muesli, Peaches dear.' But not soy milk, Merryl detested the stuff. Peaches had slung a woolly cardigan over her flimsy gear, Merryl was pleased to see. She handed her a bowl for her muesli.

'Did you sleep well? Cup of tea?'

'Yes and yes. Herbal, please,' giving Merryl a sweet smile.

'How's your mum, Mandy? And Xanthe, how is she?' asking as the girl sat at the table.

'They're fine. Mum and Dad live in the same street in Lonnie as Gran.'

'That's handy. Both teachers, aren't they?'

'Yes. Pretty ordinary family, really. I'm the creative one. Mum let me do my bedroom pink with black animal footprints and red trim.'

'Very nice. Your brothers?' Merryl poured the tea. 'How are they?'

'Good. Studying building at tech. Gonna be builders. So boring.'

'And you, what's your university course?'

'Fine arts. You want to see my portfolio? My focus is street life, photos, prints, and stuff.'

'Very nice, but not right now. Here's your tea.'

'Thank you. Love your house, Merryl. Where's Alan? Such a great view!' And she was up, dancing over to the living room windows.

The back door opened and Alan came in from his morning walk, Daisy bounding about him. He shrugged off his waterproof, his boots discarded outside the back door.

'Oh, I so love her!' Peaches ran to the dog, and she jumped around, her coat bouncing, pink tongue out, little eyes lost in curls, almost laughing. 'Gorgeous girl.'

'Did you get the paper, dear?'

'As always,' Alan's tone was ironic as he slapped it on the table. 'Has the Empire State Building fallen down?'

Merryl almost snapped and stopped herself. Alan's joke that he'd forget to get the paper when the Empire State Building fell down was so tiresome.

'Breakfast on the go?' Merryl hurried to get the pan out for the bacon and scrambled eggs. She was running late, due to Peaches. Then stopped. Running late for what? They were both retired, that was one reason why they'd agreed to help the girl.

'Daisy, get down.'

The dog was jumping around while Peaches laughed.

Alan grabbed her by the collar. 'Outside.'

'Oh no,' Peaches pleaded. 'Leave her in. You'll behave, won't you, Daisy?'

To Merryl's surprise, Alan relented, and the dog quietened down.

After breakfast, Merryl planned to continue planting a strip of garden down the side of the house. It was shady, getting sun only early morning, and she wanted white blooming plants to lighten it. A camellia japonica with overlapping white petals, white flowering scabias, impatiens and lobelias in pots, and so on, she had all the seedlings in their trays ready, and the camellia shrub. When they were planted, she would mulch with a layer of woodchips to finish it off neatly. She went out and left Alan cleaning up the kitchen and stacking the dishwasher while Peaches sat at the table, playing with Daisy's ears. After fifteen minutes, they came outside.

'Just taking Daisy out.'

'But she's had her walk this morning.'

'Come on, Daisy.' Peaches was already out the gate with the dog on a lead.

She was wearing Alan's waterproof, Merryl noticed.

'Peaches wants to see Lindisfarne Bay,' Alan said.

'What about university? Doesn't she need to get down there, enrol and all that?'

'Hasn't she enrolled already?'

Merryl shrugged. 'Orientation, do they still do that?'

But Alan had turned to go. She watched them depart together, leaving the gate open. Irritated, she walked down the garden to shut it, and saw them heading down to the bay, talking nineteen to the dozen. Was this good for Alan, or not? He'd grown so inward, is how she put it, with retirement. Depressed? Surely not, but it worried her. If someone like Peaches could take him out of himself, well, she should encourage her.

Merryl knelt on the padded rest to protect her knees from the concrete and dug with her garden trowel. The soil was moist, friable, and she quickly dug the holes and planted the seedlings along the length of the bed. The camellia could wait. Aching, she stood and brushed herself down, took off her gardening gloves and looked about. The house was silent, the street too, the air cool under low cloud and she had that feeling that she was the only person alive in the world and therefore what was the point of an all-white garden? What was the point of anything at all? In this mood, she wasn't surprised that Alan and Peaches had not come back. They might have fallen off the edge of the world for all she knew. A cuppa. She must go inside for a cuppa. That would shift this mood.

The kitchen was neat, well organised. Alan had done a good job of cleaning up, he always did, and they got on well performing household chores, like all old retirees, nattering on, their conversation no longer focusing on the state of the world. That was behind them, the anti-war moratoriums, abortion rights, equal pay for equal work, not that they had participated but it was there, a backdrop to daily living then. And it was up to the young ones, now, to fight on – there was always an issue. She put on the jug and wondered how much had Peaches helped Alan clear up, probably not at all, and caught herself. That was a mean thought.

The cuppa over, the cup washed up and put away – nothing ever remained out on her benches, Merryl went out and watered in her new plants with diluted seaweed extract, and then put the gardening tools away in the shed up the back. Back in the kitchen, she started the evening's soup. She got the stock she had made from boiling up chicken bones from the fridge, and a selection of vegetables from the crisper. She had an idea that Peaches might be vegetarian, so she decided to keep the chicken stock secret. She was cutting up the vegetables when the front gate banged and in they came on a gust of cool air, excited, lively, wanting to share their morning.

'How's the garden going? Get it all done?'

'Yes,' she started to say but Peaches interrupted.

'Oh god, I really need to get to the university. It's your fault Daisy, you're such fun…' and off they went again, chasing around the table.

Merryl reached up to a shelf and extracted a bus timetable from behind jars of dried beans. 'Here you are. The buses are regular into the city, then you catch the uni bus.'

Alan looked at Merryl, astonished. 'That will take her hours. I'll take her. Be ready in a jiffy.'

'Cool. You're such a sweety, Alan,' Peaches said as he left the room, glancing at Merryl, just a sideways flicker, but Merryl understood. Alan is my friend, you are not.

Merryl went into the hall and took her coat off the hook. She pulled it on as she returned to the kitchen. The vegetables and the soup stock went back into the fridge.

Alan came in. 'We'll be off now.'

'Just get my bag.'

'What, you're coming? No need, dear.' His moon face concerned.

Merryl thought of making an excuse, like, something at the shops to pick up, but no. She could do what she liked. They went out to the car, Merryl in the passenger seat, Peaches in the back, backed out and drove away. They were all silent, but accelerating down the East Derwent Highway towards the bridge, they saw someone hitching.

'Stop! Stop!' Peaches cried. 'Someone needs a ride,' and Alan swerved over.

'Oh, really, Alan,' Merryl protested. They never picked up hitchhikers, could be dangerous.

The hitchhiker ran over as Peaches opened the car door, and a woman got in beside her. Short hair, jumper, jeans and boots and a backpack which she hauled in with her. 'Oh, thanks! I was walking between bus stops, the bus went past, it didn't stop.'

'Bummer,' Peaches said.

'We're going into town,' Merryl said, craning to get a better look at her.

'Me too,' she answered.

'You live around here?' Alan asked as he drove off.

'Yes. I came to Tassie fifteen years ago to be with my dying mother,' she said.

'Heavens, where from?' Merryl asked.

'Melbourne.'

'Cool!' Peaches said. 'I love Melbourne. Mum took me over to see the art gallery, a really famous exhibition, Monet. Amazing!'

'Your mother…' Merryl gently reminded the woman.

'She died. But I was never able to leave. I tried and tried, got to the airport and came back. Tassie's so beautiful it kept me here.'

'D'you have any other family here?' Merryl asked.

'An adopted son. He's twenty-four. I was told I couldn't have children but then, after I adopted, I got pregnant.'

'Oh, wow!' Peaches exclaimed. 'That is so good.'

'I had three babies, one after the other. I didn't try to stop, it was meant to be.'

'It was, it was!' Peaches gushed.

Merryl twisted round to look at this woman who was so sure that all that happened to her was good.

'I'm catching up with my son. We're heading down the Styx to the protest.'

'What's that? Alan, what's the protest?' Peaches demanded. 'What's the Styx?'

'Down the south-west, I believe,' Alan said. They were going over the bridge now, he needed to concentrate.

'On the edge of the World Heritage area, actually,' the woman said. 'We've got to fight to save the forests, it's a war on nature, the clear-felling.'

'War on nature,' Peaches echoed. 'Wow.'

'Where do you want to be dropped off?' Alan's voice so calm, like a dash of cold water.

'In the city, Barrack Street, if you're going that way. A group of us are meeting there.'

'Can do.'

'You're saying, because you were given these babies, now you must fight for the forests?' Merryl was unconvinced.

'That's right.'

'That is so cool. You have to do what's right!' Peaches insisted to Merryl.

Do what's right? All her life she'd done what was right, hadn't she? So now she spent her time planning a white flower garden up the side of her house. This woman, probably uneducated, had at a whim of fate had a family, and at a whim of fate was fighting for something she believed in. She'd never managed anything like that. Their life, what had it been?

'The most beautiful forests,' the woman was saying. 'Paperbarks, celery top pine, native beech, blackwood, sassafras, King Billy pine, man ferns, mosses, fungi…'

Listening to the voice behind her, Merryl felt ignorant and felt again that this woman, this unknown hitchhiker, knew so much, was prepared to do so much.

'It's being bulldozed and burned. Napalmed.'

'No! Why are they doing that!' Peaches protested. 'Alan?'

'For woodchips, I guess. Export dollars.'

'Napalmed?' A memory came to Merryl from the Vietnamese War, the girl running, her back on fire. 'I don't believe it.'

'It's true,' the woman exclaimed. 'They're bulldozing the environment, like they own it. Too bad about climate change.'

'That's right!' Peaches joined in.

'And the right of the forests to stay as they are.'

'Every single tree,' Peaches said, and Merryl felt herself agreeing.

Alan was cruising through the city now. He turned into Barrack Street. A group of people with backpacks and gear was clustered outside a health food shop.

'This is it,' the woman said, and Alan slowed and pulled over.

'Thank you so much.' She got out, dragging out her pack.

A tall young guy left the group and hugged her.

'Oh, wow, that's her son,' Peaches said. 'He's cute.'

'What a story,' Merryl said as Alan left the kerb, and they turned and waved.

At the university, they dropped Peaches off, arranging to pick her up after an hour.

Alan drove down to Long Beach, parked, and discussed buying an ice cream. 'Vanilla, dear?'

Merryl wasn't listening. She watched the passers-by. How did they live their lives? Were they happy, or did they feel the dissatisfaction that she felt? Because, what had she done with her life? Kept a good home for her husband. Prepared for the six weeks they spent overseas every year, and the regular breaks they took around Tasmania, staying at only the best bed and breakfasts. Only the best, that had been their mantra. Wednesdays, she volunteered at the local church coffee and chat mornings for old people who needed company. As she took orders for drinks, she overheard the conversations: my sister-in-law's sister, she passed; diverticulitis, your colon is cut; my knee replacement's been cancelled… How long would it be before she joined them in their obsession with illnesses and death? Alan's life centred around Daisy and she felt a rush of impatience. A dog is a dog, after all. Her husband occasionally met his former engineering mates for a drink at a pub, but he had no other life outside the house, either. Children, they'd decided against them. Why? If only she'd got pregnant accidentally! Or adopted?

Alan got into the car, holding two wrapped ice creams, and she started. She hadn't noticed him getting out of the car.

'Here you go, dear.' He thrust the vanilla ice cream topped with chocolate at her.

She gazed at him. Was this all they were now? Where was the passion, the debate, the commitment to something other than themselves and their day-by-day comfort? She got out of the car, walked over to a nearby bin and tossed the ice cream in. 'Let's go,' she said, ignoring his astonished face. 'Pick up Peaches.'

Back home, sitting on the comfortable twin leather lounges, they watched the news on television to see if there was anything about protests in the Styx Valley. Nothing.

'No wonder,' Peaches said. 'The men who control the media don't want everyone to know about the protests.'

Alan scoffed. 'You're seeing conspiracies now.'

'I think she's right.' Merryl got up.

Peaches followed her into the kitchen.

'That woman we picked up, she's amazing. Her story should be on the news, hey, Merryl?'

'Absolutely. She's an example to us all.' Merryl got the soup stock and vegetables out of the fridge and together they got the soup on the go.

'I checked out student accommodation,' Peaches said. 'No worries, I can get a flat.'

'Oh! Right. You're welcome to stay, Peaches dear.' Surprising herself at how much she liked the girl's company.

'Thank you, Merryl. I don't want to be a bother.'

Merryl suddenly saw herself and Alan as Peaches did: two old fuddy-duddies. Why would she want to live with them?

'You can always come for a meal, stay overnight. Any problems, come to us…'

'Mmmm… Thank you, I'll have to come see Daisy.'

After dinner, Merryl asked Peaches to fetch her laptop. Could she find pictures of the Styx?

'Sure.'

Alan snorted as Peaches darted to her room.

Merryl turned on him.

'I want to see what's being destroyed,' she said.

'All right, all right!'

'Here we go.' Peaches set up her laptop on the table and Merryl sat close by her.

The girl tapped away and the pictures came up. Beautiful forest, a tree so massive a person, arms outspread, still didn't reach its span, a waterfall cascading. It was almost ethereal in its beauty and must once have been the home of Indigenous myth, legend and fairy tale, maybe like European forests and it belonged to all of them, just as Peaches said. Then a scene of terrible destruction labelled Styx Valley Holocaust.

Merryl gasped, her hand to her mouth. 'That is wicked!'

'Like a war,' Peaches said.

Indeed, it was just like the pictures Merryl had seen of the aftermath of war.

'That cannot be justified. Alan?'

Reluctantly, he came over.

'We have to do something.'

'Do no good, the government's backing it for jobs and votes,' and he went back to the leather lounge.

'It doesn't belong to the government or the timber industry. It belongs to us all,' Merryl cried.

'Exactly right,' Peaches said.

Next morning, while Alan was taking Daisy for her walk, Merryl went up to the shed where her old camping gear was stored. A sleeping bag, the thick green type, was in its bag still. An old backpack, gardening boots. Would they be enough? What should she do about a tent? She lifted down the sleeping bag and buried her face. It was musty, damp and a hint of her old self was in it, that girl who'd once gone camping with Alan and the university walking club, and she sensed lost potential, a different way that she could have lived. Was it too late? She thrust the bag back on its shelf and walked back around the house to her little white garden. Petals like little faces turned to the light would grow and bloom now. Alan would be fine while she was away, coping with cooking, regular walks with Daisy. In fact, who really needed her here? She went back into the shed, took out the sleeping bag again. No, this would not do for camping in the freezing wilderness. She must stop at the outdoor shops in town and get all new gear. And food, freeze-dried food, to stock up.

She went back into the house as Peaches came down to breakfast. 'I'm going into town directly,' Merryl said. 'I can drop you at the university.'

Peaches looked up. 'Oh, thanks, Merryl.' Sleepy, her hand curling a strand of hair.

'Now, Peaches.'

'Oh, right.' The girl got up, went upstairs and came down dressed and ready to go.

As they were leaving, Alan came trudging across from Anzac Park, Daisy trotting obediently on the lead.

Merryl slowed the car and retracted the window. 'I'm dropping Peaches at the university,' she said. 'Won't be long.'

Alan watched her drive away, his bland face surprised, and Merryl saw in the rear-vision mirror her husband receding and diminishing into a tiny figure. She was going, but further than the university, back in time almost, to herself as a different person with different friends. And deeper, into a wilderness of heart and a willingness to experience forces beyond her control and to try to change them. That woman, the hitchhiker, had shown her what was possible, crossing her path almost as fate. She would join her and her son, and when she came back, splattered with the mud of the Styx Valley, imbued with its scents, its beauty, its sounds, she would go on as a fighter for the right of the forest and all of its inhabitants to live safe from the massive machines of exploitation and capital. For the generations to come, for all the children to be able to know and treasure, these forests. And she so looked forward to it!

Pentimento

Driving around the hook of the South Arm Peninsula, Pete slowed to look north across Ralph's Bay. Sunlight dazzling the water snared fleets of seabirds in its net of light and far off the blue-hazed slopes of Mount Wellington/kunanyi slumped against the sky. Ah, that view, the backdrop to his childhood!

Slowing to the sixty-kilometre speed limit, Pete drove on, passing the South Arm Returned Servicemen's League club rooms set back from the road. By the entrance drive, a chalked sign advertised Asian Menu Saturday Night, but missing the 'u' instead read Asian Men Saturday Night. Fuck me! He swerved, laughing, then straightened the wheel of his Land Cruiser. Not the old South Arm he knew and he wondered how many takers they would get. Just kiddin'… Bert, his dad, used to spend a fair bit of time in the RSL with his mates from around the place, the fishermen, the farmers, the orchardists, and he'd mixed with them too back then when he'd been Peta. Nothing was as it was, he'd found in life, and as an artist he'd tried to show it as it was not. And now, late in age, he was here to revisit family history, for the old family home, his home, was up for auction.

Described as a farmhouse on acreage, most of the land had been sold off way back after the British market for fruit had collapsed. That was before he was born, and his father had got other investments to live on. He wondered if the house right now was within his financial reach. He was interested, but why? Nostalgia, for family, for the life he'd lived down here? He'd left this place too soon, moving up to Hobart to study fine arts at university. His two older sisters had left too, training as nurses. Only Jess, his favourite sister, eighteen months younger than he, had remained. What had happened to her, what had she done with her life? Bronwyn, Amanda and Jess, the sisters with himself as one of them, Peta.

At their parents' funerals, for they'd died within a few months of each other fifteen years ago, Jess had ignored him. Looking cured like leather by chain-smoking, dog hairs on her black jacket, she'd had little to say to anyone, and that in a whisky-deepened voice. She was no longer the bright perky person she had been. His other sisters had barely acknowledged him either, and he felt such rancour. What was hardest for them to swallow, his sex orientation or his art? All that naked flesh, the unseemly religious references, the controversy. Mum and Dad hadn't deserved it, they seemed to imply. In turn, he was cold and haughty, cloaking himself in his persona as an artist, keeping their censure at bay, consolidating his break with them. A history underlying the present, the lines of his earlier life showed through in forms and emotions, shadowy outlines and streaks of colour. Pentimento came to mind, where earlier efforts on a canvas showed through to the surface of a new painting, as his birth gender showed through in his current gender identity and he smiled: himself as his own work of art?

The past informed the present, too. His name was one of those of the first settlers, ex-convicts most of them, given land grants in the early 1800s. Taken the land of the Indigenous people, but whose presence was still visible. Down at Shelly Beach, the coast of Ralph's Bay was edged with half a metre of shell midden, and on top another half metre of soil, the division between the two cultures' knife-edge. The pasture created when the settlers cleared the land of its ancient forests overlay in less than two hundred years the tens of thousands of years of Aboriginal life. And everywhere emerged this evidence in shell scatter, along the bike paths and drives, by house foundations, gardens. People living on this land, he reflected, were illiterate to its Aboriginal history. And their own history was as mutable as a river, carrying stories from one generation to the next with the ebb and flow of time. Lies and half-truths and misunderstandings, too often the facts of the matter jettisoned, along with the real-life feelings and experiences, the pain and the longing such as he had felt. So much for words and language, let alone sex orientation, body image, self-image and the words that did not describe them.

Before Pete drove to the auction, he stopped the car at the jetty, and got out. Birds were wheeling and calling, and down at the end of the jetty two fellows were fishing. He walked down, the salty breeze buffeting him.

'How's it going?'

'Not much happenin.' The old guy looked up at Pete.

'Way to spend the arvo,' his younger mate said.

'That's right.'

So many times he'd gone out with the Balcombe boys, Joey and Mark, fishing for a feed of flathead, diving for crays around Betsy Island, even as far as Tasman Island, where basking seals had barked. Good times with the Balcombes, he'd fitted in with them, until his mother had put a stop to it. No, you aren't going fishing with those boys, you're staying home, there's plenty to do around here. What had she thought would happen? Sex? Rape? Or was it snobbishness, the Balcombes too lowly in that stratified rural society? Where were they now, Joey and Mark, still living locally, fishing these waters? Probably, their lives embedded in this environment, and Pete took a deep breath, sensing again, as he had back then out on the water, the deep tolling of an aeons-old existence, and felt an answering response in his old body. His old body, yes, that had returned to the chunkiness of his youth. In fact, he had a heart murmur. But, not to worry, everyone had something wrong with them. He breathed deeply, enjoying the moving, sighing expanse of water, far off the hills of the Channel, Tinderbox and Flowerpot, and Bruny Island poking its nose north.

Their parents and grandparents before them had used the Derwent estuary as a road, going to dances and celebrations on Bruny, across to the hamlets of the Channel, and across Storm Bay to the Forestier Peninsula, sailing back at dawn to get stuck into a hard day's work. He'd never painted these views and this history, rarely this life. His art was described as 'sensual neo-expressionism' by critics who knew fuck all. It was his particular vision he put down in oil paint, as both Peta and Pete, the feminine and the masculine. How could they hope to understand that? Was it time to let this sense of place seep through in his works, like pentimento? This place on the edge of the world with its dinky shop and post office, its memorial to war an obelisk with a lit cross in its point, the wars named, and the names of the soldiers from local families listed on a brass plaque. He loved its shacks decaying into the dunes, less substantial than the timeless middens, but also of this place. And not much had changed over the decades. He'd only seen a few new houses, a few renovated shacks.

Yet, when he'd started to make it in the art world, he had left here, left Tasmania. He'd found a place in the country, Bairnsdale, bought land and created a studio and house. A mud-brick big-windowed place completely off the grid on a few acres, including a spa and a sauna, the landscaped gardens right up to the windows a retreat for his soul. So why was he leaving? The area was too popular, Bairnsdale and the little towns around it like Hepburn Springs going alternate with llama studs, Buddhist retreats, karmatherapy workshops, aromatherapy studios, health farms, wholefood shops. He'd lost his sense of privacy, the distance from the great centres of power he needed to create his art. After all, Melbourne was a city of several million and spreading north, not the few hundred thousand of Hobart. The end of his long-term relationship with Katya five years ago still hurt, so much he'd had to shell out to her in separating, pulling the strands of their lives apart. Values in the Bairnsdale area had escalated, he needed to cash in for his old age, seventy not being old in his terms, but it was heading that way. So his presence here in South Arm was propelled by his need for money as much as nostalgia. The family had left him nothing; he'd wanted nothing after they'd sold up. So to the auction, and no, he wasn't getting even, nothing like that.

Pete got back into the car, backed away from the jetty and drove up to the road, and turning left cruised the half-kilometre to the house. A few cars were already parked in the drive, and Pete drew to a stop across the road. He looked over at the house and was shocked, it looked so run-down. The grand lines shabby, its 1930s style – California deco with its arched Spanish-style entrance – looked out of date, but a winner to someone, surely. The garden, his mother's pride and joy, had gone, just a couple of scrappy rhododendrons lost in hillocks of grass and bracken. Bracken! It had never dared push its curled fists through the soil in his mother's garden. The house needed a new roof, the stucco needed a coat of paint, the downpipes and the gutters needed replacing. And the window frames? Who knew? But so much was left, the allure of better times showing through. Pentimento again but the word also meant to repent, and he started. Repent about what? Jess? What about Jess?

Where Pete had parked the car was a row of shacks, half fixed up, subsiding in wild garden, then bush and beyond it, the dunes above the beach. The Kincaids, the Wilsons and the Morgans had owned these shacks, coming down every summer to his and his sisters' delight. With their kids, they were a gang roaming the beaches and the bush. Family barbecues, the games, the ice creams on hot afternoons, his older sisters filling the house with the hit parade, the mooning American songs of teenage obsession. He'd loved black singers, humming to himself: *I was born by the river in a little tent, and just like that river I've been runnin ever since, it's been a long time comin, but I know-ow a change gonna come whoa yes it will…*

He knew back then the change was coming when he developed breasts and tried to flatten them, the pubic hair he'd tried to cut off. What did he want, to be Peta Pan? It was about that time that skinny red-haired Jimmy Kincaid had tried it on, kissing him, Peta. He'd pushed him away, revolted, and Jimmy had sneered, calling him a bitch, so he'd kicked him hard in the crotch, then run for it. Jess had been upset, because he hadn't waited to make a joke of it and she'd thrown a fit. She had a crush on Jimmy? That squirt, he'd teased her, only too willing to torment this sister whose femaleness affronted him. The smell of her, of them both, the time of the month, the hated menstruation, the self-hatred. How bitchy he'd been to Jess, back then as Peta. Oh god, repent!

Right where he was standing, pines, gums and coastal wattle formed low scrub. He bet there was still the track they'd pelted along to Half Moon

Bay, avoiding the blackberry brambles, thumping their feet to scare snakes, to haul themselves up the dunes and fall straight down to the shore and into the water, screaming with delight, and he almost felt again the breath taken from his body with the cold shock of it, and he shivered.

Across the road, people were wandering about, so Pete mooched over as if he were just a bystander and not too interested, a local having a sticky-beak. A couple more cars arrived, slowed and drove in. There was interest, then.

Pete walked up the wide gravel drive, a path between nothing but scrubby bush, no landscaping left here. He climbed the steps and paused in the hall. Oh, good heavens, all the beautiful woodwork had been painted thick glossy white, even the art deco features above the doors and windows. The walls were white, the lovely grain of the wood-panelled doors his mother had been so proud of, blotted out with white paint. The agent, interrupting his horrified response, introduced herself as Margot and thrust a clipboard towards him, asking for his name and phone or email address. He filled in the details absentmindedly, giving her no additional information about himself, and then hurried away.

The floorboards had been carpeted, the windows were intact, the rooms as large and open as he remembered, but silent to the sounds of their life there. He didn't go into the bedrooms, he knew them so well, large, cold rooms which had been hard to warm. The bathroom looked like it had been modernised in the 80s with green plastic fittings, a shower over the bath, a toilet, a handbasin, unpainted pine walls and a small window. It was awful, so small, how had they made do with it? Back then, no one worried, you just waited in a queue or went outside to pee behind a tree. The hall opened into the long lounge room, also painted white, with a big window at the far end. A fireplace, an open fire, not even a wood stove? Ah, those cold winter days when he'd curled up in an armchair with a book right by the fire, the flames dancing, logs subsiding with a shower of sparks. And in everyone's way because this was the direct route from the front door to the back, through the hall. His dad coming in with muddy boots, his mum yelling at him from the kitchen, Bert, not muddy boots on my floors! A couple of dogs bounding by, Blacky and Socks, he'd loved them, and Jess had, too. And his mum coming in with a tray of cupcakes straight from the combustion stove, the warm icing dripping as he pushed one whole into his mouth and getting told off, that is not a ladylike way to eat, Peta!

The kitchen was a long galley, just as he remembered it. The cupboards and drawers tatty pine, the floors covered with some cheap lino tile, and a low pine ceiling with fluorescent bars. A round table and some chairs were squeezed in at the end under the windows where they had all sat for their meals. The space between the kitchen and the laundry had been filled in by his dad, creating a lobby where wet gear, boots, raincoats and the dogs' bowls were kept. It was so shonky, Pete could see stains on the walls where the rain had come in. The whole place needed work, and saw that estimation in Margot's apologetic eyes, as she followed him around, her clipboard held to her breasts.

Outside, the old packing shed where they had spent so many hours grading, wrapping and packing newly picked apples into pine boxes, listed to one side. He paused, remembering those hot days, sunlight falling through, motes dancing, the Kincaids yelling for them to come for a swim… The past seeping through the present in his mind.

In the back garden, scrubby geraniums had gone wild and weeds covered the beds and the paths. Beyond the rough wooden fence rails, everything a metre up was covered by Spanish ivy reaching to the orchards, rows of apple trees, all dead, he could see that from here. Then, a memory. Jess. He'd seen her going into the orchard with Jimmy Kincaid and he'd sneaked after them but the dogs had bounded around him, and trying to send them back he lost sight of the two, till he heard the screaming and crying and the dogs had rushed down the orchard, barking and he'd fled back into the house. Memories, once as dead as this place, re-emerging to haunt him. What had Jimmy done to Jess? Exacted revenge on his sister, retribution for his rejection of him? Oh god, what had he done! Jess was never the same. The cheerful girl had retreated into a silent, brooding presence whom he was relieved to forget when he eventually left home.

Pete bolted round to the front of the house where the auction was taking place, the grating voice of the auctioneer rising, describing the house, the land, the view. Brushing away Margot and her clipboard, he hurried down the drive and across the road, heading along the track to the beach, brambles catching at his ankles. He struggled up the dunes, one step sinking deep after another, panting, sweat running, reaching the top. And then there it was, this long blue vista up-river to Mount Wellington/kunanyi, the view he'd loved. But what did it mean now, he who'd buried his memories? Because Peta, in becoming Pete, had become utterly self-absorbed, convincing everyone of his genius with bravado, eccentricity, flare. Yet what did he really have to say about life, when he couldn't even face the truth about what had happened to his little sister? Not in all the years since…

He half-fell down the dunes to the shore. What had really brought him here, what had made him change his mind, when long ago he'd decided never to return? The need to face what he'd done, to reconcile himself to a tragedy, to his sister? I was innocent, he cried to himself. I didn't know! Surf broke, swirled and rushed away from him, the glare of late afternoon sunlight snared him, and wincing, he scanned the bay. The figure of a woman was silhouetted on the sleek shore, walking away, two dogs bounding around her. Jess? Walking Blacky and Socks? He started after her, longing to dispel the rancour, the bitterness, resurrect the good and the beautiful they had shared here. He staggered, listing in the wet sand and fell as a wave broke, dashing against his unwieldy body. He clawed back upright, frantic to reach that figure and this time the image he saw was of himself as Peta, walking in the past. He started after the image, desperate to merge with it, for Peter and Peta to become one. Sudden pain, his vision tilting, the bay rising up, Bruny sliding away to the south, the deep blue of kunanyi looming. His heart! The pain deepened and he fell back into the swirling water where voices called, and he strained to see Peta and Jess playing on the shore together. But as the sun drew down into darkness, Pete went with it, knowing at last, this was why he'd come back, this was why he'd returned home.

Sasha

The funeral service was over, the drinks and titbits to follow were damp, the bubbly flat. Gerard, Sasha's younger brother, had died, passed, as everyone said, a word for which Sasha had nothing but contempt. Massive heart disease. Dead. Edward, her older brother, had 'passed' years before. Lung cancer. Dead. He'd been a chain-smoker. Sasha had seen that, when she'd stayed with him in Sydney that time. Heart disease? Cancer? What was in line for her? Well, not preventable lifestyle conditions, that was for sure, and she wafted her hand over a plate of cream horns proffered by Anna, Gerard's youngest daughter. His widow, Shelly, looked on, looking good in mourning, and Sasha entertained the spiteful thought that she had a lover. She checked the room for talent and with a frisson of horror found bulbous noses, cratered necks, slumping bellies and hairlines in full flight. Patting her own grey-blonde hair swooped up and frothing over a loose knot, she arranged curls about ears studded with fat pearls, not hearing aids, and loosened her silk scarf.

Ironically, Gerard was being farewelled in the former college they had both attended, now converted to a funeral home. An ugly pink and cream stucco edifice, it caught the winter fog flowing from the Derwent Valley through the streets, making the lives of the students even more miserable. Frozen hands. Chilblains. Breath puffing on frosty mornings spawning her desire to flee to a warmer climate. She'd left only a year after graduating from here, had she actually graduated? Flying to her brother Edward in Sydney, where she'd discarded Sandra and become Sasha and continued north, finding her preferred ambience in Byron Bay. Now she was back again, as Gerard's only sister, his children's only relation from that side of the family, all gone like leaves falling from the family tree, and glimpsing bare branches beyond the windows, realised that she was the only bird left singing in it.

Why had Gerard chosen to die in winter? She hadn't wanted to leave Byron Bay, its verdant colour and warmth, her house so entertaining to the arty elite of the area. Yet, lassitude, introspection, depression had taken hold recently, curling around her mind like those cold fogs of the past. Marcus, her partner, had opted out of attending the funeral, despite her wish, she reflected bitterly, and smiled brightly around at no one in particular. People were chatting away, about what? She wondered if she could introduce the topic of her latest book into their conversations. Some informal promotion, just to let people know down here that they could purchase it at their local bookstores or online.

Amour in the Cane, set in the sugar cane fields of northern Queensland, had not been a success. She'd written her usual romantic magic, she'd thought, given that she had found the sugar cane fields to be hot, dirty places, and as for sugar, she avoided it. Had she depleted the gold she'd mined from this seam, romantic fiction, for so long?

Critics? Well, no problem there, they'd never reviewed her books anyway, despite the care with which she wrote, a stickler for correct English expression. Worse, she'd had to contend with opinions that her books were nothing more than upmarket Mills & Boon, an accusation made by rude young journalists, unpaid interns, their bylines restricted to local rags. As for that woman at a party in Byron, carrying on about mercury in the pesticides used on the cane fields, kidney damage and neurological impairment in children, for heaven's sake! She didn't deal in messages, she dealt in escape from such horrors, that was her schtick. Didn't anyone appreciate her style, her characterisation, her descriptions of landscape and setting? The drama? People – yes, mostly women – read her books and that was how she liked it. But why not this time? Was it time to reinvent herself, to write a serious work? She remembered the advice she'd heard from a writer on a radio book show: whatever you are writing about, stare it in the face. A puzzling admonition. Stare what in the face? And then her concern surfaced: Marcus, was he tiring of her?

The fallings out! The fiery reckonings! The passionate reconciliations! Disputes she could only view through the lens of romance. Maybe now was the time to take another slant and write a magnificent novel that reviewers would critique favourably in lit mags and weekend lifestyle inserts, discuss on book shows, press invitations to chat shows and festivals onto her…

'Sandra?'

Hearing her former name, Sasha winced.

'Are you okay? I know, it's so sad for you. The loss will ease with time, dear.' Shelly's face was concerned. 'Don't be so cut up, I'm always here, you can always, you know.…'

'Thank you, Shelly, I'll manage.' The woman was crazy. She didn't feel that much for Gerard, hadn't even seen him for years. Her mobile buzzed. 'Sorry, Shelly, must get this…' and backed away to a quiet corner. Positive news from her publisher? She listened. No, a contact from the airline. Her flight to Sydney had been delayed. How long? Twenty-four hours, for heaven's sake. She'd thought one day and return, that would be enough here, but another night it would have to be.

She tapped on the phone and rang Marcus's number. 'Hi, darling…' No answer. She left a message explaining the problem. 'Love you, darling!'

Marcus had been a late romance, an Indian summer of love, someone to enjoy her architect-designed statement on her landscaped hectares, and she longed to get back to him. There was no need to let the family know of her change of plans, and making airy farewells and condolences, regretful that she had a plane to catch, Sasha left the funeral home.

Standing on the steps outside, Sasha hugged her Italian-styled coat around her and lifted the collar about her face. Through the bare trees, the old houses opposite huddled in the cold air. Would she have been happy living in one of those if she'd stayed here, as Gerard had done? She knew the answer was no, as cars passed, their tyres swishing mournfully, and she shivered as if the ghost of another life had passed her by. Descending the steps, she walked to her hire car and drove away through the cold city, back to her smart hotel overlooking the picturesque wharves.

The next morning, Sasha took a cup of coffee and a slice of toast in the hotel dining room. She didn't believe in big breakfasts and looked distastefully at the guests piling up their plates at the breakfast bar. Scrambled egg, baked beans and tomatoes, omelette, fried potatoes, sausages… The smell of the food was enough to make her vomit. She was as elegantly dressed as for the funeral for the simple reason that she hadn't brought a change of clothes, intending to fly in and fly out, with only a clean change of underwear. And she wasn't about to search the city for decent leisurewear. Her hair was brushed back now, showing off her tan, her careful make-up, dark eyebrows and blue eyes. Marcus would have been pleased with her looks, as their image of a groomed and sophisticated couple when seen out and about helped the business, when she wasn't writing. There was so much money to be made in property in Byron, but so many sharks, you had to do everything to beat your rivals. Marcus was firm about that, and she always followed his advice.

As Sasha waited at reception to check out, she picked up a tourist pamphlet promoting the East Coast Drive, the wineries, the beaches, boutique holiday retreats in historic homesteads, fresh seafood, classic Tasmanian wines, Freycinet National Park, Maria Island… Yes, she would spend the day hitting the East Coast. And then the thought came, she could look for a setting for a new romantic novel. Perhaps the change would be all that was needed for her to write the next winner, and she left, full of anticipation.

Accelerating out of the underground parking, she joined the traffic heading for the Tasman Bridge, crossed it and sped onto the freeway through suburbs of welfare housing, reaching Midway Point and then Sorell. Well, so far nothing much out this way, she rang to tell Marcus, but this time the phone rang out. No worries, the sun was out, warming everything, giving life to the landscape, and she relaxed and drove on.

Turning left for the coast, Sasha cruised through farmland, degraded paddocks, scruffy stands of trees, weatherboard houses needing paint. Taking the outer lanes, she climbed several ranges of hills called of all things, Bust Me Gall Hill and Black Charlie's Opening, arriving at Buckland, another nothing sort of place. She sped away, reaching the narrow, winding road above the Prosser River to Orford, and at last here was the East Coast proper. She took a right to Spring Beach, a lovely curve of shore above aqua shallows. Smart holiday homes edged the road and rose up the hillside, half hidden in the bush. Positively Malibu! There no one was in sight, no restaurants, only a corner store café, no signs of holiday activities, fishing trips, kayak tours, mini golf, surf or fashion outlets, nothing.

Sasha angle-parked and gazed over the pristine beach, across the bay and there, floating along the horizon, blue and dreamy, was Maria Island. Magic! Such a selling point, this view, she thought, but on another level, this can't be bought. It is too special. And her thoughts went back to Marcus.

Sasha had met him when she was out riding. Not on horseback, as in a Jane Austen novel, but a bike she'd hired from Sunshine Cycles. Pedalling along the road to the lighthouse, she'd hit a clump of grass and the bike had dumped her on the verge. Swearing, she'd staggered up, and a guy had wheeled around her, and there he was in full bike riding gear. Lycra pants, a T-shirt tight over his tanned chest and shoulders, brown muscled calves, and studded sneakers, helmet and goggles, like a knight in armour coming to her rescue. He'd helped her up and they'd chatted, finally taking the bike and helmet back to Sunshine Cycles, where Marcus had insisted on a refund. That was the start of their Grand Romance, exactly five years ago, she reflected as she got out her phone, tapping his number. The answering machine this time, his smooth voice welcoming callers to Byron Investment, and its catchphrase: Home is an emotional concept. So true!

Sasha checked the local real estate offerings on her mobile and found a couple of properties, one in Walpole Street, another in Charles Street. She located them, thinking, probably nice enough at low prices by mainland standards, but holiday and retirement only; you couldn't commute to work from here. The Walpole Street property was a four-bedroomer:

She forwarded it to Marcus's email address and placed her phone on the passenger seat in easy reach. Then took it up again. She rang Marcus's private number. Listened. Simone, the PA, answered. What was she doing there? Couldn't wait to move in! She flung the phone on the car floor.

Twenty kilometres on, she reached Triabunna. She remembered it from her childhood as a working town. Logging, woodchips, that sort of thing, not a good option for people following their dream, and she didn't slow her speed. Past Triabunna, the road veered away from the coast into bush and pastoral, old cottages, slumping wooden shearing sheds, beautiful properties, grand stone houses. History? Sure, but it too was there in bucketloads back in northern New South Wales. Bangelow, Clunes, Rosebank, Eureka, all the little villages of the Northern Rivers, the roads following old bullock trails through the verdant landscape, fabulous ambience for a sale. More to the point, she used history often in her novels to pad out a thin plot, giving interest and colour to the reader.

A sign pointed to a property, Lisdillon, one of the exclusive retreats she'd read about at the hotel. Could she set a novel there? She'd have to stay for a break later. Maybe even that night, given she had time to get back to the airport for her flight. She stabbed at the car radio but someone had left a disc in the player and sound burst out. What was this? A man singing, music so strange and so beautiful, she gasped and increased the volume. Voices, almost a chant, then a woman singing so ethereal it seemed more than human, like the song of hunchback whales.

Sasha wound down the windows and, as she drove, the music seemed to rise out of the landscape. Cruising up the cambered bends of Rocky Hills, winding above beaches edging aqua and navy waters, those sublime islands floating offshore, she felt a strange sensation, that she was driving into another realm, unhooked from everyday life, of such intensity she almost cried out.

Spiky Bridge, the convict-built bridge with its jagged crown of stones, appeared on her right, a hint of a dark and bloody past. She averted her eyes, wanting to know nothing of blood or horror, cruising on through forested hills to Swansea, a pleasant town seeming to gaze across the waters into infinity.

A few kilometres beyond, a signpost indicated Dolphin Sands, and on impulse she veered off the highway. The dirt road went through paddocks, farmland, an air strip with its sock limp, another turn-off to the right, a few more kilometres, ten maybe, along a roughly asphalted road past properties hidden in the dunes, with names on their entry gates: Drinkalot, Shell Seekers, Driftwood. Then, sighting a track into the dunes, she turned into it. The car bounced along sandy ruts for five minutes. She stopped and sat there, bathed in music, sunshine, peace. Leaning over, she opened the glovebox and there was the CD cover: *The Essential Philip Glass*. Philip Glass? She'd never heard of him, but his music!

Slipping off her heels, Sasha let her coat hang lose and started along the track. She checked her pamphlet, this bush was boobialla and coastal wattle, and up a sandy rise, across the bay was the peninsula of Freycinet. Smoke or cloud was drifting away from the pinnacle of Mount Freycinet, the granite mountains of the Hazards a dark orange, and to the south its consorts, Schouten Island, Isle des Phoques, and further, Maria Island. What a place!

Sasha wandered down the track to the beach, finding a warm dip in the sand, and lay there, her coat flung away, her hair drifting. Stretching out her hands, she stroked the sand, and lifted and let fall a cascade of shells, the midden of the people who'd rested here, like her, thousands of years before, but maybe only two hundred years ago too. This had been their view, their music had risen into this sunshine too, and now they were gone. Her thoughts merged with the rhythm of the waves which, sliding over the sand sounded like tearing paper, text and context, texts and texture, the script of her life being torn away page by page, and a new story being written. Here, in this place, she might have been a serious writer, she might have written great novels, but she'd spent a life behind a persona as frothy as her romances. She looked up, her eyes fixed on the Hazards where the lowering sun was gilding them in a fury of colour.

Sasha stood, wandered along the shore, her feet sinking into wet sand, waves catching her toes in a net of foam, and finally grief at her brother's death rose as acid in her mouth and she choked. Poor Gerard, leaving all of this beauty behind. Well, she would find a place, a holiday home in Orford for Shelly and her grandchildren, she would be able to do that. Now, it was time for this all to come to an end, Marcus and Simone. Had known, without wanting to know, back at Byron, the reality before her eyes and the climax, the fight yesterday morning two hours before she'd left to catch the plane.

First, a short message to her lawyer to put her property on the market because, as Marcus had come, so he would go, with nothing. Would she face this disruption fearlessly, put it behind her and write that serious novel? It really didn't matter. Here, just being here, was where Sandra wanted to spend not one night, but the rest of her life.

Slip Yards

Years later, I went back to that time, to try once again to find the trigger to my father's disappearance. Death? Suicide? Attempted abduction of me and my brother gone wrong? Or was it as a man on the run, looking for a new life? Was he giving the slip, slipping away, or slipping up? My mother's take was the latter, because, she said, he was always sailing close to the wind. No regular job, a windfall here and there: buy a car, fix it up, sell it; or a dinghy, or a trailer… On a larger scale, schemes and scams mostly connected with the water, that ever moving, dynamic environment his natural habitat, but a flawed relationship to reality. Slipping away from the truth, I created stories about Dad skippering a billionaire's luxury yacht in the Mediterranean, taking tourists on Antarctic cruises, drug running, holed up on a remote Pacific island or exploring the further reaches of Arctic seas… None were true, that was the point.

Soon as I'd got through college, I headed off, hitching across the Nullarbor to the sun-blasted sand-scoured West. No shadows there where people could disappear without trace. Or so it seemed to me, holed up in Fremantle in a hot little room with a tiny veranda, walking the white limestone streets and Indian Ocean-washed shores. There, I tried to get over the loss of my dad, writing, writing it out, living hand to mouth. Finally hitching trucks north, Geraldton, Carnarvon, and in Hedland I got a job on a prawn-fishing boat. Loved it out at sea, like living an illusion, so brilliant, the colours, the ocean life, the stars at night out on the deck, barnacles clicking on the hull, waiting for the prawns to run. But tough! Wore me down to skin and bone, scorched my skin black, my hair bleached white, you'd think there was no room left for sorrow, regret, anger in my soul. It's all in my book, the story of those years. Got to two hundred thou words, finished but not finished, because the story isn't over.

I came back home to Tassie when Mum was ill. I was with her through it, as she died of liver cancer. Six weeks, and she was gone. Did the loss of Dad bring it on? Part of the ongoing tragedy, yes, you could say that. So, thinking back to that day when he disappeared, I've gone over the events again and again, starting from the night before. Forgive me for including the details, but everything's important when you lose someone.

I was fifteen. We rented a terrace – you don't get many terraces in Hobart. This one was in a semi-industrial area north of the city, handy to the slip yards at Prince of Wales Bay where Dad picked up work and his yacht was moored. Yacht? An old fishing boat Dad bought for a coupla thou off a mate of a mate who'd died. Thirty-footer, faded blue, rough as guts, no amenities, but it got us about the harbour and south out of the Derwent estuary to the bigger seas. Anyway, lying in bed, I overheard a fight that night, slamming doors, Mum swearing him out.

'You're a do-nothing know-nothing waste of space…'

You know how it is when your mum and dad fight, the ache in the heart, pain twisting your guts, as you lie rigid in the dark. When it was quiet, I crept downstairs and prised open the front door. Dad's old car was parked at the kerb. It'd been raining, slicking the road, the roofs, the duco, and as I watched a side window wound down.

'Come 'ere, mate.' Dad's voice, sleepy and hoarse.

I padded down the front steps in my bare feet and crossed the footpath. The side door swung open, and Dad was slumped along the seat with a rug around him.

'What're you doing out here, Dad?'

He pulled me in and slammed shut the door. I huddled into the rug, snuggling into his smoky warmth.

'I'm in the doghouse, Adam.'

'Why, Dad?'

'Your mother wants her own house.' Was that all? 'Like now.'

'Buy this one?'

'What with?' and he sighed. 'Gotta work at getting somethin' like that. Every hour of the day and night. Or scam the money somehow.'

I felt a twinge of anxiety. Dad, I love you, I wanted to say. He seemed to know, and hugged me close.

'We'll be right, mate. Don't you worry about shit. Hey, you want some Indian?' He reached down and brought out a takeaway carton. Stale chicken fat and spices tickled my nose.

'No, Dad.'

'Wise boy. They've lost their touch down at the South Indian.'

Out the window went the chicken pieces, bones clattering on the roadway.

'Dad, you're littering.'

He ignored me. 'Hello, what've we got here?'

Cats emerged to sniff at the bones, Romeo from across the road, black as velvet in his red collar, no sign of his sister, Juliet. Honey the marmalade from up the street hobbling on three legs and then Sam, his grey and white patches showing in the dark, he'd adopted Chloe down in the furthest cottage in the street.

'Which'll take the prize, mate?'

'Romeo, for sure.'

The cats circled, swearing at each other.

'Nah. He's all good looks, that cat. My money's on Sam.'

At that moment, Sam made a dash, carrying off a chicken thigh.

'Hey, what did I say!'

Romeo pounced after Sam. They swore at each other, and Honey took her chance, sneaking in and hobbling away with a bone.

'Honey's got hers.'

I laughed. 'Poor Romeo.'

'He's all right, top of the shit heap, that cat.' Dad ruffled my hair. 'Not like some of us.'

'Dad?'

'Life's law of the jungle, mate. Don't you forget it.'

It started to rain again and we dashed inside. No Mum. I knew her scent, her warmth, her presence, and she wasn't there, I'd never known her not to be there. My mum, so smart, so cool, working a few days a week in the shop around the corner, I was so proud of her. Liked to think I was like her, tall and fair, to Dad and Andie my brother's short and dark.

Dad stood still in the hall, listening, then he pushed me on the shoulder. 'Off to bed, mate. I'm hittin' the sack.'

Next morning, still no Mum. Dad said she was at her sister's. That was it. Had she left us? There was no knowing, not after what happened. Anyway, Dad roused up me and Andie and we went down to the slip yards, Prince of Wales Bay and its floating marina and industrial yards. What a scene! so much going on, workers in fluoro, tiny in the huge Incat sheds, the Seamaster workshops, cranes loading fish-farm gear, trawlers, Georgetown Seafoods, Tassal trawler moored next to it, a ferry being worked on, bobcats and trucks working away, and boats! Moored close in, others parked at angles or up on cradles for work on their hulls. Dad drove down a laneway between sheds and parked, and went off to talk to a bloke greasing the workings on an old Sydney Harbour tug, the *Farm Cove*. I got out of the car to wait, but Andie stayed in the car, reading.

I loved the slip yards, possessed like Dad by the dream of owning a smick boat. I had my eye on a two-masted black-hulled schooner way over, high and dry, probably rotten. I loved the salty air, the stink of diesel, the blue and rust colours, the slap of the greasy water, the seagulls out on the bay calling and diving…

Dad came back, we got in the car and drove over to the Gepps Parade Marina. Boat sheds of patchy galvo and salvaged materials were built out on the jetties, water washing beneath, walkways to moored boats, a whole different way of living, and I'd love to crash down here once I left school.

We parked. I took the oars for the dinghy, Andie took two life jackets, and Dad the other life jacket, and two bags of groceries. We walked across the broken, weed-invaded asphalt. Our boat, *Celestis*, was bobbing in the bay, the dinghy pulled up high. Andie ran to beat me to it, and we pulled it down to the water. We rowed out to the boat, and I climbed on board and then Andie. Dad threw up the life jackets and handed up the groceries, threw up a rope which I caught and tied up the dinghy to the stern. Dad got on board, checked the engine, a Gardner diesel, got it warming up, checked the instruments inside, and we pulled on our life jackets. Standing at the rails, Dad at the wheel, we chugged out of Prince of Wales Bay, heading for open water.

'Where're we going, Dad?'

'Jimmy's shack on Bruny.'

'How long for? I'm gaming with Shaun tonight.'

'We'll be back in time.'

So why the groceries? Did Dad have different ideas? We headed towards the bridge, smooth going at first, but it was gonna take hours to get down to Bruny Island, especially when, out in the river, a south-westerly hit us. So rough Andie was sick, and the diesel fumes didn't help. I gave him a Kwell with a glass of water and we battled on.

It was late afternoon when we reached the jetty at North Bruny, made fast the boat and staggered up the path to the shack, up from the beach. Pushing open the door, a smell of dust and ashes from the wood stove hit us and it was freezing, wind whistling through that makeshift cabin. We dumped our gear on the bunks, Dad got Andie into dry gear and I got the shopping in. Dad lit the fire and we relaxed in these comfortable old chairs and ate hot pies. Cold, but what could be better than that?

Dad had a beer, then another. He dropped the empties on the lino with a clatter. I watched him, like kids do watch their parents, and I knew something was off-course. He looked different, pale, like he was getting sick. Anyway, I did what I always do down at Jimmy's shack, went for a walk.

I powered up the hillside, leaning into the gale off Storm Bay, the headlands distant brushstrokes in the saturated air, away to the horizon.

South Arm, and further over Forestier and Tasman. I leaned against the wind, it filled my lungs and tore at me, and I turned and let it buffet me back down to the shack. I burst in, the door slamming shut and I knew something was wrong. Andie was asleep in an armchair, rugged up, the fire was low, but no Dad. I went to the window. The bush was too thick to see down to the jetty. I waited for a bit, walking backwards and forwards, was he getting wood?

I shook Andie. 'Where's Dad?'

'Dunno… Gone to lay the cray pots.'

'In this fuckin' weather!'

'He'll be back, he told me not to worry.'

'Crazy!' I got out my phone and rang him. It rang, sure it rang, on the table. He hadn't taken his phone with him? Shit!

'Maybe he's on the boat.'

'What would he be doing out on the boat! Gonna check. You stay here.'

I ran out and down to the shore. The boat was gone. I ran around to the next bay, nothing. Then climbed up a bit to get a wider vision, no sign of anything, because who'd be out in this weather? What to do! Took me ten goes at least to get to Mum, shouting against that gale roaring through the trees. She was furious! She didn't know Dad had taken us out on the boat. She said to make sure Andie was safe, she'd get onto the police.

'Get them down here!' I shouted but her phone had fallen out of range.

We waited, me and Andie, jumping up at every sound that long dark night, huddled by that fitful fire and the wolves are out there, howling in the wind. Hours later, the police turned up, got us off the island and back to Hobart by road. Mum was at the front door, frantic, pulling us to her. What she had gone through, wow. Joe her husband, our father, was missing.

The police asked us again for the details. We had nothing to tell them. I was out, Andie was asleep. Dad had gone out. But why did he take the boat, instead of just the dinghy to lay the pots? Why had he gone out at all? Who knows? The dinghy turned up, beached on South Bruny, but no sign ever again of *Celestis*, or my father, despite a massive search of Bruny Island and the waters south. So many little bays, he could be anywhere. So much wild weather in the south-west, anything could've happened on that unseaworthy little craft.

We went through this weird phase, not knowing, trying to adjust, numb. Death by misadventure was the finding and that seemed fair to everyone. But me, I just couldn't believe it. Like I said, I headed off soon as, but Andie, his drive to succeed, was that his way of coping? Because he went straight through with medicine while I was over in the West, is now a top oncologist. Top rung in the medical world, I'm on the bottom rung. Ironic? Well, he got me the job in the hospital as a wardsman, after Mum died. He has Dianna, a lovely wife, two kids, did I mention that? Yep, succeeding for Mum, that's how I see it. Me? A loner, I live on my own, a weirdo writer. Suits me.

I went back to Prince of Wales Bay, thinking to search out the old guy Dad had been chatting to, that day, the day he disappeared. I didn't even know his name, just asked around. I came across an old bloke, yes, he'd known Joe Torenus, my dad. Knew nothing. But what he did say? Dad was in trouble. Yeah? Didn't surprise me but that wouldn't have been the trigger. More important, that he had an old mate living way south, far as you could go, south of Southport. Gave me an address. He might have some idea. See, I'd never given up wanting to know what happened, what had led to his disappearance, and what if Dad was alive somewhere?

I got onto Andie. He was reluctant. You mean, reset my schedule? People wait months to see me, and you want me to just take a day off? An afternoon then, I said. We've got to follow this up. Suggested I go, but it had to be us both, so he agreed. The next day, it wasn't looking good, the weather. Overcast, introverted, psychotic, I'd say, being a writer. Andie picked me up in his Beamer, I took the wheel, and we headed off. As we drove south, the rain started, through the Huon, Franklin, Geeveston, Dover. Main streets empty, coupla pick-ups, old people shuffling with shopping, dogs ambling, log trucks thundering through, and along the Huon River dingy boats moored up bilgy backwaters, and that backdrop cloud tangling with black hilltops, reflected in gunmetal-grey waters. A morose journey, with Andie on the handsfree the whole way, rearranging appointments, giving urgent advice, taking calls, and I felt bad just listening to him.

South of Southport? Last stop Lune River, and we reached the road in the address, halted and stared. A rough gravel track rose steeply and disappeared into the bush.

'Sure this goes somewhere?'

'Yep, Andie. GPS says it's correct.'

'Get it over with.'

So I started off, bouncing up the overgrown track, taking care with the Beamer. Bush, and more bush, towering gums, glimpses across a grey sweep of water, dirt tracks down to occasional small holdings on acreage, rubbish littering, not looking good! Ten minutes later, a sign, private property nailed to a tree, and before Andie could protest, I barrelled on. The track rose steeply and after twenty minutes of driving, we were at the end of this high tongue of land licking the ocean. A two-storey house stood there, rough brown vertical boards, small windows, a deck, looking weather-beaten and run-down, but with solar panels covering the galvo roof area. A place off the grid, in hiding, a retreat? Wanting to be out of touch, clearly. We stared. So this could be where my father had holed up, all these years?

Emotion welled and I turned to Andie. 'He could've let us know.'

'Christ's sake, Adam, get a grip. It's the mate here, not Dad.'

As he spoke, the door opened and a tall old fellow came out.

'Christ!'

He waved us over. I got out, Andie following me.

'Come in, have a coffee,' he said as if he were expecting us. Red strands of hair across a bald blotched head, skin weathered and white, an old jumper hanging off his caved-in chest. 'I'm Martin A. Jones.' He held out a hand. 'You're welcome.' Old bloke with old-time manners.

I took his hand, it was limp and cold. 'I'm Adam Torenus, this is my brother, Andie.'

He nodded and we followed him in. There was a study on the left with computers, I saw as we followed him up a short flight of stairs. We entered a small living room warmed by a wood-burning stove. A little kitchen to the right, bench tops, a gas top, a sink, cupboards.

'Welcome to my very humble abode,' Martin said as he filled the jug and put it on.

All around were windows, and what a fabulous view! More than one-eighty across to the dog leg at the very end of South Bruny and straight out to the horizon, a knife edge slicing water from sky.

'Amazing view, Martin.' Andie was polite.

'You can see everything from here,' I commented, to myself as much as to Andie and Martin. 'Nothing would escape you.'

'There's so much we don't know, I can tell you,' Martin said.

'You know a Joe Torenus, sometime in the past?'

Blue eyes blank, a hand going to his chin, but he shook his head. 'I don't believe so.'

'See a little thirty-footer go by, ever? Called *Celestis*? Seen it around Southport, or further?'

Martin pondered, eyeing us. 'Celestis, meaning celestial, relating to the stars. A code?' Absently reaching for three cups on the bench top.

'No, the name of the boat.'

'Then who are you?'

'Adam and Andie. We're looking for our father, Joe Torenus. He went missing…'

'Missing or searching?' Martin said as the jug boiled. 'So easy to con-fuse one with the other.'

'Ah, we're doing the searching,' Andie said.

'Celestis,' Martin repeated. 'Starry. Our friends from Venus can tell us so much about the stars.'

I went rigid. Andie gave me a look, meaning what the fuck have you got me into?

'Coffee's smelling great,' I said quickly.

Martin poured in the hot water.

'Milk? Sugar? A biscuit?'

And I forced my high-class oncological brother to stay while we drank the coffee and Martin rabbited on about how you can tell a Venusian – they don't have belly buttons, and he has a guardian angel, another Venusian, called Mifune, who helps him whenever he needs advice, and had told him to expect two visitors from Venus today. Us?

That was too much even for me, and we gulped our hot coffees. Then, looking perfectly sane in his old jumper and worn jeans, face bland, Martin informed us that an intergalactic event was taking place on Ayer's Rock (he was too old to call it Uluru) on 21 December involving the Venusians.

Explaining that we had to go right now, thanks for the coffee, we were out of there and into the car.

Martin stood at the door, watching us go. 'Everyone wants the final truth,' he called out. 'Can't be found! Doesn't exist!'

'Christ's sake,' Andie muttered, but his words struck home.

I was silent, anger and grief welling as I drove back down that track. This lonely point, those tall eucalypts, their black shapes reflected in the leaden bay, that monotone sky, it was like one of those places where you walk to meet your death. And I had seen death in that old guy.

'Fuckin' false trail. Waste of a fuckin' day.' Andie was furious.

'We had to give it a try, mate.'

'You want to find our dad like that poor sod going mad with loneliness?'

'Shut the fuck up, Andie! You never wanted to find him, you the gun oncologist! Nothing stopped you in your rise to the top.' I wrenched the steering wheel over bumps and the view lurched.

'What! You chose your life, scraping along the bottom, Adam, not me.'

'I chose it, did I?'

'Yes. Over Mum. You ever think of her?'

''Course I thought of Mum. I was with her…'

'Before. Never knowing was he alive or dead, would he turn up, would the police turn up? No. You fucked off soon as you could to WA. Chasing what?'

'Bullshit!' I braked and stopped the car. 'I came back here. For her.'

'Never faced up, just like Dad, making nothing of your life.'

'Get out!' I shoved him.

'What!'

'I said get the fuck out!'

'Won't help, Adam.'

'I wouldn't care what he was like, just to have him alive. But nothing stopped you, did it, your career…'

He stared at me, my brother. 'I did what he'd have wanted me to do.'

'Fuckin'…' I dropped my head onto the steering wheel, shaking.

'Adam?' My brother's hand on my arm.

'I want to find him as he was.' I reared back against the seat.

'For sure. Good and bad, mate. Good and bad. Not like that bloke. Better dead.'

Better dead? I looked around this bleak wet bush. I loved my Dad, Andie did too, that we could think like this? What the fuck were we doing in this benighted place, but facing the truth. Dad had taken the boat out, the sea had grabbed him, he'd gone that night. For the first time, I wept, grief flooding through me, while my brother waited.

'Okay, mate?'

I took a breath. 'Yeah, okay. Let's go.'

We bounced back down that track to the Lune River Road, the hands-free kicked in and Andie was the professional again, on the job. And me, still the lonely writer. Joe Torenus, my dad, there was no trigger, he just slipped through our fingers. He would've wanted me to do my best to find him, and to tell a good story, I knew that now as Andie and me, his sons, started the long drive back home.

Stillborn

Melanie remembered when she first realised that dreams, wishes, ambitions aren't enough in the world. That endings come before beginnings. That nothing can be guaranteed and that the dark will snuff out the light. The yachts on the harbour that Friday evening told her that. Sitting on a bench at the end of Elizabeth Street Pier eating fish and chips with Jack. Just beyond on the water, the yachts turned and turned about a buoy, jostling for position, black mainsails taut against the aluminium masts, looking majestic and evil all at once.

'Don't feel bad about it, love.'

She edged away from him. 'Don't know how else I'm meant to feel.'

'It's not your fault.'

'You're going away, what else?'

'I'm not just pissing off on you.'

'Pissing off on our baby.'

'Melanie…it was just a scare, you weren't really that pregnant.'

'You'd know?'

The yachts jostling for position around the buoy, the deepening sky.

'Is it me you're leaving or Hobart?' Trying to force him to say.

'Choice? That's crap.'

With an explanation, you can move forward.

'You know?'

He wanted her to absolve him.

She'd made a choice when they'd first met as teenagers. They'd bunked off school one warm afternoon and hitched to Seven Mile Beach, found a place in the dunes and huddled down, messing about, smoking, getting their gear off as seagulls cried and the waves slid along the shore as he slid along her thighs and she'd rolled away and was off into the pine forest, the sighing spreading pines a refuge. She'd climbed up branches like stairs and saw beyond the dunes the waves sweeping the shore, ocean to the horizon and she felt safe. Did she feel the need to be safe from Jack, or with Jack? He was trudging off along the shore, the way he walked, hunched, she read hurt, and jumped down, resin gum on her hands and gym tunic, stumbling down the dunes, and caught up with him. They'd stuck together, fallen in love, shacked up, coming so far, and falling so hard. Herself through university, then falling, that was how it was put, more like a crash: falling in love, falling pregnant, falling down… Jack loving sailing, and now the water taking him away from her.

Melanie hugged him to her then pushed him away. The baby, that was the reason he was going. She'd wanted this baby. Little Sammy, Jack had called him from the word go. She hadn't expected tenderness. Promising her he'd find a block of land and build, putting down roots, all the while his eyes returning again and again to the water. Neither had much of family, both parents single, her mum, his dad.

Watching the yachts jibing, black sails scissoring the sky like the fabric of their future, he offered her the cone of chips and she extracted a squid ring and he put it on her ring finger.

'We're good together, Melanie. You know that.'

They were. Her mum had said to her, don't believe there's always more pebbles on the beach. In life, there's only one or two. Hold it in your mouth and savour its smooth cool texture. That was her Jack. But she'd said you're worth more than that, when Jack had first turned up in the decrepit Ford he'd fixed up with his uncle Max, who lived two doors away in North Hobart. That was Jake's family, distributed through the northern suburbs as mechanics, labourers, tradies. Her mother had wanted a career for her daughter and an upmarket match after she'd scrimped and saved as a hairstylist to send her to St Mary's, nothing less. Jack had threatened all that her mother dreamed for her, she knew that. Well, here they were, on the point of splitting up. Going their own ways.

His choice, her decision.

The yachts were flying down river now, black sails like scimitars slicing through a silvery expanse of sky and water as vast and empty as the future lying ahead of them.

Jack the joker, her first love. He threw a chip to a seagull and immediately dozens flocked, so he threw the rest in the air and they jumped up from the seat, mobbed by feathered wings, deafened by screeches, running back along the pier to the car.

Melanie, with her Bachelor of Laws, didn't have the money to get accredited further. Evenings, she hung around the Ice House bar where the lawyers hung out and listened to talk about society's toerags – blokes bashing their wives, drunk drivers, women shoplifting on wet Friday afternoons, land disputes, warring neighbours. Life at the bottom of the barrel, the footy, and lots of beer drinking. This scene and therefore the law weren't for her, she realised, but she needed a job to pay the rent. Her mother had helped her out with the bond and the first month's rent in a cottage, and she'd moved in.

Melanie called in on Anna, her next-door neighbour, walking along the brick path overhung with daisies that linked the two old cottages.

Anna was pottering around in the little conservatory, a cigarette stuck to her lip. 'Come in, come in. Sit down.'

Melanie sat at the little patio table. From the kitchen came a sweet beetroot odour.

'You're busy?' Stubbing out the cigarette, Anna went inside to wash her hands at the sink. 'I have made the beetroot soup, you have some. Here, here.' She ladled a bowl of soup from the pan. 'Eat now,' insisting with a motion of her hand.

Melanie shook her head.

Anna placed the bowl on the table. 'Why you are sad?'

'Give it time, people say.' Meaning the miscarriage.

'Ah. Time.'

Melanie lifted the bowl and sipped straight from it, the clear soup red as blood.

'Healthy, strong, good.' She encouraged Melanie.

But why be healthy, strong, good, what was the point?

'I want to believe them, I really do.'

'Words, those people. Huh!' Anna dismissed them. 'I will punch them on the nose.'

Melanie smiled: her friend would, to defend what she loved.

'What you are afraid of, beautiful girl?'

'Of going on living without…what I had.'

'Life is losing what you have: innocence, belief, health… Look at me.' Anna, so gracious in her age, so sure, so…unassailable.

'But then, what is left, Anna?'

'Love! You must go on, for love.'

But that was Jack. He was her love, but his love was the ocean. Not so many pebbles on the beach, but where was she to find another? Like one of those feats demanded in fairy tales: to win the prince, you must search for the right pebble out of thousands on the beach, taste each one, roll it around in your mouth, feel its texture. Find it, and only then you would win his hand.

Anna took Melanie's empty bowl, stained red, to wash at the sink inside. Melanie stood and followed her in. The lumpy crocheted seat covers, the little paintings on the walls of folk dancers, forests, peasant houses. Wolves would be lurking in the undergrowth, and she glimpsed herself in Anna's fancy mirror, ivy twining over it twisting around her image, locating her right there, in a forest glade. Inside, shelves with home-made tinctures lined a wall, the glass bottles and jars glinting in the dim light. All in this little house was created with love.

'So. You have job now?' Anna's theory was that work would take her out of herself.

Melanie shrugged and looked out at Anna's pot plants profuse in the muted green light, thinking about Little Sammy, and the flavours of babyhood, milk and baby poo, powder and the softness of skin on skin, the small sounds and caresses, all stillborn. No one talked about it, so how could she? Not even to her mother, definitely not to her mother.

Who, on her visits, was wary of this woman next door, so friendly and yet so, well, different.

Anna understood. She was always ready to listen, and then to remind Melanie that she had a life. But her degree was useless, years of study and ambition had taken her up another dead end, to a stillborn career.

'Heading off now, Anna. Thanks for the soup.'

The old woman walked with Melanie to the door. 'I tell you, a house, its walls, its spaces say you live here. You leave the house, sunlight falls, sand fills the house, the walls fall, the roof, the people are gone, the children grown… It is the past, a memory of the past. Don't look back, this I know, Melanie.'

I won't forget, I can't forget little Sam! she wanted to say. Instead, repeated, 'Thank you for the soup. See you next time.'

Melanie got a job with a local council. When people came in to pay their rates and water bills, they came to her, sitting in an office behind plexiglass, open to everyone passing by, handling bits of paper, taking bank cards, handing out receipts. It was boring, repetitious, but it kept her going with rent, bills, food. One of the council staff was an arts officer, Dezzie, younger than she was. She organised visiting artists, writers, musicians in the community. Melanie wanted that job and tried to think of ways to get it, coming up with nothing, but made friends with Dezzie anyway.

She took to attending gallery openings on Friday evenings, often with the girl. One rainy evening at a gallery in town, she met Alex, an artist. They chatted and, huddling below an umbrella, left for a drink. Later, he led her through Hobart's old streets to his place, a two-storey house with wide verandas set in the middle of a large garden. He pushed open a rickety gate. A streetlight threw shadows, the house lights showed here and there. Silence, rain dripping.

'What is this place?'

'Flats. Rented from the Ed Department. I'm upstairs.'

They followed the path round the back, brushing through wet overgrown shrubs. An iron fire escape zigzagged upwards and clanged as they climbed up, going in through a heavy fireproof door.

It was a long room, a room that shocked her, with its charcoal and pencil canvases spotlighted against the walls. Dismembered animals from fairy tales: twelve headless geese wandering a stony slope; a bear agonised, with a suppurating wound in its side; a bird, an eagle? chained to a rock too sharp for it to land on. A canvas with a small form showing through a black leafy surface. A lost child? Anguish, fear, despair were caught there and she felt both appalled and mesmerised. She took out her mobile and snapped pictures of the drawings. He led her to a bed, but she resisted. He caressed her, she felt only cold, and turned to go from this place. He stopped her, easing down her top and her tights, kissing her, and she succumbed, falling into the dead blackness of his persona.

'Why?' she whispered. And knew the answer.

At work, Dezzie caught up with Melanie in their lunch hour. The girl looked up to her, was it her LLB? Melanie didn't set out to influence her. Actually, she envied her bubbly self-assurance in these chats, usually one-sided. The Monday following the art exhibition, she was full of talk about her good time at the gallery opening. Told Melanie that she'd set out to walk from Salamanca to South Hobart, slogging her way up the Davey Street hill.

'A car cruises along the kerb, and thinking it's a taxi, I get in, give my address: ninety-three Denison Street, like, sit there, thinking about the opening. Like, did you pick up Alex, he's right up there in the art world…'

'Go on, Dezzie!' Melanie brought her back to her story.

'Okay! We're like cruising along, he says, wanna go for a ride up the mountain? Weird, a taxi driver wanting a ride up the mountain. Thanks but no thanks, I say, staring straight ahead and, like, we get to my street, I indicate my place and he pulls over. How much, I say. Nothing he says, I'm not a taxi. Yes, you are! No, I'm not! I don't have a sign on my roof and I don't have a meter! He was so offended!' Dezzie collapsed in giggles. 'Melanie, I was out of that nothing cab like a shot!'

'Jesus, Dezzie, don't do that again!'

Huffy, now. 'I didn't set out to get picked up by a kerb crawler.' And gave her a stare, as if to say, what about you!

'Look, I'm busy,' and got rid of her.

Was it true? Was Alex as dangerous as a kerb crawler she'd just let pick her up? Was this what women do, seek out danger when… When what? They've lost faith in themselves. Or was it simply men sniffing out the vulnerable and needy?

Melanie showed the pictures of Alex's art work to Anna. She was making chutney, stirring a pan on the stove. Scents of Indian spices, vinegar, fruit filled the room and drifted out, almost like the essence of Anna herself.

Wiping her hands on her apron, Anna peered over Melanie's shoulder as she flicked through the shots. 'Why he makes like that?' She went back to her stirring. 'It is not good, to make the evil pictures. Where is the hope, the love, the belief?'

'That's the point, Anna. They're not in this world.'

Anna threw her a glance. 'You love this man? No. You hurt yourself to take in his darkness like the poison.'

'It's not like that.'

'So what is like?'

Melanie didn't have an answer.

'This…' she gestured with her wooden spoon,' brings bad, something terrible, maybe the death to you. Of the soul.'

'Anna!' Melanie half-stood, angry, scared, fearing her words. Who was she to say that, bringing her own torments to lay on her.

'Sit, sit down, be still, now.'

Melanie sat, wanting to go, not wanting to hurt her friend, and then saw the newspaper. It lay on the table, the front page a picture of a yacht under full sail, the leader of a fleet of maxis racing around the world. She glanced at it, then at a small picture inset, of the senior strategist. It was Jack. She shoved the paper away from her. Grabbed her head against the pain, eyes shut.

Anna turned. 'Melanie! What is wrong?'

She couldn't answer, but indicated the picture of Jack.

'So, is him? Ha. The boys with the toys.' She swung away. 'Is not life!'

Melanie ached with the pain of their life together, a stillborn life.

'I give you something, you take.' Anna took down a jar of dried leaves from a shelf.

'What is it?' Trying to look up.

'Lemon balm.' She sniffed the leaves. 'Make you strong, the tea.' Getting down two mugs, Anna made tea with boiling water. Lemony odours filled the room, and filled Melanie's nostrils as she sipped. 'Better?'

Melanie nodded, yes, better.

'For the other one, Alex, yes? Stronger, I think, to dissolve like detergent on oil, the oil slick that covers life…'

'Anna, he isn't that bad.'

What more could she say? When she was at work, she imagined him working away in his studio, with clever hands, his dark face absorbed as the pictures emerged from his imagination. Or down at Salamanca with his friends, drinking on and talking about life and art. Was it a fantasy? Should he be drawing women like her, all the women caged behind the Plexiglas of their lives, performing acts that warped their minds, deadened their feelings, left them bereft?

From a wicker basket, Anna took a cigar-shaped stick of leaves tied together. 'Cedar, sage smudge-stick.' She handed it to Melanie. 'You take.'

'Smudge-stick? What do I do with it?' She sniffed it, recognising the scent of sage and a woody smell with it.

'Light like incense. Let it…' Anna wafted her hand around. 'In the room, to lift your feelings, the bad goes, you two are one, yes?'

'Sounds good.'

'Hawthorn tincture I can give, heal feelings?'

'Thanks, Anna. I'll try the tea, and the stick thing first.'

'For you, Melanie. For you.' A plea as Melanie left.

Anna's experience of men wasn't hers, but was she right? She wasn't a victim, helpless against the secret signals exchanged between predator and prey, the perpetrator and victim. The strong and the weak. But then…

The night Melanie decided to light the smudge-stick at Alex's, she had her period. She wanted its protective barrier, its hormonal firing up of her determination. But Alex wanted sex, rushing her, easing off her clothes, her holding back firing him up, his mouth on her neck, her breasts, her nipples betraying her with their rubbery engorgement. She moved back as he eased his hip into her, his hand reaching, his head in her hair, kissing. She murmured, 'Alex…' and she slid away, but he used her movement to pull her body against him, his hands pushing her tights down, her thermal top off, her hair flung to one side, his face on her shoulder and they collapsed forward like that onto the bed, and he was bare-legged now, hard legs scissoring her body, his hand reaching between her legs to remove the tampon, and he was into her now as she trembled on the bed, liquid in the rhythm of their movements together.

Sighing, they lay in bed, drifting in and out of sleep, her feelings fleeing into darkness, and a dream image of the black-sailed yachts scything the expanse of sky and water that time pushed her into wakefulness.

Melanie got up as Alex slept, took the smudge-stick and the matches, struck a match and lit it. She wanted to assert her intentions, to consolidate her place in this room, and so in Alex's life. First, a thin tendril of smoke, a dank weedy odour catching in her throat, and then it burst alight. Melanie shrieked, dropped the burning brand to the floor.

Alex started awake. 'What the fuck!' He leaped from the bed and grabbed the glass of water from the bedside table, dashed it on the flames, smothered the mess with a pillow. 'What is going on, Melanie!'

Acrid smoke filled the room and they choked.

'Is it out?'

'Why did you?'

'I can't breathe!' He pushed open the door and freezing night air flowed in.

Melanie dragged on her clothes. Alex kicked the mess out of the door, pulling on his coat over his sweat shirt and trackpants. He pulled on his boots and together they staggered out, and down the steps to the dark garden.

'Incense, that's all, I couldn't sleep.'

'Come on, let's get out while the smoke clears.'

They walked down to the wharves. People were out to welcome in the leading maxi in the race, cars lining the foreshore, arc lights lighting the maxi yacht coming up river.

Sitting on the bench at the end of the Elizabeth Street Pier, Alex took off his coat and draped it over them both, for a dawn wind had risen. The yacht progressed, its sails livid white, looking vast and heraldic against sky and water, its multicoloured spinnaker bellying out to catch the wind, car horns sounding, people cheering.

'Wow,' Alex murmured, hugging her close.

Watching the yacht coming in to port, Melanie felt light coming into her life at last, chasing out the darkness of despair. She and Jack had once sat here, like this, and he might even be aboard this yacht, sailing in to harbour, but she felt nothing for him now.

The wind picked up over the houses beyond the shore, lifting above the streets and through the open door of Alex's flat, where a tiny ember glowed red, and lit spilled paint in a join between the floor boards, a stream of fire trickling towards the canvases stacked against the wall. Melanie decided, as they cuddled against the wind, that she would be able to introduce Alex to Anna as her man now, and tell her with a laugh how her smudge-stick had worked so well, for them both.

The Dead Zone

When Anne Marie's friend Don dropped Liz and Anne Marie off at Waldheim, rain was starting. This was the exciting beginning to their walk on the Overland Track, in the Cradle Mountain-Lake St Clare National Park, seventy-five kilometres, north to south. She and Liz were both early childhood teachers and she'd talked Liz into coming, partly to get her away from her home life, prey to a demanding but dependent mother. So the Overland Track, she'd done it before, but for Liz, it would be a new experience steering her life into a new direction, Anne Marie hoped.

Cradle Mountain and its glaciated surrounds were blurred in rain as they set off. Stepping onto the duckboard crossing the button grass plain, just as in a story they might tell their students, they were entering the wilderness as trusty friends to face danger, perform feats of heroism, and make boon companions. Following one after the other, they trudged around Lake Wilks and climbed up through a pocket of rainforest at Crater Falls.

'How are you going, Liz?' She was a novice bushwalker, keen on aerobics, so somewhat fit.

Anne Marie had checked her gear and provisions thoroughly, made sure her boots were firmly tied and her pack was strapped tight on her back; it made walking so much easier.

'Good, good,' Liz panted.

By the time they got to the top of Marion's Lookout, the rain had turned to sleet, then wind-driven snow.

'God, this is a blizzard!' It was hitting them sideways. 'You okay?'

'Yes, fine, these gusts are barrelling me along.' Liz turned rosy cheeks to Anne Marie.

'We'll get everything on at Kitchen Hut.'

This was a shelter below Marion's Lookout, set in rainforest. Bent against the driving snow, they descended an hour later to Kitchen Hut, where they took out gloves and beanies from their packs and pulled them on. Anne Marie got out her flask of hot coffee and they had a drink, and rested, then set off again, descending into Waterfall Valley through lovely forest of King Billy pine, native laurel and myrtle.

'This is gorgeous, Anne Marie.'

'Sure is. There's Waterfall Hut.'

The roof of the wooden shelter showed below. Reaching it, they staggered in, slamming the door behind them and dropping their packs in the lobby. It was crowded, steamy, a noisy scene with about thirty walkers sitting around the table talking, drinking, playing cards, reading or writing. A stove was burning, food and cooking gear was strewn across bench tops. Some walkers had come from the south, others were setting out, like themselves.

'G'day, where've you walked from?' a guy asked them.

'Just starting out,' Anne Marie said, 'from Waldheim.'

'Weather closed in about then,' he said, stating the obvious.

'Hope it will fine up.'

'Anything could happen weatherwise,' and turned back to his card game.

'Sleeping bag,' Anne Marie said to Liz. 'We need to find a space on the sleeping platform, bottom level.'

'Oh, right.'

They pushed through and found a space to lay out the two sleeping bags against the wall. Anne Marie was tired, and she knew Liz would be exhausted. Time to get the food on the go. She yanked her pack to a space on a bench and took out the fuel stove, matches and the container of kero, filled the cup and lit it. Liz had already got out their first meal, rice and freeze-dried vegies, each meal packed separately.

'Go find a seat, Liz, I'll handle this. Like a cuppa?'

'You bet.'

While the water was coming to the boil, Anne Marie got out the mugs and tea bags. Looking up, she expected Liz to be chatting with the guys – they were always interested in her, she had those looks, soft and blonde, but with firm abs and biceps due to her aerobics. Instead, she was sitting by an older woman still wearing her outside gear, a smart red gortex jacket. She had her pack by her and two walking sticks, and looked a seasoned walker.

Anne Marie took over her mug of hot tea, reaching to hand it to her.

'Oh, thanks.' Liz took the mug and clasped it with both hands. She looked up. 'Anne Marie, this is Judith.'

'Hi, Judith.'

'Welcome. You had a rough walk in.'

'No real problems.' Anne Marie made to move away, but Judith was speaking, as if answering a question from Liz.

'I've always been independent. Financially, physically, emotionally…'

'Right. Food. Coming, Liz?' But the woman kept talking.

'Leading my own life, with my companion, Hilary. We skied, we sailed, we kayaked, we walked, we climbed. Our business was Wild Women Travel.' Judith's speech was precise, sounding her sses as sh with a slight New Zealand accent. She was whip thin, with greying brown hair, neatly curled.

'Liz, food!'

Liz got up, and edged past the crowded benches, squeezing onto a seat as Anne Marie opened packets and tipped them into the boiling water.

'She's fascinating,' Liz appealed.

People always told stories while bushwalking, it was one of its pleasures, doing without television, radio, computers and phones. Anne Marie also knew people like Judith who had a compulsion to talk, and she tried to steer clear of them. 'Aren't you tired? We should get an early night.'

'Exhausted, actually. Hit the sack straight after eating?'

'Sure. I'll clear up.'

'Going to be hard, missing a shower.'

'That's bushwalking! Make sure you get into your sheet. You don't want to carry mud into your sleeping bag.'

They finished their bowls of rice and vegetables. Liz gave her dirty bowl and mug to Anne Marie and pushed across to the sleeping platform. Others were also settling down to sleep, and pretty soon the room was quiet, the few staying up around the hot stove talking in low voices, respecting the sleepers. As Anne Marie cleared up, the wind howled, snow smattering against the windows. She left the fuel stove out on the bench top with the clean bowls and the mugs for breakfast, covered them with a tea towel and crept across to her sleeping bag. She undressed, pulled off her damp tights and thermal top, put on dry thermals, got in and immediately fell asleep.

Next morning, the wind had dropped, it was snowing outside and the hut was freezing. People were up early, dressing and putting on breakfast to laughs and chat.

Anne Marie sat up on the sleeping platform with Liz. 'Sleep okay?'

'Like a log, not even a dream.'

'Me too. Nothing could keep me awake. How's your gear?'

'Everything's damp.'

'Put your dry thermals on.'

'My over-trousers, my jacket, my gortex?'

'Put them all on, dry socks, boots outside, gaiters, you'll be okay. I'll get tea going.' Anne Marie dragged on her own clothes, plus dry socks and indoor slippers, and returned to the bench, pouring water into a saucepan to heat.

'You've had a good night's sleep?' Judith joined her there. 'I sleep like a dead thing when I'm walking.'

'Yes, fine. I'm making tea. Like some?'

'No, no, I have my water.'

'Sure?'

'Quite sure.' Her words almost terse, she left.

Anne Marie and Liz drank their tea and ate muesli and hot water for breakfast. They stacked the gear in their packs and went out, pulling on their boots, socks up tight under gaiters and heaving on their packs. They set off for Windermere Hut by Lake Windermere, a three and a half hour trek.

The duckboard was snowy, and every so often marked by large wombat poos topped with snow, looking like Christmas puddings.

'All they need is a sprig of holly,' Liz joked. Claw prints were left by currawongs. 'They look like animal claws,' she said.

'No thylacines here, I'm afraid.'

'Such an ancient landscape.'

Pandani groves were hung with snow, forests of dwarf pine and native beech in the mist, were so atmospheric.

They reached Pine Forest Moor. Here, the duckboard ended and a track of dazzling white quartz chips stretched away, glistening in the mist.

'Much of this moor resulted from Aboriginal burning long ago,' Anne Marie said.

Far off, black pencil pines bent by the winds seemed to traverse the landscape like an ancient line of nomads. What were the legends and myths the Aborigines associated with this place? She would never know, but felt wrong to impose European myths. She saw this northern end of the national park, Weindorfer's vision, to be positively Wagnerian in its dark grandeur, but wasn't that equally Eurocentric? Imposing an alien culture on place that had been country to Aboriginals for so long, forty thousand years?

'One feels tiny in the face of nature.' Judith had caught up with them.

'And history,' Anne Marie said and they fell in with her as she marched along the boardwalk with her two sticks.

Windermere Hut was not far off, but it took them another hour to reach it, Anne Marie shooting on ahead. Two green bins, and then the hut appeared at the edge of the lake. With relief, she dropped her pack. After using the long-drop toilet, she took out the fuel stove, washed her hands at the tap, got some water and went inside to get lunch going.

Judith and Liz arrived, dropping their packs by the sleeping platforms. As the packet soup heated up, Anne Marie sat at the table chatting with other walkers. Outside, she saw a rufus wallaby with a joey in her pouch nibbling the marsupial lawn. One leg poked out of the pouch, then a head.

'Oh, look!' She ran to the window and walkers crowded.

A shaft of sun broke through the mist and they dashed out to warm themselves, sitting on the steps, where she joined Liz and Judith.

After lunch, Anne Marie washed her socks out in a bucket, wrung them out and draped them over a branch in the sun. 'Liz, want to do yours?' Offering her the bucket.

'Oh, okay,' she agreed, reluctantly it seemed to Anne Marie.

With evening, more people arrived, filling the hut, and Anne Marie was glad they'd already spread their sleeping bags in the prime spot at one end of the lower platform.

Sitting around the table with the stove going, Judith dominated with her talk of Wild Women Travel. 'We organised local and international trips for women from New Zealand, Christchurch. You'd be surprised how many women prefer their own company and we made so many friends. So many destinations. Kilimanjaro in Africa, Kanchenjunga, Annapurna Circuit, yes, the wonderful Himalayas...'

A noisy card game started up by candlelight on the top platform. Someone was whistling an endless tune, and after cleaning the fuel stove and plates of their latest freeze-dried meal, Anne Marie decided to hit the sack. She lay dozing until Liz crawled into her sleeping bag beside her, but sleep didn't come. It was a night of snorers, swearers, gigglers and shoe throwers and she got up sluggish and grumpy in the morning.

They had breakfast. Liz, quite sparky and cheery, got the fuel stove going. The cup of tea cheered them.

'I should've done mine,' Liz moaned as she eyed her filthy socks.

'Wash them now, they'll dry as we're walking. Haven't you a clean pair?'

'No, I missed packing them.'

'Have my spares.' She pulled them out of her pack.

'Thanks.'

Anne Marie took Liz's filthy socks, found the bucket and went outside to wash them. Sharing was not unusual on the track. A couple of young guys sitting around the table last night, Mark and Stewie, didn't seem to have much food at all. She wouldn't be surprised if they came looking for spare morsels. Another, Gavin, seemed only to eat porridge. This morning he'd been stirring it with a twig. He'd lost his spoon and no one had a spare.

Liz came out, all packed up. 'All set!'

Anne Marie draped the wet socks over Liz's pack. 'There we go, dry in no time.' She heft her pack and they set off for Pelion Hut, six hours away.

'I've aches on aches in my leg and back muscles,' Liz said. 'Dare I hope I'm getting fitter?'

'You'll get there.' Anne Marie strode away along the duckboard.

The sun was out now, lighting up a terrain of moorland and forest, views of snowy Pelion West and Barn Bluff. Ahead were the hanging cliffs of Mount Oakleigh, reached via the infamously muddy swamps of Frog Flats, which Anne Marie hoped were now duckboarded.

Half an hour beyond the Forth Valley Lookout, Mark came back along the track. 'Landslip ahead,' he said. 'Track's disappeared.'

Fifteen minutes later, they found it. Twenty metres had been carried down in a tumble of boulders and uprooted trees. Stewie was on the other side, both men helping walkers across as they came along. Anne Marie queasily followed Mark, picking her way across, her body at an angle, gloved hands grabbing low, mud-smeared bushes. She looked back to watch Liz set off, Mark helping her at that end, Stewie at this end, having edged a short way back to grab her. She was going all right when halfway across a boulder dislodged behind her, cannoned into a heap of mud and debris and careered down the mountain. She took a run and, with Stewie, got across.

'Well done, Liz!'

'Nothing to worry about,' and tossed her head.

Anne Marie smiled. Her friend was doing well.

Frog Flats wasn't too bad, a lot of sloshing through mud but at last they reached Pelion Hut by late afternoon. It was a minimal structure of galvo and chicken wire, boarding and louvre windows painted dark green.

'Grim,' Liz said.

They went in and Anne Marie rested on a bunk, her pack sliding to the floor. Rousing herself, she took out her sleeping bag and stretched it out, Liz doing the same beside her.

Two more walkers arrived, a tall woman hobbling with a short, muscular man. She sat on a bunk, easing off her boots, and he rushed about, lighting the stove, getting some water on the go and setting into cleaning their boots.

'Army,' Anne Marie murmured. She roused herself to get a late, cold lunch.

Mark and Stewie arrived, Gavin and other walkers, but no sign of Judith yet.

After sunset, the temperature dropped and Anne Marie snuggled into her sleeping bag, dropping off to sleep to the quiet crackle of the stove and the murmur of voices, jokes being told, laughter, chat, Liz amongst them.

Next morning was brilliant, a dazzling day even though it was only two degrees Celsius inside the hut. They had breakfast outside where it was warmer, and set off for Kia Ora Hut. It was a long and muddy climb through myrtle forest, roots trapping boots and ankles. They lurched and tripped and stumbled their way out of the valley. Where the path sank into swamp, there was duckboard and little bridges to help, such a relief! It was dark under the trees, but the limbs were outlined by encrusted snow, the blue sky high up, the sunlight shafting through, brilliant in contrast.

'Magic,' Liz breathed. 'So glad I came, Anne Marie.'

'Still a way to go,' she answered.

'You know, Judith has climbed in the Himalayas? She was telling us last night.'

'I heard her.'

'In this region above 26,000 feet, the air is so thin that even with oxygen every minute, you are basically dying. It's called the Dead Zone. Mark said, aren't we basically dying from the moment we are born? Johnny told him not to be an ignoramus and listen.'

'Who's Johnny?'

'The ex-army shoe cleaner with Joanna, she a basketball pro.'

'Oh, right.'

'Judith said in the Dead Zone there's about two hundred climbers and sherpas frozen in the snow. An Indian climber died near the summit of Everest's north side. Green Boots they call him, after his neon-green boots. Climbers have to step over his legs on their way up and down.'

'Charming. Did you get any sleep after that?'

'Sure. Stewie made mulled wine, we played charades.'

'You mean I missed a party?'

'Sorry, I didn't want to wake you.'

'Doesn't matter. Where's Judith now?'

'She gets up so early, like, it's still dark.'

'Uh huh. She should be at Kia Ora by now.'

They climbed up to the plateau, Pelion East to the east, mounts Doris, Ossa and Thetis to the west, and beyond them was the Labyrinth and the Acropolis in Pine Valley. It was so warm now, they stopped to put on shorts and sunhats, peeling off and stowing their gear and rubbing in suncream on their faces, arms and legs. They strolled along the duckboard, enjoying the hum of insect life, the brilliance of the colours, the views, as they journeyed to Kia Ora Hut. Made of new pine boards, it had a pitched roof which also formed the ceiling inside. The Kia Ora River pooled nearby and Anne Maria and Liz dropped their packs, dragged off their clothes and waded into the freezing water.

'Oh, it's so cold!' Liz laughed and splashed Anne Marie.

She dunked her head, splashing water.

'Your hair!' Liz said.

'Who cares. 'S funny. Bushwalking with no mirrors, no reflecting glass, you forget what you look like.'

'Not so much forgetting, more disremembering,' Liz said.

'Disremembering.' Anne Maria considered the word. 'What, our personas as early childhood workers? More, facing our true self.'

'No, us. Me, Liz.'

'Me, Anne Marie,' she agreed. 'Back to basics. I like it.' Shedding society's image of herself, her role, the wild environment demanding only that she cope with it. She took in a deep breath of cool, crisp air and felt herself expanding.

'It could be confronting, don't you think?' Liz said.

'You mean, if you're not sure about yourself?'

'Something like that.'

'I tell you who'd never be unsure of herself: Judith.'

'You think so? She reminds me of my mum, so certain, but underneath, not.'

'Oh, shit, here come the fellas!'

Mark and Stewie appeared, discarding their shorts and T-shirts, yanking off their boots and socks. The girls sank to their shoulders as the waves splashed up from the men's impact. Anne Marie laughing, Liz looking nervous, as the men horsed about. Anne Marie waded out, Liz too.

'Aw, come on, girls, we won't duck you!'

But the women grabbed their clothes and ran, back along the boardwalk to the hut, laughing as they dried themselves and got into fresh clothes.

Teatime, Anne Marie offered Judith a cup of tea.

'No thank you, dear, I've had my water.'

What was she surviving on, Anne Marie wondered. She wasn't eating, just drinking cold water.

'Over here,' Liz called to Judith, and the woman sat there with her.

Joanna and Johnny came in. Joanna sat on a chair and eased off her boots. Johnny took their boots outside to clean, and she lay back, then extended a long leg and eased off her socks.

'Just look at my blisters. New boots did this.' Her heels were rubbed raw.

'D'you have bandages?' Anne Marie asked her, as she got the fuel stove going.

'We've used them up.'

Anne Marie pulled out her medical kit and looked through it. She found two round antiseptic pads of cotton and gauze, meant for eye-patches. 'Will these do?'

'They'll do just fine.'

Joanna took them, and when Johnny came back in, he carefully washed, dried and bandaged her blisters.

Mark came over to them. He'd accidentally pulled the cord from his tracksuit pants and was holding them up with two hands.

Anne Marie rummaged in her sewing kit and found a safety pin. 'Here you go,' hooking it through the cord for him. 'Feed it through and out the other end.'

He sat down to do this.

Gavin came in. There was still the problem of his lost spoon. Stewie was hanging around again, sniffing the food. She dived into her pack and handed him a packet of instant chicken and rice curry, thinking, had she become the old woman of the tribe, patching and feeding and healing its members?

'Hey,' Mark said, 'what d'you do when the safety pin opens?'

'Oh, god, you blokes are hopeless!' Anne Marie exploded and turned to Liz. 'Food's ready.'

She was in deep conversation with Judith and gave a look, a wave of her hand. Anne Marie dished up and took the bowl over to her. She didn't offer food to Judith, she knew she would have her few crackers and cheese. After eating, Anne Marie went outside to enjoy the last of the daylight.

'Hey, look here,' Stewie called.

She went over.

'Give us your finger.'

'Why?' She bent to look. 'Eeek!'

A leech on a twig was waving about. Stewie took her hand.

'No…' She wrenched it away.

''S okay.' He took her hand again and lowered her finger towards the leech. It stiffened and rose up, bringing the twig with it.

'Levitation,' he laughed. 'Show that to the yogis.'

'How does it do it?' Trying it herself.

'Antigravity. If only you could commercialise it, you'd make a fortune.'

Walking back to the hut, an object glinted below the boardwalk.

Anne Marie bent to look. 'Hey, Stewie, look here.'

He came over and leaned, his hands behind his back. 'I would say you have identified a superb example of the species cutlery, subspecies spoon.'

'No! Get it out, Stewie.'

He found a short branch, reached under the boardwalk and scuffed it out.

Anne Marie picked it up and rubbed it clean on her shorts. 'Brilliant. Gavin's spoon…' She dashed inside and presented it to him.

'Thanks, Anne Marie, I'm back in society, no more twigs,' and they hugged.

She looked for Liz to tell her, saw her sitting by the sleeping platform with Judith and went over.

'We were ascending Kala Pattar in Nepal for the sunrise,' Judith was saying. 'Hilary started to complain. I took her pack, I made her rest, gave her a boost of electrolytes in water, made hot tea. She seemed to improve. True, she perked up.'

'Right…'

'This is the very gortex jacket. I was wearing it back then.'

Anne Marie stood by, waiting to catch Liz's eye.

'We adventured all around the world together. But with age…'

Anne Marie gave up and joined the crowd. The night was noisy.

Johnny was sitting on the sleeping platform, Joanna popping chocolates into his mouth, her long body curled around him. So this was love, Anne Marie mused, the coming together of opposites? Her relationships had never developed this far, maybe she was looking in the wrong direction? Stewie and Mark were playing cards, Gavin was writing in a notebook. She stayed up a little later, then crashed.

Next morning, Liz and Anne Marie didn't get moving until nine thirty after a late, slow breakfast. They were climbing Mount Ossa today, and staying at Kia Ora another night. They took only daypacks with them with plenty of water and snacks, and walked back along the duckboard.

'Where's Judith today, heading off?'

'Don't know. Her pack's still here but her sticks have gone. She must be up ahead.'

'Thank goodness, a day free from her.'

Liz turned on her. 'You shouldn't be so harsh. She was telling me this awful story. It was so sad. She's really sad, you know.'

'Oh, well…' Anne Marie felt uncomfortable. She just didn't have Liz's patience, her kindness.

Turning off to the left, first to climb up to Mount Doris, then Mount Ossa, they walked on duckboard through low cider gum and pandani groves, up rough-hewn timber ladders and stone steps as they ascended.

'This is so beautiful,' Liz paused and looked around.

'Look at that.' Anne Marie indicated ahead a low cliff of broken granite columns. Each column was topped with a plant, sending a cascade of greenery over the dark stone.

'Like a planting for an amazing garden,' Liz said.

At about four hundred metres the gravel track levelled and curved south, and as they rounded the mountain onto the saddle between Mount Doris and Mount Ossa, a gulf opened out. Across the gulf stood the spires and columns of Mount Massif, Geryon, the Acropolis and Wall Mountain, blue beneath their shawls of snow. They stopped to take it in, standing silently in awe, before walking on stone slabs through an alpine meadow of sphagnum moss, mounded lime-green cushion plants, wild flowers. Boulders were laced with lichen, driftwood, and sprays of grasses and reeds fanned beside tiny tarns looking deliberately placed for effect, rills and pools spanned by stone slabs, the whole exquisite.

'This is like a Japanese garden,' Liz breathed, 'a natural place, a Zen place.'

'A place where you come to reach out and forget yourself,' Anne Marie said.

'Or end things from the past,' Liz added.

Mount Ossa reared its pronged peaks, and they made their way up past drifts of snow. At the very top, below the granite prongs was a tiny tarn of pure water edged with reeds

'The Pool of Icarus,' Anne Marie said.

Beyond, blue valleys fell away to the south-west.

'Gorgeous.'

Arm in arm they stood there, breathing it in, not bothering with photos as other walkers edged and jostled with their cameras to capture the scene.

A sudden commotion.

'Down there, look! Somebody's down there!'

Stewie came stumbling across the rough ground.

'What's happened?' Anne Marie grabbed his arm.

'Someone's fallen. Gotta get down to Kia Ora. Satellite phone.'

'Oh, god.' Anne Marie started forward.

'Don't go there.' Mark stopped her. 'Hey!' Calling after Liz.

'Who?' Liz called.

'There's a red jacket!' Gavin was there.

'It's Judith! Anne Marie, that's her jacket!'

'Wait, Liz.' Anne Marie stumbled after her.

'Whose are these?' Gavin held up a walking stick.

Liz stood at an outcrop, looking down. Anne Marie got to her.

'SES!' Johnny called out. 'Impossible to get down there to get her out.'

'Helicopter the team in?' Joanna said.

'She must've fallen.' Anne Marie looked around. 'But how could she, here?'

Liz grabbed her arm. 'She told me. She blamed herself, Anne Marie. Poor Judith!'

'Told you what?'

'Her partner, Hilary. Pneumonia, on that trek she told us about. She died.'

'That can't be right. She was so competent, Liz.'

'Hilary never wanted to go, she made her, she said she had to take flight from ordinary life.'

'Oh, shit.'

'She never forgave herself.' Liz was weeping now.

Joanna joined them. 'Must've been an accident, hey? It happens.' She put an arm around Liz to comfort her.

'Pretty steep, fifty metres down,' Johnny said.

'I couldn't help her,' Liz wept.

'Liz, let's go back to Kia Ora.' Anne Marie tried to guide her away.

'I want to wait!' She broke away.

'Okay… But SES will be hours yet.'

'By the time Stewie gets to the hut, then the rescue helicopter,' Johnny said.

'She was your friend?' Joanna asked.

'We met her at Waterfall.'

'Yes, my friend,' Liz said.

No one asked, is she still alive? Ann Marie knew why. It was too far to fall.

Anne Marie stood by her friend, then gently eased her away to try to find some shelter beneath the prongs of Mount Ossa. All the while thinking that while she was running around being the top walker, fixing trackie pants' cords and blisters, her friend Liz was giving time and comfort to a lost woman.

'You did your best, Liz.'

'This beautiful place, it's like, it's her dead zone. It's why she came,' Liz wept.

Anne Marie, silently agreeing, hugged her friend to her. 'Liz, you did your best,' she murmured as they waited together for the rescue team.

Taken out of themselves? Misremembering? Anne Marie wouldn't forget this walk, ever, when she returned to her normal life. Neither would Liz, and she hugged her friend.

The Quad Squad

Beyond Derwent Bridge on the Lyell Highway, Samantha encountered snow. Driving her Alfa 75 manual five-speed, chipped up for extra power and economy, she had no problems. In fact, she was able to enjoy the flakes smattering her windscreen, trees hung with snow, the black peaks in the distance marked with lines of white where the snow had drifted in crevices. It made driving to Queenstown and Strahan to assess the market for a new car yard all the more of an adventure. She had a lot to get through: check sites, assess the competition, cost establishing the yard, check local council rates, government regs. In fact, feet on the ground, she needed to get a feeling for the market for high end vehicles. If good, she and Fortune Status Wagons were on the up and up.

Ossarian had objected. His reason? They already had two premises, another would stretch the business model too far. Samantha guessed that he feared a relocation to the West Coast, if a new car yard was viable. He had objected to her even driving there; it would be much more time-efficient to fly. The cost! she'd said and overrode him. That's what you can do when you're the boss. Anyway, it was years since she'd ventured to the West Coast. Before, she hadn't wanted to go there, put off by the period of the protests when, her parents had told her, they should've dammed the rivers. Didn't they need more power, how else would development go ahead in little Tassie? At least the Hydro meant jobs, because if people didn't have jobs, how could they get ahead? Start a family, get a roof over their heads, educate their kids. Tell that to the Greens! Now, the stats said tourism was booming, despite the constant rain, and there was money on the West Coast. But if she came across any Greens, well, she'd wouldn't be standing on the brakes!

Her hands-free rang.

'Ossarian. What's the schedule?' Though she knew it. 'CLA reps at ten? Good. Go for it. Secure their car fleet, plus six-monthly maintenance. What do they want, Toyotas? Go Korean, they don't need the grunt.' She listened as she cruised along. 'I know we can cream more, Ossarian, but think reputation, think fair dealing, think integrity…' Did she have to spell it out? 'I said Koreans, Kia. Neat, fast, nippy for getting around their city outlets, fuel economy will win them over.' She listened. 'You're worried about image? An outfit like theirs doesn't need image. Sell it to them, Ossarian, it's in your corner.'

A young bloke, Ossarian. She'd picked him out of a line-up from the employment agency, thinking his dark looks might get in the migrant buyer. Plus, he did have experience, unlike most of the hopeless lot coming her way. Maybe she should've gone for an older woman, they were so much more trustworthy and hard-working. Image, though. There was the dilemma, as Ossarian had pointed out. Still, what was done was done.

She switched her attention to the landscape. Dense forest highlit with snow, branches hanging, looking gorgeous with the weight. But then a few kilometres on, clear-felling. It was an almighty mess and she speeded up to get through it. A log truck thundered her way with a massive trunk on its jig, looking like a felled giant, the gust as it passed shaking the Alfa. She hated the sight. Wasn't old-growth logging out the door? She certainly supported that ban.

Earlier, she had seen water flowing in a concrete canal. A sign on the left indicated Butler's Gorge. Hadn't she heard of it? On impulse, she'd turned off the highway and driven past the power station, all pylons and wires behind a cyclone wire fence. She continued along a gravel road, following the canal. Power lines linked towering pylons standing against the sky, and rounding a bend she came to a dam face. Its great curved arc was black, marked with streaks of white, and beyond its edge was a huge stretch of water, a tiny boat floating on it emphasising the great grey space stretching to low hills. Wow! What was this dam?

Leaving, Samantha had spun the Alfa around and come up with a jerk to three metres of solid black rock face, its dense planes shining with water. Her little white Alfa looked like a petal floating on air beside its presence. So this was what underlay the above-ground feats of engineering! Incredible what they'd had to carve through.

She drove back to the Lyell Highway, and again, the road wound through overhanging forest. A noticeboard indicated the Tarraleah Conservation Area, then a metre-high metal pipeline barrelled parallel to the road, crossing a hillside and then between two great pipes upended as towers at the entry to the Hydro's Tarraleah Village. Then came Wayatinah, another Hydro village, then Tungatinah Power Station. From power station to power station, six-legged pylons strode, arching across the forested landscape. This might be the Central Highlands, but she was well and truly in Hydro country!

Now, the forest each side of the winding road looked untouched, dense and beautiful, such a variety of foliage! She reached a blue Parks and Wildlife sign, stating that this was now the Franklin-Gordon Wild Rivers National Park. So here it was, the great achievement of the Greens, who'd stopped the Gordon Below Franklin power scheme! Her parents had told her about the civil disobedience, the rallies, the fall of governments, the campaign on the mainland, people writing No Dam on their ballot papers, the blockading, thousands camping on the Gordon river banks, every wannabe celebrity rafting down the Franklin, the intervention of the federal government and the final High Court decision. For five years, it went on, because how could the Hydro be denied their country, the state its power? Her mum and dad were simple small business people, did all this fuss benefit them? No way! Or her, she humphed as she drove past a forest lookout point, and then a trail to walk. But the beautiful forest, this was what had been saved, and for once she understood the conflict.

Samantha powered up the hills, snowy mountains in the distance, and reached the outskirts of Queenstown. The hills around the town were no longer bare, but green, clothed with low growth. That was an improvement; she'd hated that poisoned look. Entering Queenstown, with a shock she saw smoke rising from the chimneys of a row of hovels.

People actually lived in them? They needed demolishing. She drove through the streets, so shabby! Peeling paint, stained concrete and houses made of some awful board. Broken down fronts, rusting cars and trucks, just a few nice public buildings, the library, a museum. Okay, there was some parkland and landscaping, but this was not the place for a car yard of her quality. She didn't even feel like stopping for a coffee!

Signage indicated the route to Strahan, and Samantha, with relief, turned along it. Traffic was light, mostly tradies rocketing past in trucks and four-wheel drives. The road again rose through beautiful deep forest, lit up with the occasional shaft of light through the snow clouds.

Evening was deepening when she cruised down the hill into Strahan and entered the main street. Ah, this was better. Nicely renovated houses, the long veranda of a heritage hotel, an information building and a heritage interpretation site. There were fishing boats in close, and two large tourist boats moored one behind the other at the dock, one dark grey hulled, the other white. Samantha looked for her accommodation, Harbour Views, with no luck, so she parked, getting out her mobile to ring for directions. She was hoping it would be warm and comfortable, she'd paid enough. She could see a large hotel or motel complex up on the hillside. Was Harbour Views up there?

As Samantha was thumbing her phone for the number, a wagon towing a trailer loaded with two quad bikes – red, squat, fat wheels, cruised past and turned into a large open area off the road. As she waited for her call to go through, another wagon towing a trailer with two quad bikes joined it and backed into a space. Then another, and another, backing and turning, engines rumbling, lights sweeping. She studied them. Trade names on the doors of the wagons: MJ Renovations, Plumb the Depths, CDElectricals… In all, seven four-wheel drives with two quads each, made fourteen tradies? Oh, god, she just hoped they weren't booked in anywhere near her. Fears of partying, drinking, drugs, noise, all went through her head.

'Harbour Views, Narelle speaking, can I help you?' a voice trilled.

Samantha asked for directions and Narelle sent her along the waterfront. She was only a hundred metres from her destination. Welcome to Strahan.

Food. Samantha hadn't eaten, being on her twenty-four/seven diet, but she needed something. She got out of her car, looking along the esplanade for a takeaway, not the best choice, and glimpsed a pizza sign. As she was locking her car, three men appeared and stood there. Young, shaven heads, jeans and sweat tops, tradies she guessed. Locals?

'Alfa 35.7, get a handfulla that!' the guy nearest her commented.

'Black leather Momo steering wheel,' his mate added. 'Classy.'

'Italian styling, that red duco, real style.' Another joined them.

'Black Recono bucket seats, I kid you not.' The first bloke turned to his mate, who'd joined the crowd.

'Simmons wheels…' They bent to look. 'And yes! Billy Stein shockers. Am I right or am I right!'

They all turned to Samantha.

'This your wagon, lady?'

'You bet it is.' Flattered, she patted her blonde bouffant 60s style and did a double take. This was the quad mob.

'Sick styling, that Italian flair,' the first one who'd rocked up said, and she gave him a look.

Not bad, she could go for him. But she was here on business, don't get distracted, she told herself.

'You boys locals?'

'Nah, down from Lonnie, Devonport. Goin' quading with our Can-am 4x4 ATVs Scramblers.'

'Where, here?'

'Ocean Beach. We've done Granville Harbour, south.'

They shifted, reliving the experience, she could see it in their eyes, shrugs, arms across their chests. You had to be able to read the signs to sell cars, but she wouldn't be selling to these bogans.

'You mean, along the beaches?'

''S right,' but they were already shifting as two of their mates arrived, handing out folders.

'Room keys. Straight up the hill, plentya parkin' behind the villas.'

They gave her a glance, the Alfa another, and headed off, back to their wagons to drive up the hill.

Samantha watched them go. They were well away from her accommodation, and with relief she headed down the esplanade to the pizza take away. She'd eat, watch a bit of television, have a shower and get an early night.

An hour later, Samantha, having showered, was in bed. The room was quiet, clean, smart, the double bed comfortable. Tired after the long day's driving, she drifted off.

Morning, and Samantha was up and about early, dressed in a warm fake leopard skin jacket and thick ski pants, thick socks and walking shoes. The air was freezing, though the roaring forties weren't blowing, not today. It wasn't raining but was misty, closed in, giving a remote feeling to the place. She had a hot coffee in the hotel, no breakfast, she wanted to get moving. Standing on the footpath, looking up and down the main street, she knew at once this was not the place for an upmarket car sales yard. There just wasn't the population, so no need to waste her time checking with the West Coast Council, which was in Queenstown anyway. But what now?

'G'day.'

Startled, she turned. 'Oh, hello.'

It was the first guy from the evening before. He looked even more reasonable this morning. Fit, smiling, good-looking. 'No Alfa?'

'No… I feel like walking, it's so easy to get around.'

'Follows. Tourist?'

She thought for a minute. 'Well, in a way.'

'Guess you're takin' the cruise?'

'Cruise?'

'Gordon River. Everybody does it. Up to Warner's Landing, where the protesters camped.'

'Suppose I could. What are you doing today?'

'Headin' off when the fellas get their act together.' He looked about for his mates.

Samantha looked over as wagons with the trailers and the quad bikes entered the street. One or two were backing and shifting.

'Looks like they're making a move.'

'Havin' drinks later, up the hill, Room 4216. You like to drop in? Ask for me, Matt.'

'Oh, okay. I'll see how today goes. Thanks, Matt. I'm Samantha.'

'Have a good day, Samantha,' and he strode over to the wagons.

Samantha looked over at the cruise boats. She read the name, *Spirit of the Wild*, and, making a quick decision, she hurried down to the office, went to the counter and paid for a ticket. They were already boarding, so she dashed out, climbed up the gangplank and a young fellow welcomed her.

'I'm Josh, I'll show you to your seat.'

'Thank you, Josh.'

It was in the front of the boat. She made herself comfortable and looked around. Not a big crowd, but still about seventy people at the cost of the ticket, it was profitable. Should she think about this game? Shuddered. Living on the West Coast? No way.

Almost at once a voice announced the cruise, details about safety and toilets, and lunch. Oh, so lunch was included, that was nice. Now they were crossing Macquarie Harbour, six times larger than Sydney Harbour, to go through Hell's Gates. They would come back to the Gordon River, cruise up to the Heritage Landing, where there was a delightful rainforest walk, and over to the convict settlement on Sarah Island, back by three p.m. Fine, her day was mapped out for her. She was happy to sit and take in the views as the boat left the dock and cruised into the vast stretch of silvery water, dark forested hills rising to black mountains. Normally, she was busy running the two car yards, so this was a treat, and after a while she closed her eyes and drifted off.

Samantha came to with a start. They were at Hell's Gates now, edging through and back, everyone standing to see the boat navigate the narrow gap. She jumped up, went up the stairs and joined them. It was cool but not cold, the boat so well built, the passengers calm and chatty, a nice experience.

The *Spirit of the Wild* powered back across Macquarie Harbour, past distant fish farms, past Sarah Island, where they would be calling in later, to the entrance of the Gordon River. Samantha had heard about the colour of the river, darkened by the tannin coming off the button grass plains, so what? Well, she hadn't realised the effect. As the boat slowed, and the engine switched to electric to save the banks of the river from erosion, the water in its calm reaches acted like a mirror, creating an exact image of the forest above. Samantha was mesmerised. The slow silent cruise through this amazing landscape was like journeying into a dream where sky, water, land merged, and she felt its power, its timelessness, and then such a wave of gratitude that this had not been lost. But then sad that the jewel of the south-west, Lake Pedder with its white quartz beach, had been drowned. Tasmania had been described in tourist brochures as a natural work of art, and she had scoffed. Now, she sensed the truth of this statement and mourned all that had been lost, and for the forests right now being destroyed so wilfully. The walk through the forest at the Heritage Landing was exquisite, with signs identifying the rainforest species. Celery top pine, native frangipani, the ghostly stands of sassafras, leatherwood, but missing was the great Huon pine, logged almost to extinction.

Lunch was a smorgasbord on board, tasty and pleasant as they cruised, the engine a gentle throb, back down the Gordon River. Entering Macquarie Harbour, they crossed to Sarah Island and moored at a walkway. The wind was blasting now and Samantha was almost blown off the long walkway. How wild this place was, and how harsh living must have been here. They started off on their walk, led by a fun guide, Frank, who got them to join in his spiel.

There were the brick remains of cells, the oven, the Old Penitentiary, the New Penitentiary, remains of jetties and the stories that went with them. Out of the wind, it was pleasant, a charming little island with its own historical walk and Samantha was impressed. The alternativee history of the island, that it had been industrious, the convicts building boats out of Huon pine, and other activities, and that they were not the down-beaten rascally lot portrayed, and therefore weren't given the cruel punishments by the regime later in charge at Port Arthur, was fascinating.

The group met for a last chat in a shelter shed where on the walls was a wooden display board listing convicts who had absconded, most of whom were captured again, topped by Matthew Brady's name. Running her eyes down the list, Samantha gave a start, her eyes falling on one name, Joseph Fortune. But that was her father's name! She felt such a shock, and such confusion, for heaven's sake! So this was the result of her journey to the West Coast? To find her own family history, her own beginnings, that her great-great, how many greats, grandfather had been a convict? She sat on a bench, oblivious to Frank's talk.

A woman guide sat by her. 'Are you feeling all right? You'd like some water?' She handed her a bottle.

Samantha took it, and drank. 'Thank you,' and handed it back.

Frank came over. 'We're done here,' he said. 'You need help to get back to the boat?'

'No, I'm fine.' She stood shakily and looked at the display board again. 'It's that…' and then hesitated. Should she be telling them what she had found? No, she quailed at their response. It was private.

They left, following the group, staggering back across the walkway to board the boat.

The cruise back to Strahan was quiet, Samantha deep in thought. Did her father know about his convict forebear? She'd never been interested in local history, or her family's Tasmanian past, her mother having been born in Manchester, England. Her father, a quiet carpenter who had his own woodturning workshop, loved Tassie's woods, especially Huon pine. Was that his inheritance, a talent for using the wood? After all, over a hundred boats had been built from Huon pine on Sarah Island itself. Maybe it was in his blood. And in hers? What else?

The *Spirit of the Wild* cruised into Strahan and docked, and Samantha filed off the boat and walked back to her hotel. Blown about and cold, she threw off her clothes and dashed under the hot shower. She didn't know what to feel, but as she stood there, she felt the first stirrings of well, not pride, but interest and the need to know more about this man. Also, that the family in the past obviously didn't feel shame as they had kept his name. Dressed, she lay on the bed and slept.

For dinner, Samantha walked over to the heritage hotel. It was full, the tables taken by the tourists. A waiter ushered her to the last table in the corner. As she sat down, she glimpsed, through a glass door, a crowded bar. Was that the quad squad? There were Matt and his mates, drinking on; they must've had a good day roaring up and down the beaches. Thinking back over the journey along the Lyell Highway, the high rainfall resulting in this wild and unique country also had led to the development of hydroelectricity, its power stations, pylons, concrete dam, canals and races, and massive pipelines that, she saw now, was wilderness bound and shackled. A terrible clash, the need for power for the island and the preservation of this spectacular place made so obvious by the unique beauty she'd seen today, in the Franklin-Gordon Wild Rivers National Park. And her family history? Was bound up with it, for her forebear was right there on Sara Island, building boats from the Huon pine cut out of the forests along the Gordon River.

After a meal of hot soup in the hotel, Samantha walked back to her accommodation. A light rain was falling now, misting lights and outlines. She looked for the quad squad wagons, and there they were, parked in the same area off the main road, the four-wheel drives, the trailers and the quad bikes' duco shining under two street lights high up. Should she take up the offer of drinks later with Matt and his mates? Definitely not. Samantha reached the house where she was staying and stopped. Noise, male voices. She walked up the drive, and there they were. The quaders were in the parking area behind the house, standing around the Alfa. What were they up to?

'Hey!' she called and hurried over.

Matt turned. 'G'day! Had a good one? Just checkin' your wheels.'

'Smick, fuckin' smick,' his mate said and ran his hands over the duco.

Samantha shivered. It wasn't quite as if he were running his hands over her, but she didn't like it one bit.

Matt nudged her. 'Great cruise, hey, Sam?'

She was Sam now? She backed off, wanting to leave. But what about her car?

'Fantastic, the cruise, the wilderness, and Sarah Island,' she gabbled as she tried to edge between them and the Alfa.

'Headin' off tomorrow?'

'Yes, early. How was your day?'

'We rocked it, eh, Jeff? Those dunes, Henty Beach, friggin' massive!'

Jeff chortled and she smelt beer on his breath. 'We friggin' fanged it, eh, down those middens.'

'Well, I need to go in.'

Matt turned, his face wide and smiling. 'Comin' up later? Few drinks?'

'No. I've a long drive back to Hobart.'

'Cool. Mind if I take a turn of the Alfa, see how she runs?'

'What!' she started.

'Round the block. See how she runs,' he repeated. 'Come on…' Almost a threat, that smiling face, the mate, Jeff, moving close.

She handed over the keys. 'Straight back,' her voice frail in the cold air.

'Yeah, no problems. Jeff, get your arse in here.'

'No, reall…' she protested as Jeff slouched over and slumped into the passenger seat.

Matt gunned the car, it jerked back, almost colliding with a brick wall and they hooted. The Alfa shot past her, Matt waved, and it was gone with a roar of the engine into the night.

Samantha stood alone in the cold and the rain as the sound of the car engine faded. What was she without her Alfa? For the first time seeing herself as she was, just as she had on the boat, gliding up the Gordon River, its reflections mirroring life, her life. And then a rumble of engines approaching and alarmed she ran down to the road. Across the way, the buildings were lit with dim security lights, the water black with reflection from the lights of the boats. A line of quad bikes came barrelling along the road, each loaded with blokes shouting and drinking from stubbies. And there, right behind the leading quad bike, was her Alfa! The hood was back, Matt and his mate shouting and laughing, filling its tiny space.

She ran into the road. 'Stop! Stop right now!' Her hands flailing.

'Cheers, Sam!' Matt yelled as he and his mates roared past, the quad bikes veering around her, their drivers jeering, and off they roared down the road and on around the far bay.

Samantha watched them go, the lights of the vehicles dimming, catching a last glimmer of white in the distance, the Alfa captive in the middle of the quad squad. Samantha stood in the road and waited as the dark night came down over Macquarie Harbour, the rain pelting now. It seemed like the wilderness was rearing up, throwing off its shackles, intent on obliterating this little settlement on the edge of the vast waterway. As with time, Samantha understood now, it would, this place as frail as her Alfa before the immensity of its force.

Surface Tension

Tumbling in a roar of white water, arms flailing, chest bursting… I surge upwards and surface from the usual nightmare, my unconscious in sleep tormenting me. Blinking gummy eyes, I flex my arms above my head and shift my upper body, my soul self, deepening my breathing, relaxing, relaxing as the physiotherapist advises each time. Pre-dawn light lapping at the windows saves me from the night errant with its jousting defeats, deceits and regrets, in a tournament of dreamtime guilt.

Pre-dawn becomes dawn, reassuringly inexorable, the earth turning, promising warmth and heat, for the sun also rises as I rise and turn, lift my body and allow the room to show itself, its reassuring, rectangular reality. A daddy-long-legs is stringing a line from the edge of my book on the bedside table open at page fifty, across to the windowsill edging the open window through which floats a banner of garden scents above the petroleum glaze of the streets. A move, a shift, and off the spider staggers, spare legs clawing the air, terrified, because that's what we do, us top predators, frighten the lights - pre-dawn, dawn, day and night - out of every living being. And we are the chosen of God? No one would say that in these nihilistic, narcissistic times except crazy penteostals proliferating like cancer. Yet we still act as if we are the gods of the world, bulldozing, destroying, blasting, bombing our own kind as well as the whole of creation, leaving only rags and remnants of the great phylogenetic universe that we so unwillingly share.

Excuse my rant, but my mind is springing whole like Athena from Zeus's head from the formless nothingness that preceded my birth, recreated every night in sleep, and which waits for me at death, which has to be the ultimate unknowingness.

I go on like this to delay. What, living another day? No, to delay throwing back my sheet and angling myself out of bed and onto my commode to expel the night's waste. The moment comes, though, when it's make the move or burst the bladder, and I do so with a heave and a gasp without the grace and elegance of the spider which spools away on its web to freedom. And I long to be like it, skidding above the shallows of sentimentality, skating over the deeps of depression, floating away into the biosphere of possibility. Words words words, that's all you'll get spooling from me, locked into my half body's half-life.

Sitting on the commode, I curate the sounds of the house awakening, the people with whom I share my living, breathing journey through life. Firstly, Krishna and Mardhi, orange people, Westerners converted to Indian mysticism, yoga and meditation, murmuring mantras before breakfast, after which it's the daily gardening routines because, of course, they are vegetarian. Upstairs, bare feet patter across the floor, the two little boys playing, before one of them, Teddy or Bertie, will skip down the stairs and come peeping around the door to visit me in my room, fascinated as they are with my ambulatory shortcomings and goings. Dave the Prophet would've been up at dawn, working in the garden to demonstrate how to save our world from the industrial production of food and factory farming, fossil fuel emissions and other desecrations. Ethics grounded in an immense depth of knowledge is the needle steering his moral compass. And me? I follow their course, loving these three as they create a verdant garden where I spend so much time in my wheelchair. They embody reason and faith, a bulwark against the endgame, a world they are unwilling to let immolate in either Armageddon or Apocalypse.

Two others. Mike, a rationalist architect of sustainable building, a long-haired sinewy bike rider, so good-heartedly maintaining my wheelchair, oiling, greasing, keeping the tyres pumped, picking out pieces of Lego wedged in the rubber, cat fur clogging the sprockets. Simone does the same for me, Teddy and Bertie's mum, a registered nurse and a writer, and so carer and the scribe of our lives here in our urban republic. Together in this gracious decommissioned rectory above the city, receptacle of the good and the holy, she attends to my useless legs, rubbing in the cream, massaging the dormant muscles, cutting my rampant toenails, getting me to physio at her friend's practice. Simone is lovely, a visual miracle. Yesterday, mustard tights with multicoloured splotches, and a billowy yellow tent that she ripped off in the garden's heat down to a bra, her bright hair covering her shoulders; salve and solace to my sight.

Oh yes, one I have failed to mention, Monar, a tall, beak-nosed house member. Always in black, the mirror of his inner state, he is the termite gnawing at the foundations of this dwelling. Only I can see the threat he poses from his bleak, nihilistic redoubt, challenging with reductive logic the mores that allow us to live in harmony with ourselves, with the world. From my own darkness, I watch, wishing him nothing good, willing him away with acerbic bile that rises in his presence. I had put it to the house members that we evict him, but they, with good-hearted tolerance, declined, pointing out that he always pays his share of board and rent on time. God help us, is that all that's important?

I curl my body and reach between my dead legs, reaching where you have to tell the ladies to place a beloved hand to massage the organ that joins the spine for a magical cannonade. It helps, waking, to keep me alive, in my progress down the vista of time to my eventual suicide. Don't be shocked. With half my body gone, I'm halfway there, aren't I, in this ground-floor room with its faded wallpaper, bare boards and bleached curtains edging its wide windows looking deep into its greenery and garden, the backdrop of my daytime wheelchair life.

Late nights, I sink into the past. Alex, you idiot! The kayak! And to evade agonising remembrance, I wheel through moonlit rooms, mourning in the tides of darkness the missing parent who was lost when I fell from the kayak into turbulence, but who was never with me, anyway. Why the hell did he force me into that kayak! My anguish is terminated by the cry of a child upstairs, kookaburras going for it, a rooster calling the dawn across the valley, all helping dispel my black and suffocating emotions.

My legs? Psychological. No evidence of physical damage is the summation of the congerie of counsellors, consultants, specialists, psychologists, psychiatrists, all the other psychos who, in the past, lined up to take my mother's money and reveal the truth of my condition, on which is dependent my disability pension. The truth is that we all enter adulthood with a wound, harm, damage physical, psychic. As I tell my mourning mother, whom I no longer will see. A truth she and they are unable to accept, because what does that make them? Purveyors not so much of lies as belief in the false prognosis, the shallow assumption. For what is obvious is not obvious, the capacity for love, a consoling soul, and I like to think I share that capacity.

Self-pity! I can do without it. I have help, daily, from Nicklas, my Greek carer. A black water beetle scudding into the house on a passing current with hints of garlic and bouzouki – he plays nights at his family's restaurant and comes trailing encores and admiration. Nicklas is good for a chat and a trip out, a visit somewhere, the museum and art gallery, for instance, seeing that I'm a learned man. Yes, I got through the self-education jag, ending up as far as I could go with my mind while hobbled physically, for the university did its best to make the world of knowledge accessible to me. Some recompense, I suppose. Sex? Ah, the big one. I suggested to Nicklas he tee up a prophylactic exchange, a warm body, warm feelings, and skin! Don't neglect our largest organ. Abused and used, it deserves recognition, tenderness, care. I couldn't convince him, me the would-be satyr. Sex worker, he said, rubbing his shaved head in laughing disbelief. You asking me to pimp?

But get this! Last Tuesday, Cassie, my cousin and stand-in for my mother, glided in on her long water-strider legs, sporty in shorts, T-shirt tight across square shoulders, flying blonde hair and scents of cinnamon and nutmeg. She brought me Narelle, a hairdresser, blessed with an angel face above a body slumped on solid legs in pyramidal concession to gravity. They wheeled me outside into the sun, muffled me in warm towels, and Narelle clipped and shaved and tweaked and rinsed with gentle but firm massaging hands. Ah! The wonderful sensations of the hair salon were mine, while the two women chatted on in their ditzie ways. Freakin' bliss!

Through the french windows, I see Simone. She is sitting on a bench while her boys play under the walnut tree, throwing the green nuts at each other. Distant cries, a flash of red jumper, a pink face, the blond hair of the little guy, his older brother's chestnut curls, I love those little dudes. Monar appears from the laundry, and I watch him walk across the grass and sit by Simone. What the fuck is that stick insect up to now?

A car door slams out in the street. Nicklas is here, so I wheel about to welcome him, and that's it for now.

Late afternoon, I'm parked just outside on the patio, soaking up sun dappling through the trellised wisteria, its purple racemes irresistible to bees. Rowing my wheelchair across the watery surface of life with powerful arms, shoulders and, I like to think, mind, I'm in control. But once parked, it's hard to move. It's not an off-road vehicle, my chariot, so I spy on what's going on. Dave, I can see his head down the garden. He is planting the lettuce seedlings which he propagated in the greenhouse which the house members built, with a chook run attached. We have three white chooks – Pinky, Perky and Pauline – and one black chook, Ebony, and she's the boss. Sometimes, Simone wheels me along the path, taking the kitchen scraps to fling them into their run. The boys collect eggs from the nests, and I feel the warm round smoothness of a newly laid egg against my cheek. I can see that the corn is ripe now, fat green and yellow cobs showering silky fronds. Lettuces, tomatoes, cucumber, zucchini, peas and beans. In the trees, apricots, plums, lemons, a cornucopia! If I hear the chip chip from the workshop, I will wheel along the path to watch Krishna at work, busy making the little inlaid boxes out of the local woods that he takes to a gallery to sell. I sit there and watch him at work, this former boatbuilder, no need to talk, his wisdom manifested in silence and the beauty of our Tasmanian minor species.

So here I am, the sentinel of the garden, getting some healthy vitamin D. Simone has left, gone to bring the boys, Teddy and Bertie, back from childcare. Footsteps down the path along the side of the house? Monar. I wrench the wheels to shoot back inside, but too late.

'Getting the sun, Alex?'

'Hnnn.' I give him a stare that he ignores, confirming my assessment that he is narcistically unaware of his own superfluity.

He drags up a wicker garden chair, sits and eyes me. I know what he wants – to plumb my psyche and search the darkness in me to see if it corresponds with the space where his heart should be. For I sense a loveless childhood, a private school boarder, dispatched at the age of five to an institution of torture. For his own good, of course. It always is.

'If you, I could, you know…'

He is asking me for something? 'What?' I glare.

'Screen beats, David Byrne, St Vincent, Stranglers, your room…'

What! Muscling in on my music? He's been listening in evenings when I float away from my disabled body on jet streams of sound, the sneak. I know what he wants, for me to share his chancre of bitterness, just like a drinker needs someone to drink with, validating their addiction, his to nihilism.

Mahdi, sweaty in shorts and singlet saves me, stepping onto the patio holding a bunch of fat carrots and beaming orangely. 'Carrot salad with orange juice tonight.'

A car door slams and the boys are here, hurtling down the driveway, followed by Simone. I brace myself for two small bodies throwing themselves on me, like frogs onto a leaf.

'Hi, guys. Had a good time?'

We trail inside as Simone comes in, lugging two bags of shopping, and dumps them on the table. It's time for my afternoon rest, if I don't get it, my legs suffer, so I leave them to it and head down the hall to my bedroom.

Lying on my bed, the weight of me subsiding onto the doona in the shadowy afternoon stillness, I don't think of much, certainly not activities associated with legs. They are what they are; force of will makes no difference to them. What would it take to get them working, some sort of crisis? I want no freakin' drama, hell no, had enough of that, and no happy ever after either, to my life. With all of its routines – massage, exercises, physio, therapeutic swimming – in this house, with these people, it's mine.

I lie here mourning my last sexual love, Rebecca. Two years ago now. Short, dark, ebullient, her skin the colour of chocolate ice cream, vanilla in the hidden places, soft hands massaging me, and me her. Cassie brought her around to a little flat I had then, across from the beach. Was that their plan, that sex might fix my legs? I suspect it was, but in the end the ice cream melted in the heat of lust, and she left, leaving a sticky pool on my skin that I licked away. No one since, only the kids' hot little bodies and an occasional cuddle from Simone, but I can relive the experience…

Hold it, what's happened? Screams! the kids! I heave off the bed and into the wheelchair, get to the bedroom door and slide across the hall, through the living room, just as Teddy bursts in through the open back door.

'Snake! Alex, snake!'

He's asking the cripple for help? 'Where's Bertie! Simone, the kids!' In one movement I shoot out onto the patio.

'It went there,' Bertie, holding Teddy's arm, is pointing into the garden.

'Get the spade!' That's Dave hauling up the garden, intent on finding and dispatching it, no room for a snake in his Garden of Eden.

'Kids, come here!' Simone's frantic.

'What is it?' Krishna bumbles out of the workshop.

'A snake, probably after rats,' is Mahdi's calm assessment. 'No need to worry.'

'Put the body in the compost,' Mike's arrived on his bike.

'Why are you talking about killing it? Leave it, let it be!'

'It's dangerous, Alex,' Mike says as if I'm a retard. 'The kids.'

'Fuck's sake, it's a living creature.' I shunt the wheelchair forward, and then it happens.

The snake, a black tiger, slithers through the green and red bells of the fuchsia by the path and it's right there, scales like coal, its tongue forked, flicking, tasting the air, a black eye gleaming, and it's giving me this look and for a moment, for me, time stands still.

Bertie shrieks. Mike's off after it. Teddy stumbles after him.

'Teddy!'

Simone reaches to grab him, I lurch to grab her and the wheelchair slips off the edge of the patio and the whole of me tumbles over into the fuchsias. Pitching forward, for the first time for so long I smell soil, rotting leaves, insects, see red blossoms up close, like I'm joining the snake in the worship of mother earth.

'Alex, look out!' Simone's shouting and I'm back there.

Alex, you idiot! The kayak! I'm struggling to get up when two strong hands grab me under the arms. Monar's heaving me upright, and I'm up on my two scabby legs, clutching the veranda post, the wisteria racemes in a violet dance with my trembling body. I fix Simone with my eyes, take a breath of the cool air of this upper stratosphere and feel the trauma falling away.

'Hold on, Alex, you're doing just fine.' She's placing a hand on my arm to steady me and I look down at my wasted limbs, bare feet crooked crabs clutching the concrete path.

'Mummy. Alex is standing right up!' Bertie shouts.

'Thtanding up,' little Teddy lisps.

Monar moves away, off the patio, hands in pockets, his black back to me. He turns, we're eye to eye, and there he is, his face trying on a smile, that hooked nose, those sardonic lips, eyes as black as the snake's.

The tension is broken by Mahdi pelting up the path. 'Alex, you're standing?'

'Hey, man!' Mike, abandoning his hunt for the snake.

'Krishna, come see!' Mardhi calls.

Dave, with a shy smile, presses a fat, newly pulled leek, dirt hanging on its roots, into my hand, a trophy. I hardly notice, because I can see so much. Our garden bursting with leaf and flower and fruit, chooks clucking, the sunlight falling through the trees. Our world and I'm upright in it, buoyed by the goodness of the people in this house. Simone, by my side, sees what I see, knows what I know, the boys pressing against me. And Monar? Maybe it had to be someone like him with darkness deep within, to help me upright, to break through surface tension and enter the sunny world.

It's too much. My legs give way, I flop back into my righted wheelchair.

'You did it,' Simone murmurs, 'for my boys.'

I wheel around, and Simone, with Bertie and Teddy, pushes me back into the kitchen, and I wheel through the house to my bedroom, my shelter, my refuge to face myself with tears. For I know what Monar has seen, that the loss was of a father who wasn't a father, a truth only he can recognise. And I know what Simone has seen, that, in an instant, I was willing to give myself, and in doing so, found what everyone in this household knows: that to sacrifice the self is for a greater reality, love.

And now, affirmation, a tentative stirring, my legs demanding agency, the ache of muscles wanting to be used, to take me back into this world, to float away on the currents and rhythms of life. My encounter with the snake, with Monar, has given me back the upright world, the promise of a future on two feet that is now mine to take. And I take up my neglected phone to ring my mother.

The Shore

Brady

'I told the police, I had nuthin' to do with it. If I hadn't've been hanging out with me mates, pissin' on last night, I would've got down to the shore earlier, for sure. I surfaced about ten, dunked me head under the cold water tap and went down to check the surf. Waves grumbling across the cliff platform, dragging at kelp bundles, you haveta look where you put your feet, shells can cut 'em to pieces.'

'Get to the point,' they said, Officer Jones, DI Marney.

'Lighten up! You want the truth? Tellin' yer.'

It hadn't looked good, sea fog blottin' out the bay, greasy surf ratsarse, waves slidin up the sand, hissing along the shore. Needed an off-shore wind to shift the fog, get some surf pumpin'.'

'See anything at all, anything might help?' Jones said.

'Heard someone puttering out on the bay, pro'ly a tinny headin' out to one of the yachts out there.'

'Who?'

'Don't ask me.'

'A local? Fisherman? Divers?'

'Couldn't tell, no way.'

'What boats were missing?'

'Wouldn't know.'

'You tell us what you know,' DI Marney said. 'And fast.'

'I don't know nuthin'.'

'Who lives here?'

'Just me and me dad.'

'Your old man is all?' Jones is lookin' around like I got something to hide.

'Yep.'

'What's he do?'

'Works lookin' at things, you know? Studying.'

'Studyin'?'

'Marine stuff. Fish.'

'Poncy nutter, eh?'

'Nah. Not really.' I'm proud of my dad. He used to be an ab diver and got out of it, took up university, did all right.

'Who were you drinking with last night?'

'Snapper, Codfish, Koota…'

'You taking the piss?'

'Me mates. Oh, Birdie turned up later with Chelsea.'

'Woman?'

'Nah, dog.'

That floored 'em.

'Tellin' yer, we jammed a bit on our guitars, got pissed, mucked about till late…'

'Your mates… They can confirm your movements?' Jones is onto it.

'Check the pile of bottles in the recycling. Couldna drunk them all meself.'

'Write down names and phone numbers, all of them.' DI Marney, he's cold as ice.

'Chelsea too?'

'No lip from you, mate.' Jones arcs up.

They went off for a walk, the two of them. Had a smoke.

Thing is, there was somethin… We did races down the cliff path, timing it. Sick! Chelsea was fastest, jokin'… Koota made the best time. I reckon I coulda broke the record, I'm so used to goin' up and down, but I'd had too much grog.

Anyway, I get down there, dark coming on, seagulls crying. I turned to head back, then I heard it, not a cry, more a gasp, as if somebody had hurt themselves, mm, like that. Hurt, real bad.

''S goin on?' I yelled.

Everything's still, as if someone is listening. I start across to check it out but a racket breaks out up top. Chelsea's barkin' like crazy, the guys yellin, what's goin' on! I'm up to the clifftop. For shit's sake, Chelsea's treed a possum! They've got the car lights on the tree, Birdie's eggin' her on, Koota and Snapper are yelling go Chelsea! There's this little possum clinging to its mum, big round eyes starin', scared to death. Koota aims a beer bottle, it thunks right by them.

'Cut it out, you bastards,' I yell, and boot Chelsea a good one.

Well, that's it as far as Birdie's concerned. 'Fuck you, Brady! Kick my dog, you kick me!'

'Have some fuckin' respect,' I yell.

Birdie's out of there and the others too, into their cars, doin' donuts down the drive to the main road.

Shit, the cops are back. Marney squints at me, Jones circles.

'Reckon you know something.'

'Nah.'

'Tell us again.' Jones checkin' his notes.

'Told ya. I come down after ten to check the surf. Then I noticed it.'

'Noticed what?' Marney scruffs me. 'Spit it out before I whang your balls...'

'The gulls...'

'What about the fuckin' gulls!'

'Fightin' over something at the water's edge.'

'What!' Marney's right in my face.

'Kelp.'

'And what else.'

'Rubbish. Tossed over from a fishin' boat.'

'You're gonna be rubbish.' Jones is losin' it.

'So I headed back here.'

'Who was here?'

'Me dad...usually.'

They eased off. 'Stuck here with your dad? No girlfriend?'

'Nah. Here's where I wanna be, catchin' waves, keeping a count of the mutton birds breeding in the rookery, right whales travelling north in spring, dolphin pods…always something happenin' out here…'

'Fucking Greenie!' Jones says. 'Greenie dole bludger, eh?' He's circling again.

'I work, fishin' with Reg, on the *Lazy May*.'

'Last twenty-four hours, fill us in,' Marnie interrupts.

I give it a go. 'Big swell, storm out at sea, caught some rippers, one monster, three steps, crest at take-off, then middle, nearly lost it there, 'n' at the bottom. Sick!'

'Stick to the point.'

'I rang around me mates, got them over last night, show them some shots, here look…'

'Ditch the fucking phone.'

'Rest of the day cleaned and filleted a bucket of trevally put them in the freezer, then trawled the internet until me mates turned up.'

'No one else here? Like a woman?'

'Nah, no woman.'

'Where's your mum?'

'She's got her own place down the dunes.'

'You're gonna have to make a statement down at the station,' Marnie says. 'Informing you, we'll be taking a DNA sample.'

'DNA? What for?'

'Evidence,' the tall one said. 'Count you out.'

'Or in,' the fat one said. 'You touched anything down there, we'll nail you.'

I watched as they got into their car and drove off, went back inside and took a swig of Dad's whisky, trying to calm me nerves.

You see, down on the shore, it was like I said. This morning, gulls screamin' over that bundle on the shore. I sprint through the shallows, yelling, driving them off. Turn it over and oh shit shit shit! It's a body, a girl! Face dead white, black hair like weed over her face, eyes starin'. Ooof! I heave away, throw up. Look back, I know that face! Who is she, what am I gonna do! Get back up here to Dad. He's not around, car's gone, where the fuck is he? I hear sirens along the road to the beach, and I know they've found her. Then those two dudes turn up, doin' door to door. Questioning.

I'm outa here. Don't say it: if I'm innocent, no worries. But I know how they look for a suspect to get a conviction. If only Dad was here. Shit, I can't get her face outa my mind, it's like, she's lookin' at me for help… Doin' my head in!

Thing to do, take out the boat, head off. Stupid? Yeah yeah… Put yourself in my shoes. Get myself outa the picture while they find out what happened, yeah. Maybe she was partying on a yacht, fell off, no one noticed her missing? Mates'll come forward, she was with us, went for a swim, we couldn't stop her, tried to hold her back and then… Or, or she had a fight with her boyfriend, walks away into the surf, rip catches her, nah, he catches her and then… Oh shit, gotta move! Right, key to the moorings. What the fuck, the tinny's out already? Hang about, the outboard I heard…was Dad? Mobile, outa range! Oh shit, no tinny, no this can't be happenin'! I gotta find Dad, now!

Joeley

You like my work? Stand back and take a good look, immerse yourself, the great Joeley Henderson's work in mosaic. My friend here, I call her Venus, after *Reflections on a Marine Venus*, a book I read once. Taken me a few months flat out but what a body, hers or mine, ha! These silver and blue bits of china, they'll do for eyes, just blank pits at the moment. You got any china you don't want, toss it my way.

You need strong hands for all that china chipping. Look at these nails, Christ almighty, no man'd look at me. Certainly didn't last night! Who gives a fuck, I tell myself, and I'm telling you this: how do you know what you're getting with a man anyway, darlin'? An income, security, paid for with a regular fuck and a bit of home management, debit and credit, all accounted for? Or do you fall for the angel dust of romance lighting on a dark star, a short course delight, wham bam no complications? No, I lay my cards on the table, the black queen's trumps, and it was for James and me.

I say was, because that chaotic *pas de deux* has ended. Passionate, wild for sure, but any bloke can impress a sexy nineteen-year-old, me, Joeley from nowhere, aspiring, desiring, lusting, who caught the big one, an ab diver with his own licence. Licence to what? The scene, living the dream, all the brands on display? All of that until he fell for mega money, got rumbled, a blazing star fallen to earth barely avoiding time in jail. Lawyers creamed it, a dream case so it was repro time and James had to sell his abalone licence, the house, the land, and all the accumulated toys to pay for them. He took up study, camouflage, hiding in broad daylight where he found himself, a marine biologist over at the Marine Studies Centre. Hard to believe, heck yes! He's still screwing around, sometimes dropping round here looking for what? Solace, quiescence and aqua vita, too, la dolce served up free? In his dreams. Yep, I can do words, just look and listen, you lifeless beauty, Venus.

Me and my son Brady, we're still hangin' here. He's good, not making the best of himself, but there's time. Me? Oof! A quick-mouthed scrag left behind with a bunch of weirdos. Alcoholics, single parents, loners hooked on online betting holed up in sand blasted shacks along these shores, sand piling at the doors and windows… A life with the tide going out, jettisoned to the future, that's my life.

Got its moments, like last night, just savouring it this morning, when two cops are strolling down my path, knocking on my open door.

'A few minutes of your time, ma'am?'

'Sure, come in,' but they are already in, Officer Jones and DI Marney, introducing themselves and having a good look around. 'What's the problem?'

'Name?'

'Joeley Henderson.'

'Ms Henderson, did you see or hear anything unusual last night?'

DI Marney puts the questions, Jones makes the notes. Marney's short and fat, gravity had its way with him. Jones is more elongated, in body and tone.

'No, officer, can't say I did.' Like, the onboard entertainment on the *Nadir* last night? But you've got to be careful what you say to the officers of the law, find out what's what, the way the land lies before talking facts.

'Where were you last night?'

'I was right here, officer.' Hedging.

'For the whole evening?'

'Well,' I concede, 'I had a few drinks at the Rock Lobster. Walked back about eleven.'

'Late for a little local bar?'

'Not really.' As if other things could be going on. Drugs, money laundering, human trafficking… Maybe he's right. 'It's friendly. Everyone knows everyone. Nice.'

'And this morning?'

'Got up, matter of fact late for me. I usually go for a walk, check the surf, look out for my son, Brady.'

'Ah, Brady.' DI Marney cocks an eyebrow at the other, and they circle.

See what I mean? Just one loose name and they're onto it like dogs with a bone.

'You find him?' DI Marney says.

'No, matter of fact. What is this about?'

They ignore my question, for now. 'Out in the bay. See anything unusual, out of the ordinary?' Jones, this time.

'Sea fog rolled in, can't see more than a few metres…' Surf was slick and flat, I knew Brady wouldn't have rated it.

But DI Marney can see I'm on edge. Still, they back off, Jones writing in his notebook. They go checking around the place, the veranda while they have a smoke.

Thing is, there was something. Rock Lobster's rocking, I'm cruising over a gin and tonic with Charlene, my sister in crime, and see… Uh oh, the fuzz is back. Where did they stub those cigarettes? Not in my garden pots!

'Tell us again, where you were last night, Joeley?'

Joeley? I didn't allow them to use my name. Hope to Christ they haven't sussed out me and James, our unhappy record with the law.

'Well,' I say, as melt in your mouth as butter, 'DI Marney and Officer Jones –' it helps to use their names – 'check with the Rock Lobster, they'll corroborate my story.'

DI Marney puts his face up close, but hey, I'm taller than him, so not dominating like he wants. 'You telling us everything, Joeley?'

'Big problem, Joeley. For you. For Brady,' Jones says, 'if you're keeping anything back.'

'Boats,' DI Marney says. 'You hear an outboard engine, for instance?'

'Someone going out?' says Jones.

'Or coming in,' DI Marney backs him.

'Sea fog muffles everything, can't see nor hear more than two metres,' I say, standing beside Venus, my glittering creation, for support.

'Dinghies, tinnies, recreational craft?' Jones is on a roll.

A mobile rings. DI Marney heads out to the veranda, listens. Waves Jones out. He gives me a warning look, as if to say, I'll be right back because I'm onto you, and goes out.

Jones says, 'Thank you for your time, Ms Henderson,' and they're heading out the gate.

I'm so relieved I stagger over to the jug and fill it for a cuppa. See, it was like this: I left the Rock Lobster about nine and walked over to the marina, see if James was on the launch. James was there all right, going for it with some chick. I headed straight back to the bar, pissed off, and told Charlene, but you reckon I could tell those police officers that? What if James is implicated? I have to suss it out, because any scandal'd screw up Brady and he's had enough shit from James's freeloading sex life as it is. Not to mention my loss of privacy. So my mouth is shut. For now.

James

Brady, my son, these oxygen tanks are half empty again. Why is it you never check the meters, or get them refilled matter of course? It's all I ask. Same with the fuel. Tell me, is Brady compos mentis? One with us crawling out of the ocean and up the beach, leaping evolution to stand and lift a beer glass? Here's to the tetrapods, four limbs and sexual reproduction. Reptiles, amphibians, birds and, last but not least, mammals. That's us, the apex species constructing the great systems of thought, philosophy, mathematics, science… But not our Brady. You hear him last night up at the shack? The racket! Had to stick it out down here at the marina, doss down on the launch, in the end.

Ah, Brady… I should've called him Boris. Might've had a better outcome in life. Boris the fossil lodged eight hundred metres up a mountain in East Greenland, three-sixty-five million years ago, well before the Devonian Extinction, you know? Boris is all our ancestors, equipped with a skull, eye sockets, a vertical column… Brady looked similar in the womb, like any mammal foetus… You, me, rabbits, cops…

Where are those students? Hungover no doubt… Give them another half hour, otherwise no in-the-field-assessment for them! Am I crazy? Joeley thinks so. You never know what you're getting, she says, with a man. With a woman, I could add. She never accepted my switch from bankrupt ab diver to academic, left her high and dry, beached in a rickety shack on a sandbank. So what, she's an artist, it's their habitat. I know, she found me out, my dark side, but we all have secrets, don't we? Nothing momentous; it's life. Like, we were all beautiful once, nothing momentous, it's youth. Time's the limit, not so plentiful as oxygen, fact we're too short of it, hurtling towards oblivion, the stump end of humanity, a prosthetic for a devastated planet. I like that… Stump end, prosthetic….

Talk about evolution and competitive advantage, this morning two cops turned up. Jones and DI Marney.

'Making enquiries,' they said. 'Name?'

'James Henderson.'

'Sir, where were you last night?'

'Right here, officers.'

'All night?'

'That's right.'

They circle, study the launch, try to look as if they know something about boats.

'Anyone verify that?'

'No.'

'Why all night?'

'I was getting out of Brady's way. My son. He was raging with his mates.'

'Brady?' They pricked up their ears. 'Brady's your son?'

'That's right. He had a scene going up on the clifftop. Mates. Hell of a racket, dog barking, shouting, cars doing wheelies.'

The tall one, Jones, turned to the other. 'Confirms his story,' he said.

But DI Marney's not satisfied. He sniffed, like he was catching a foul smell. 'Partying went on all night, sir?'

'That's right, officers. You know young blokes.'

'Certain you were here?' Marney repeats.

And I get a feeling this is a trick question. Can't go back on what I stated. 'Quite certain, most of the evening.' Not to mention my trip over to the *Nadir*. Gives me an out if necessary.

They poked about, asked a few more questions, running out of wind. So I filled them in on my research for the last few years: joints, essential to the survival of the species. Any of you with arthritis, you'd know about it. Pivot joint: neck; ball and socket: shoulder; hinge: the elbows, my favourite. Where would pubs be without the elbow joint! Try push-ups without bending your elbows. See the problem? Screwing without joints, ha, a joke…

That got rid of them, they headed back past the marina, along the shore, the long and the short of it. Good grief, I'm still cleaning up the rubbish around here, pizza trays, stubby bottles, condoms. Damned students. And where are they!

Brady

Hotfooted down to the marina, Dad? Hasn't got the launch out on the water, yet. He's at it, checking the gas bottles. Gonna blast me for not fillin' them, better retreat, wait him out. Does he know about the body on the shore? Tragedy like this, it stirs up the memories like mud on the sea floor. Who knows what links to the past are gonna surface? This I know. Someone tries to take somethin' away from you, threaten, take you down a peg, you fight back big time. When Mum and Dad split… The fight! Never forget it. I was five, I woke up. Mum was goin' for him, smashin' up everythin', yellin' You've taken everything! You can't take this away from me! Take what? I was so fuckin' frightened I wet my bed.

But Dad left, and then it was just Mum and me. So I know her, her moods, her dreams, her thoughts. No one replaced Dad for Mum. Blokes used to hang around, but nuthin'. They'd decide she was too crazy and head off. Me was all she cared about; yep, she used to say that. See me off to school, there when I come home with some nice cake or biscuits she'd made, and chattin' with a friend who might be passing by. Or my aunt Charlene, usually pissing, Mum havin' a glass to keep her company. Or maybe the freckle lady, funny little character Mum feels sorry for, she makes those round chocolate lollies called freckles, hands them out to people around the place, cheer them up. And it works! Mum was always laughing after she left. She even made a statue called the *Freckle Lady*, covered in hundreds and thousands fixed with an emulsion. Because Mum had a hard time, bringing me up, no money, an artist. The local Greeks left bags of kids' clothes out at the gate, is how I got T-shirts with maps of Athens, Greek gods, Greek islands. Love to go there, sailing around the Med and the Aegean, shit cool! Why at the gate? Respected her, didn't want to shove her need in her face. You know, she makes what she needs, and that's it. Fixed up the house with bits and pieces, found objects she says, tatt from op shops up in town…

I can't have her hurt by this, but how can I tell her what I saw down on the beach? Can't. It'll come out and I gotta protect her. Because now, she's started talkin to herself, talkin' to that torso woman she's makin,

Venus, it's fuckin' doin my head in. It's since I moved in with Dad. Betrayal, is that how she sees it? I had to make a move, live on my own terms, Dad was the first step. But Mum's fragile. Talks tough but she'd break into pieces. Soon as this police thing's over, you know, I'll look about gettin' her outa here, this dead-end dump, for sure. Leave the past behind, move to a new scene. I had enough of my mates after last night, buncha losers. Findin' that poor chick on the shore, and everyone's implicated, me too and I'm packin' it! See what I mean? Gotta make a move. Startin' with Dad. Thinkin' about Mum.

Joeley

Billennia ago, little critters eye the shore and say, that's for me, legs, arms, sex on land. Wild, hey! Better than asexual reproduction, squirting up yourself, where's the fun in that? So these little critters get little feet, claws, drag themselves out of the water, upright, and what've we got? *Homo penile erectus*, da da! Going for it, wherever, whoever… Whoor! Man the apex predator as James sees it, screwing not only women, but the whole planetary ecosystem, bringing it crashing down like the twin towers. That's testosterone for you! And you know what man, the inventor of civilisation, says to the species? Shape up or ship out: it's domestication or it's extinction, that's the choice for you, tawny frogmouth, forty-spotted pardelote, orange-bellied parrot, like they've already done to the thylacine, the dodo and countless others.

Uh oh, they're back, the police, the latest models of evolution. Eyes are switching from me to Venus and back.

'Few more questions.' DI Marney says. 'Anything unusual you observed along the shoreline, Joeley?'

'Oh yes… Carrots,' I say.

'Carrots?' Jones is sharp.

DI Marney stays cool in his short fat way.

'Yachties. Stuff they don't want, over the side! Fishnet, old rope, stale food, fucks the marine life like you wouldn't believe.'

'Or a body!' Marney makes like Sherlock.

'A body?' I almost laugh out loud.

'Party on board,' Jones says.

'Drinking.'

'Drugs.'

'A drunk tries it on, pushes her against the rails…'

'Things get out of hand.'

Things sure are out of hand: their rape fantasies. You know the police, attract all sorts, perps, sadists, bullies…

'I don't know what you're talking about,' I say, making like a cucumber. 'Why do you ask?'

They give each other a look. What are they holding back?

'Any information, you are obliged by law to report it.'

'Joeley, if you lie about one thing, you could be lying about other stuff.' Jones is a thinker, no doubt about it.

DI Marney backs him up. 'Important things,' he says. 'Did you leave the bar during the evening?' And eyeballs me.

Oh, shit, they're onto me. 'Not that I remember exactly,' I say.

'The barman reckons you did leave the bar,' Jones says.

'You can't be suggesting,' I say.

'Suggesting what?' Pouncing.

Now they've got me tied in knots. 'Maybe I did leave the bar. Fresh air, cigarette, so?'

'You smoke? No packs around here,' Jones says. 'You smell cigarettes, Marney?'

Thinking fast. 'Now and then I have a puff. Fact, I botted one.'

Marney sighs. 'You got a cigarette, who from?'

'From whom.' I'm a demon for grammar.

'Answer the question,' DI Marney snaps.

'Okay! From Charlene, my sister.' She does the smoking for both of us but I don't tell them that.

'She can corroborate that?' Jones says as he's writing in his notebook.

'Maybe. She got pretty drunk. Fact, she probably won't remember,' hedging again.

'Stop wasting our time,' Jones snaps.

'Yes, I did slip out. To check on James, my ex. At the launch.'

'And?'

'He wasn't there.'

'Sure about that?'

'Absolutely. No sign of him.' Thinking fast, the chick he was with, she can give him an alibi. If he needs an alibi.

Jones is writing again. 'Certain of the time?'

'Ten past nine. Give or take a few minutes.'

'Notice anything happening along the beach?'

'Mmm, it was quiet, bit eerie… Very still.'

'Nothing unusual?

'Nothing…'

'What then?

'Went back to the bar, had a few drinks, then I left, like I told you, and came back here.'

'On your own?

'With Charlene.'

'Who else was in the pub?'

'Bunch of yachties. Students…'

'You see, we have another problem here.'

'What?'

'Charlene's version of your movements.'

Oh, Charlene my ditzy blonde sister!

Jones leans his elongated body, hands behind his back, making like a pretzel. 'States she went out to a yacht, and you went with her.'

'She was too past it to notice who was with her or where she was, officer.' I take a breath and wonder what sort of sex Jones likes. Wham bam or a more indolent affair?

He notices, and purses his lips, like he's censoring my thoughts. Which have veered away from incriminating.

'Are you saying you did or did not go out to the yacht?'

'Like I said…'

'Yes or no?

'Yes… A very short time. To keep an eye on Charlene.'

'Now we have the truth. What's it called, Jones, withholding evidence?'

'Withholding evidence,' Marney lgowers at me. 'This yacht, what's it called?'

Jones looks it up in his notebook. '*Nadir*,' mispronouncing it.

'*Nadir*,' I correct him.

'The facts, Joeley! You're on the yacht, how long?'

'Come back, um, just before dawn.'

'Who else was on the yacht?

'Yachties.'

'Answer the question.'

'A few of us.

'Any kids?

'Girls, women?

'I suppose. I don't keep a list.'

'Who's the owner?'

'Wally. He'll corroborate what I'm saying.'

'Wally.'

'Charlene can confirm…'

'Sober enough now, is she?'

Sneering. I give Jones a filthy look. Don't diss my sister, and he sees it, backs off.

'Yacht still out in the bay?' DI Marney asks.

'All marine craft advised not to leave for twenty-four hours,' Jones says.

'How did you get back to shore?' DI Marney again.

'In a dinghy. Me and Charlene and Bigfoot.'

'Bigfoot,' Jones snorts.

'Outboard?' DI Marney snaps, turning on his heel.

'Yes… We came into the far end of the beach, close to Charlene's place.'

'Outboard motor. Confirms Brady's report,' DI Marney says to Jones, and I breathe a sigh.

Brady seems to be off the hook. But of what?

'You walk back here?'

'Yes, back along the beach.'

'Ask you again, you see anything, anything at all…'

Told you, a sea fog was rolling in… Bag of garbage, that was unusual, didn't I mention that? We don't often get rubbish dumped.'

'A body's been found, Joeley.'

'A…body?'

'This morning, at the shoreline.'

'The shore, you mean, terrible. I'm so sorry… Poor girl.'

'Girl? Why do you say girl?' Jones snaps.

'Well, it would be. It's who the creeps go for. Not an old scrag like me.'

Jones looks around. 'Anything you might remember, any little detail, report it, understood? Here's my card.'

'Of course,' and I take it from him.

DI Marney joins him, and these two officers of the law head off.

'We'll be back. Don't leave the area.'

To think! Maybe I walked straight past that poor kid. Telling you, when this is over, I'm out of this dead-end hole. Soon as… But James? Shiii… That girl he had on the launch? Stupid bastard, but he can cope for himself. The *Nadir*? It was like this: bunch of weekend yachties came into the Rock Lobster spouting boozy stories, foul jokes, fishy tales, full of it. Charlene sees a chance, she gets the shots lined up, I can't ditch her, so fuck me, we ended up out on a yacht. More drinking, chuffed some dope, got talking to this guy, Bigfoot. Green eyes, tanned, massive, and sweet as. I know, I know, I'm a sucker, when am I gonna learn.

Charlene's making out with some slippery ferret, moon's up, so beautiful gently rocking out on the midnight water… Then the beat breaks out, boom boom and oh, my god… This guy starts prancing around the deck mock-screwing to 'You Give Me Head'! Charlene, I said, we're outa here, the standard has just fallen through the scuppers. Or something nautical. Bigfoot gets me and Charlene into the dinghy and back to shore just as light's peering along the horizon, and a sea fog's rolling in. Bigfoot kills the outboard, we're over the side wading in and Charlene throws up on the sand. That woman! Couldn't she chuck her guts in the water? Look out for Charlene, I say to Bigfoot, get her home. He's reluctant, thought he'd make out with me, like I'd been giving him the come on. Guess I'd know what I'd be getting… A bird in the bush, a poke in the pig, a cock in the hand. No way, this is my very own throw-away life, on my own, right here, my refuge. Anyway, I walk along the beach, and there's a buncha gulls fighting over a garbo bag of rubbish, is all. The girl? If only I'd looked a bit closer, but I just wanted to get home. I crashed a few hours, then up and into it with you, my darlin' Venus… That's my story.

James

The police were back again, a while ago. Professor Henderson, they said, smooth as, we want to go over a few details. Namely that Joeley said she visited the launch around nine and I wasn't here. How that woman complicates my life! So I told them, I'd heard a party on one of the boats. Racket blasting out, 'You Give Me Head'. Pretty wild night all round, no chance of getting sleep, so I'd headed over there. Just for a quick snifter with Wally, he can corroborate my story. That's it.

Joeley. Where was she? Sleeping it off at her place, or with that big guy I saw her with? Brady. I need Brady. There's something…could be important. I didn't tell those officers: someone was here, on the launch. Homeless kids, they doss down, leave their cigarette butts, drink cartons, takeaway rubbish, it's a bloody pain. After I got back from the *Nadir*, they'd been here. I should've told the police… Brady might know. And here he is, talk of the devil…

'Coupla officers came round here short time ago, for the second time. What have you got yourself into, Brady?'

'Nuthin'. You were here last night, what was goin' on?' He slouches past, giving me this leery look.

'As I told those two officers of the law, nothing. Including about your mother and her detestable sister.'

He snaps around. 'Leave Mum out of it.'

'So why am I here, sleeping out? Where's my family life, food on the table, a warm bed, a goodnight hot cocoa…'

'You coulda stuck around last night up at the shack. We got the barbie goin'.'

'Joking.' But if I'd taken up his offer, I'd be in the clear. No way I can get offside with the law. Not at my time of life and in my position.

'Any students come by last night, Dad?'

'Possible.' I hedge. What's he after?

'I check the fuel, be the same level as yesterday?'

'You check the fuel? That'd be a first.'

'Mum. Where was she?'

'She wasn't home knitting and reading with a cat on her lap. Now, let me see…'

'Quit it, Dad.'

'She was with Charlene on one of the yachts out there.'

'She was safe outa the way, then.' I watched the penny drop. 'Hey, how d'you know she was out there?'

'I took the tinny over. Joined Wally on *Nadir* for a coupla whiskies. Knew him from my ab diver days, then headed back.'

'You tell the police?'

'Yep. Nothing about your mum being there with some big guy she picked up. Talk about desperate…'

'Dad!'

'Hey, cool it. I got back here. Some idiots had been on the launch, left their rubbish behind…'

'So there were students hangin' here.'

'Sure. I didn't catch them at it, Brady.'

'Okay, okay. And Mum?'

'She came back in a dinghy about dawn. Same guy brought them in. Her and Charlene.'

'Thought I heard an engine goin', couldn't see for the fog.'

'What is this about, Brady? Why so interested?'

'The cops…'

'Marney and Jones, yes, I know.'

'They question you about the body?'

'What body?'

'A body on the shore.'

Anger. 'Brady, spit it out, for fuck's sake.'

'Just listen!'

I throw up my hands. 'I'm listening.'

'I come down here, oh, pre-dawn. There's this noise…'

'Your racket. Couldn't hear anything over it.'

'Listen to me. Next morning I come down again, around ten. And Dad…I found the body.'

'You what!'

Brady's in shock and so am I.

'Start from the beginning.'

And tells me some incoherent story about what happened last night. Suddenly I can see my life disappearing down the drain after I've worked so hard to create a persona, respect, a decent life.

'Brady, listen to me, son. Get yourself out of here.'

'Thought of that, had to check with you, after I saw the tinny was gone.'

'Like I said…' I look around the marina, all looks quiet, normal, but I can see shock waves emanating from Brady like when you drop a stick of jelly into a bay and the shock waves kill all living creatures. Brady is that stick of jelly, jittery as hell.

'You get some chick here last night? Usual scenario?'

'No, I didn't. Don't talk to me like that.'

'What're you hidin'? Is it from the past, come back to bite you?'

'Fuck off, hangover's done your head in.'

'This is a chick, Dad, dead! What about her life, her future?'

'What the fuck has it got to do with me?'

'Good question. DNA might tell us, be hell interestin', hey? And if they find yours on her?'

'You're saying I had something to do with this girl?'

'Am I? You read my mind? Spill it out, we can sort it.'

'There is nothing to sort!'

'You bet there is. I sorta recognised this girl I found.'

'What d'you mean? You told the police this?'

'No, Dad.'

'Let's get this straight. You think you know her, what, from college? One of your mates' sisters?'

'I don't know.'

'And putting two and two together in your burnt-out brain, she's to do with me.'

'You listenin' to me at all? I'm sayin', there's vulnerable chicks, prey to blokes on the make. '

'I am not a bloke on the make!'

'Okay, Dad. Cool it.'

'It's a police issue, not yours, Brady. What's the point going on and on?'

'The fuckin' point? She's dead!'

'Yes! And the investigation by the police will take its course.'

'Hell, here's the scenario. Someone turns up, threatens what you got, time to fight back big time.'

'Finished your juvenile fantasies?'

'The facts. When you split, never forget it. I was five, I woke up, Mum was goin' for you…'

'You think I could forget?'

'Smashin' up everythin'. Screamin', that was my daughter! You take everything from me, okay, take it. Not her! What the shit did she mean: that was my daughter?'

'It meant nothing, Brady. Your mum was off her head. She'd wanted another kid, a daughter and it didn't happen. Now, I've work to do.'

'The past. This is about the past.'

'Our past? It's nothing. Try sixty-five million years ago.'

'Fuckin' science… You're no scientist! Just a facade. A scientist should revere life. You? You screw it. Scientists know more about every little intsy aspect of a being – plant, bird, gorilla, fuckin fungus than ever… Remnants is all we've got, oh, except in the zoo concentration camps.'

'Where we conduct breeding programs for endangered species! Look, Brady… Calm down. I had nothing to do with whatever happened last night, okay?'

'See what Mum has to say.' And off he goes. Storming off down the jetty, that stick of jelly held in his hand. For now.

Joeley

Packing up, what to take, what to leave… Why didn't I get the shit out of here before, can anyone tell me? Instead I've been a handy receptacle for everybody's dreams… Brady's, Charlene's, James's.

Brady was five when Posie broke into the house of love… An invading species like a starfish wanting to move in permanently. A threesome? Should've seen it coming. James, I mean… Loyalty, support, caring, are just not in his make-up. I couldn't up and leave back then, there was little Brady. Single mother? No way I wanted that, or living on my own. Still, shit happened, James left and I've had to make the best of it.

That woman, Posie. Black hair, black eyes, skinny… She turns up in my dreams. Here, Venus, give you her hair, black, in a fringe, black texta, black round your eyes, there you go. Like I say, shack up with a bloke, you don't know what you're getting, hey? And here's what I got, walking up the path through the garden, the professor himself.

'James. Come in. Too early for a glass of wine?'

'What've you told the police? You know Brady's been here?'

'Settle down. You're all over the place.'

'This body on the shore, it's knocked him. Smoked too much dope last night, the fool.'

Now he's gone too far. He turns on my son, he turns on me. Time for some sorting. 'Of course he's upset. So am I. Who were you with last night, James?'

'I was at the launch, couldn't sleep, took the tinny over to see Wally.'

'On the *Nadir*? I didn't see you there.'

'I saw you, pretty taken with that big bloke…'

'Bigfoot. So what?'

'It's all right, Joeley, it's your life to fuck up.'

'I don't need your permission.' This cast-off castaway telling me what is or isn't my life? 'You're lying. James. She look like this?' I draw two big tears on Venus's face.

'Who?'

'Posie.' And I watch him. The body on the shore has up-tilted his safe little lifeboat over at the Marine Studies Centre. Professor James Henderson is floundering.

'Posie… Not her again! Christ sake, it was eighteen years ago.'

'Wanting to move in, stars in her eyes…and pregnant.'

'Manipulative little bitch. It was never true, Joeley, you know it.'

'The baby…'

'She had an abortion.'

'How can you be sure?'

'For Christ's sake, Joeley, not now.'

'Face it, James. She wanted you then, now she's come back, some-how.' I'm gabbling. I know it, but then he cuts right through my flow.

'She's dead.'

'What?'

'Posie. She died in a car crash.'

The ground falls away from me. 'When did this happen?'

'Two years after she left here.'

'Sixteen years… You never thought to tell me, you fuckin' bastard!'

'And have you carry on yelling the house down? For Christ's sake.'

I'm stunned. I look around this little cottage, and it is meaningless, this place in the dunes, like, I've cannibalised the past to create a life, and if the past didn't exist, neither does the present. James is rattling on, but I can't seem to get things in focus. I'm seeing double, the past and the present mismatching.

'Can't even be fucked keeping me in the picture.'

'Joeley, remember back then? I was heading for the shit heap.'

'You survived, repurposed your life and convinced everyone. But not me. I know what I saw on the launch, you going for it and that's what I'm telling the police.' Ah, it feels so good to twist the screw.

'It wasn't me, for Christ's sake.'

'And if they do find your DNA?'

'They won't. It'll clear me. But, Joeley, keep mum about the launch. They might drag things up from the past, we have to face this together.'

He's right. I'm too soft, but blackmail is not me. The police will sort it, one way or the other.

'Just go.'

'I'm going. Don't worry, I'm going! Leave you with your latest screw, Bigfoot, what a joke. Can't do better than that, eh, Joeley…'

Nasty bastard. 'Matter of fact, he offered to take me cruising the Whitsundays. I might just take him up on it.'

He's backing out the door, and me, I'm making sure he goes.

James

'Sit down, Mr Henderson.'

'Sure.'

Just the two of us, me and DI Marney in this cramped space, bare walls of cream painted concrete block, one frosted glass window. That cold, institutional feel, everything's bared for examination like the entrails of a shark to see what's been consumed, a leg, a hand… No witnesses to the interview and I'm glad about that. There's a heap I wouldn't want to be broadcast to the world.

'Take a seat, Mr Henderson.' Waves me to a seat opposite.

'Is this necessary? I've got nothing to add to my statement.'

'As of yet, you have not made a statement.'

'Right…'

'Just a preliminary check, corroborate some facts.' Eyes sliding, no eye to eye contact here.

'Residing at 37 Clifftop Crescent with your son, Brady?'

'Fancy name for a sandy rut, ha ha.' Try humour, no response. 'That's correct, officer.'

'Age…'

'Fifty-two.'

'Occupation: maintenance officer class 2, Marine Studies Centre. Employed, ah, eight years, is that correct?

'That's right.' Thank god there are no witnesses to these revelations.

'Is that a full-time position, sir?'

'Casual on-call. The hours I put in, no way I get paid for them.' Because I love it, but he doesn't want to hear that; feelings are not appropriate.

'What responsibilities does that entail, sir?'

'Check the gear's in working order, proper procedures are followed for use of equipment, it's returned on time, oxygen bottles full and turned off, gear, rosters, make sure the students are buddied up, run them through the operational procedures, communications, water safety…'

He writes all this down. 'Take them out on dives?

'Yes, I have the experience. But it's not one of my responsibilities, The postgrads conduct the research, monitor the sites, that sort of thing.'

'Get on with the students?' Ah. Now we're getting to the crux of this interview.

'Sure. Chat with them, address any issues they bring up, requests they make, follow what's happening…'

'Any particular students. Girls?'

'Look, I know where this is going…' and he pounces.

'Where's that, Mr Henderson?'

'I get on with the students, all of them. I have to, to get the safety messages across.'

'I asked, any in particular.'

'No, I'm friendly, a friendly bloke with a job to do. That's it.'

'Right… Prior occupation, abalone fisherman.'

'That's right. Had to get outa the game, diving wrecked my joints.'

'So important the joints…'

Ha! So there is room for humour.

'James Henderson, police record, few minor traffic infringements, drink driving three months disqualified, fined eight hundred dollars…'

'That is not relevant.'

But he goes on, in his relentless monotone. 'Ten years ago charged with a criminal offence, involvement in an on-water drug cartel, major quantity of heroin…'

'I was acquitted!' Ab diver, of course I knew about the scheme. Shouldna touched it but I was at the intersection of sudden wealth and greed for more. See, you get these hangers-on, you're doing all right and they come up with schemes. Using your money, of course. I should've cut loose sooner, but young, blindsided by shit thinking…nothing could touch me? Acquitted, yes, but bankrupted, legal costs…

'University know about that?' And this time, he eyeballs me. All pretence of objectivity gone.

'There was no need to inform them. It doesn't impact on my humble position.'

'Interesting, you turn up right here.'

'I live and work here, like hundreds of others.'

'And you didn't leave the marina, that morning…'

'That's right…'

'The yacht, the…*Nadir*? A party was underway that night, you've stated.'

'"You Give Me Head", ha ha…' Oh Jesus, sometimes I could punch myself!

'Didn't head over?'

Is he punning? 'Matter of fact, I stopped by, for a quick snifter… Wally, the skipper. He'll vouch for me.'

'Any reason why you didn't inform us before?'

'Slipped my mind, officer. Like I said, a quick snort, then back to the marina.'

'Lot of drinking, drugs, carry on?'

'Drugs? No way. It was all above board, so to speak.' Now I'm punning. Must be catching.

'You state you were there briefly.'

'Very briefly.'

'So how would you ascertain the presence or otherwise of drugs?'

'Nothing being passed around that I could see. Look, I'm careful. I could lose my job.'

'Yachts coming in at night, drugs, parties…'

'Exactly! I've got a responsible position.'

'Blokes like you, Mr Henderson, always think they can get away with it.'

'I'm getting away with nothing, DI Marney. Plenty of corruption in the police force, seen it all.'

'Bit of an expert, eh?'

'It's your kids that matter. Family.' I know, the irony.

'Your family. Joeley Henderson, Brady Henderson?'

'That's right.'

'Mean a lot to you?'

Where's he going with this angle? 'Sure.'

'You've lied. About what you did and who you are. Professor Henderson, eh?'

'Doesn't make me a criminal.'

'What does it make you, sir?'

'Let me tell you, DI Marney. Something you're gonna face one day. See, society doesn't care. You, me, doesn't matter how well we do our jobs, responsible family man, brilliant scientist, artist, musician, whatever. Hard-working police officer. It doesn't care, not for one little nanosecond. Society, it dishes out the punishment, gives out the rewards, but it doesn't give a fuck. It's an entity in its own right, a great beast, a moloch…'

'Is that right?' He puts a stop to my rant. 'Mr Henderson, don't leave the vicinity.'

And with that, the interview was over. I was clear, for now.

Brady

Funny thing, people talk about family breakdown, Dad, Mum, meaning you live separate lives in separate places, and even if you don't see each other, or talk, the family is there, a net holding you together. One, you share genes. Two, you share space. Three, you share time, but most important, you share dreams. All that makes for shared history, memories, right? So a look, a song, a smell and it's there, a memory in full colour and movement baying' for blood: rage, guilt, sorrow, tenderness, a laugh, a cry… So real. Shit, he's back, my old man.

'Mum,' I shout out, 'Dad's back.' The residues of a marriage, about to do some sharing.

'Brady, what is this, a family get-together?' He's nervous as hell, and right to be.

'Mum?'

'Let's sit outside.' She's floating away in her chiffon dress and I love her, my Mum. This reckoning is for her.

We take our stubbies and go out to her rickety little outdoor setting.

'You're not lookin' too good, James.'

He's aged these last twenty-four hours, even I can see that.

'Had better days.'

He's looking at Mum different too, like, feelings are breaking through the hard shell, memories surfacing from the submerged sandbanks of the past.

'Something I've got to tell you, Joeley, about my position…'

'Your position, on what, professor?'

'He's trying to tell you somethin', Mum,' I say.

She starts in. 'Brady, it's me that's gonna be doing the telling! When I tell the police what I know. Like, who you, James, was screwin' last night down in the launch.' Nailed him. Oh boy, does he look the stunned mullet.

'I've told you, stop talking shit.'

'Disgusting. A student. You have a responsibility. Duty of care.'

'No students came by last night, Joeley, zilch.'

'You can't lie straight in bed.'

'Could've been anyone hangin' around the marina, Mum,' I cut in.

Mum looks at me like I'm the adult and they're the quarrelling kids.

'Give him a break.'

'I'm talking down at the launch.'

'I was at the bottom of the cliff, I heard it, a cry…' I try. 'Like some-one was real hurt, and the night so still as if it's listenin'…'

'She must've wanted something, James.'

'Fuck off!' Dad is losing it.

'In your dreams, professor…' Mum's not gonna let him get off lightly.

'I'm out of this dump.' and he starts out of his chair, but I push him back down.

'Tell Mum!'

'Tell her what? It wasn't me.'

'Ha!' Words echoing down history, down time, down the genera-tions. War, famine, disaster, massacres, extinction and now marriage break-up: it wasn't me!

'Tell Mum what you gotta tell her.'

'You know fuck all, my son, except smoking, screwing and surfing…'

'Koota told me, Mum. His girlfriend's a student.'

'Told you what?'

'Joeley, don't listen to him. Koota, Snapper are scum. Bottom feed-ers.'

'More honest than you, fuckin' charlatan.'

'What, Brady?'

'Him! Scientist? Mum, his job's maintenance, he keeps things run-ning. No more a scientist than me. Less. I know the fuckin' natural world, and he's like a squid hidin' in the depths, king of nuthin'.'

'What?' Mum looks at the two of us: me the avenging angel, Dad shrinking before her eyes.

'Joeley, I can explain, I needed a job, any job, you know that…'

'You aren't a professor? Professor Henderson?'

'Nuthin' but an odd fuckin' job man, Mum.' Gotta hit him hard.

'You've been lying to me, all along?'

'Lyin' to us both.'

'Brady, Joeley, I did as much as those researchers. They'd be nothing without me.'

'A big man. So fuckin' big. How can the world turn on its axis without you?' I say.

Mum jumps up, the chair clatters over. 'Pouring shit on me all these years, telling me I'm worthless, useless, you wrecked my career, James. And all along, you've lied.'

'You, career? Look at you,' Dad sneers and I get up to deck him one.

Mum holds me back and lets fly. 'I spent my life supporting you, the ab diver, the scientist. Conned me, and fucked me over.'

'Brady, don't listen to her...'

'I should listen to you? It's up in smoke your life. Come on, Mum...'

'That's right, dump me. Fucking blood-sucking parasites is all you are.'

Family. Did I say something about the web that keeps you together?

'Joeley... I had to get something back, lost everything in that court case, not just the money. Standing. I was a big man, looked up to, could pay for anything, thought the trick was to pay for nothing, it's how the rich get rich. Maintenance officer class two, I know, but the students listen to me, more than to their useless professors. Joeley! The only good thing in my life, I never saw it. Joeley! You. Brady! Is all I've got left. Is all I had.'

We're headin' out, Mum with Bigfoot, sailin' for the Whitsundays. She'll fight to save the reef, that's my Mum. And me? That night down on the beach, that cry, everything that's happened since, changed me. What the fuck am I doing with myself, pissing my life away. Koota, Snapper, Birdie. I know, Friday, Saturday nights, all around the coasts of this god-given country dickheads are gettin' drunk around fires and barbecues, on decks and patios, pissin' their lives away. It's called our wonderful lifestyle, envied around the world.

I'm headin' to the platform below the cliffs, come with me. Careful, bare feet, the shells can cut your feet to pieces, might be oystercatcher chicks in nests, so fragile this place. Kelp, see? Washed up from the kelp forests, they hold on to the sea floor, called a hold-fast, like a foot, fragile as our hold on the planet. Further round, see the middens? A metre deep, then a band of fire and dead soil – that's when us, whitey, arrived to fuck the place. Yep, they'd tell us how to live, those middens, if we only stopped our speedin' lives to read them. Every shell there was food for an Aborigine, child, woman, man. Over thousands of shells and thousands of years. Us? We'll be lucky to make it to two-fifty way we're wastin the place.

Come on, don't lag, listen to the waves surfin' the shore, seabirds calling, exquisite? You bet. Shearwater burrows up on the headland, you know… Woulda been flocks of a hundred million and all we've got now is remnants and reminders of what we've lost, in this place. In this world.

That girl on the beach. That face, strands of hair, dark eyes, she coulda been anyone, or a seal pup, a porpoise, a whale, why I recognised her. Life and death was always there along the shores, but what we done – man, yeah man – is at a whole other level, a Shoa, a holocaust on all creation. Listen to the first peoples: every creature is precious, every creature has a role in the web of the ecosystems, the breathing planet, every creature has a right! Listen and act, act and right now stop the death march of the species. Those are my words – me, Brady.